Praise for the novels of #1 *New York Times* bestselling author Debbie Macomber

"It's impossible not to cheer for Macomber's characters. . . . When it comes to creating a special place and memorable, honorable characters, nobody does it better than Macomber."

—*BookPage*

"Debbie Macomber [has a] gift for understanding the souls of women—their relationships, their values, their lives."

—*BookPage*

"As always, Macomber draws rich, engaging characters."

—*Publishers Weekly*

"Ms. Macomber provides the top in entertaining relationship dramas."

—*Reader to Reader*

"Virtually guaranteed to please."

—*Publishers Weekly*

"Debbie Macomber writes characters who are as warm and funny as your best friends."

—*New York Times* bestselling author Susan Wiggs

"Debbie Macomber is . . . a bona fide superstar."

—*Publishers Weekly*

Debbie Macomber

Sugar and Spice Kisses

Yesterday Once More **and** ***Sugar and Spice***

MIRA

MIRA™

ISBN-13: 978-0-7783-0630-6

Recycling programs for this product may not exist in your area.

For questions and comments about the quality of this book, please contact us at CustomerService@Harlequin.com.

TM is a trademark of Harlequin Enterprises ULC.

MIRA
22 Adelaide St. West, 41st Floor
Toronto, Ontario M5H 4E3, Canada
MIRABooks.com

HarperCollins Publishers
Macken House, 39/40 Mayor Street Upper,
Dublin 1, D01 C9W8, Ireland
www.HarperCollins.com

Printed in U.S.A.

Contents

Yesterday Once More

One

Julie Houser pushed the elevator button and stepped back to wait. An older woman whose office was on the same floor joined her and they exchanged smiles.

Absently, Julie glanced at her watch; she'd have plenty of time to finish unpacking tonight. Not wanting to prepare a meal, she considered picking up something from the local deli.

The elevator doors swooshed open, and the two women entered, then moved to the back, anticipating the five-thirty rush. By the time the car arrived at the ground floor it would be filled to capacity.

The next floor down it stopped, and three men boarded. Julie was concentrating on the lighted numbers above the door when the elevator came to a halt again. Another man got in and Julie squeezed herself into the far corner to make room.

The strap of her purse slid off her shoulder and as she eased it back up she felt someone's eyes on her. Accustomed to the appreciative gaze of men, Julie ignored the look and the man. The close scrutiny continued and she could practically feel his stare. Abruptly, Julie turned her head, wondering who he was.

But when she finally saw her admirer, she nearly choked. She felt chilled and on fire at the same moment. Her heart hammered wildly, and her hand tightened around the purse strap as if that would hold her upright.

"Daniel." The name fell from her lips as her eyes met those of the man standing closest to her. His dark eyes narrowed and an impassive expression masked his strikingly handsome face.

Unable to bear his gaze any longer, Julie glanced away.

The elevator stopped and everyone filed out until she stood there alone, her breath coming in uneven gasps. So soon? She'd only been back in Wichita for six days. Never had she dreamed she'd see Daniel so quickly. And in her own building. Was his office here? *Oh, please,* she begged, *not yet. I'm not ready.*

"You coming or going?" An irritated voice from the foyer broke into her thoughts and Julie moved out of the elevator on unsteady legs.

Her heels clicked noisily as she hurried across the marble floor and outside. The downtown sidewalks were filled with people rushing and Julie made her way through the crowds, uncertain where she'd parked her car that morning. Pausing at a red light, she realized she was walking in the wrong direction and turned around. Ten minutes later she'd found her car. Her hand trembled uncontrollably as she opened the door.

She felt as if she'd been running a marathon as she slipped into the driver's seat and pressed her forehead against the steering wheel. Nothing could have prepared her for this meeting. Three years had passed since she'd last seen Daniel. Years of change. She'd only been twenty-one when she'd fled in panic. He had cause to be bitter and she was sorry for what she'd done. The regret she felt at hurting the man she loved was almost more than she could bear.

And she had loved Daniel. The evening he'd placed the diamond engagement ring on her finger had been the happiest of her life.

Julie's thoughts drifted back to that night as she started her car and headed toward her apartment. Daniel had taken her to an elegant French restaurant. The lights were dim, and flickering candlelight sent shadows dancing over the white linen tablecloth. Julie tried not to reveal how ill-at-ease she was in such a fancy place. She'd been so worried that she'd pick up the wrong fork, or worse, dump her soup in her lap. She was so much in love with Daniel and desperately wanted to please him. Julie let herself remember . . .

"Happy?" he asked.

She glanced over the top of the gold-tasseled menu and nodded shyly. Everything on the menu was in French with an English translation below. Even with that she didn't recognize half of what was offered. "What would you suggest?"

Daniel set his menu aside, his expression preoccupied. Julie noticed that from the moment he'd picked her up that evening he'd been unnaturally quiet. Nerves tightened her stomach.

"Daniel, is something the matter?" she ventured.

He stared at her blankly.

"I'm not wearing the right kind of dress, am I?" She'd changed clothes three times before he'd arrived, parading each outfit in front of her mother until Margaret Houser had demanded that Julie stop being so particular. Any one of the outfits was perfectly fine.

"You're beautiful," Daniel whispered and the look in his eyes confirmed the softly murmured words.

Julie lowered her gaze. Her hand smoothed an imaginary crease from her crisp skirt. "I wanted everything to be perfect tonight."

"Why?"

Julie answered him with a delicate shrug of one shoulder. She wanted everything to be perfect for Daniel all the time. "You've been very quiet," she said. "Have I done something to upset you?"

He chuckled, shaking his head. "Oh, my adorable Julie, is it any wonder I love you?" His hand reached for hers. "I've been trying to find a way to ask you a question."

"But, Daniel, all you need to do is ask."

He sighed expressively. "It's not that simple."

Julie couldn't imagine what was troubling him. Daniel was always so thoughtful; he did everything possible to make her comfortable. When they met his friends, he kept her beside him because he knew how reserved she was. A thousand times over the past six months, he'd been so loving and caring that it hadn't taken Julie long to lose her heart to him. Slowly, he'd brought her into his world. He often took her to the Country Club and had taught her how to play golf and tennis. Gradually, his friends had become hers until, reticent though she was, Julie had flowered under his love.

But she knew that a blossom had its season and would soon wilt and droop. Maybe Daniel was trying to think of a way to let her down gently. Maybe he was tired of her. Maybe he didn't want to see her again. Panic filled her and she clutched the linen napkin in her lap, praying that she wouldn't make a fool of herself and burst into tears when he told her.

"I've been accepted into the law practice of McFife, Lawson and Garrison."

Julie jerked her head up. "That's wonderful news! Congratulations."

He smiled. "It's only a junior partnership."

"That's the firm you were hoping you'd get into."

"Yes, it is, for more reasons than you know."

Now she understood why he'd chosen such an expensive restaurant. "We're here to celebrate, then."

"Not quite yet." He leaned forward and clasped her hand in both of his. "These last few months have been the happiest of my life."

"Mine, too," she whispered.

"I know you're only twenty-one and I should probably wait a couple of years." He paused. "Julie . . ."

Her heart was pounding so loudly she was afraid he could hear it. Her eyes met his. "Yes, Daniel?"

"What I'm trying to say is . . . I love you, Julie. I've never kept that a secret. Now that I've been accepted by a good law firm and can offer you a future—will you marry me?"

Julie closed her eyes, savoring the warmth of his words.

"For heaven's sake," Daniel said. "Say something."

Julie bit her bottom lip, convinced she'd start to cry if she tried to speak.

"Julie," he pleaded.

She nodded wildly.

"Does that mean yes?"

Her voice trembled. "Yes, Daniel, yes! I love you so much. Nothing would make me happier than to spend the rest of my life with you."

The look in Daniel's eyes was enough to melt her bones. "I

didn't think anything this delicate could be so heavy," he said, pulling a jeweler's box from his jacket pocket. He lifted the lid, revealing a diamond so large, Julie gasped.

Tears blurred her gaze. "Oh, Daniel."

"Do you like it? The jeweler said we can exchange it if you'd prefer something different."

"It's the most beautiful ring I've ever seen."

"Here." He took her hand again and slipped the diamond onto her finger . . .

Julie fought to suppress the memory of that night. She pulled into the apartment parking lot and turned off the engine. Her fingers toyed with the gold chain that hung around her neck, seeking the diamond ring she'd kept there these past three years. She'd continue to wear it this way until it was back on her finger where it belonged. But after seeing Daniel today, Julie realized how difficult that would be. Daniel wouldn't forgive her easily.

Determined, she climbed out of her car and walked to her uninspired furnished apartment.

The bright, sunny place she'd left in California had been shared with good friends, people who cared about her.

The most difficult decision she'd ever made was to flee Wichita three years ago. The second hardest was to come back. But she had no choice. She loved Daniel, and if at all possible, she needed to set things right with him.

Julie hung her coat in the closet. She entered the living room to find several stacks of boxes, but felt too exhausted to unpack.

Until today, everything had happened exactly as she'd hoped. Her job had been lined up before the move, and she'd managed to locate an apartment with no lease that was within her budget, and in a relatively good area. The transition had been smooth.

But running into Daniel after only six days was something she hadn't counted on. She sat on the couch and rested her head against the back cushion for a few minutes.

Julie moved onto the floor, then crawled along the carpet until she got to the box containing their engagement portrait. She stared at the two smiling faces. They'd been so much in love. As tears filled her eyes, the happy faces swam in and out of her vision.

She traced her fingers across the image of Daniel's face and recalled their encounter that afternoon. His carefree smile had disappeared. The years had added a harshness to him, an arrogant aloofness. Even his sandy-colored hair was no longer casual but styled.

Julie's finger idly moved over the lean, proud jaw, pausing at the tiny cleft in his chin. She smiled sadly as she recalled how she'd loved to kiss him there. To tease him with her lips. And he'd been so wonderful, so understanding of her need to take things slow. Julie wondered if he regretted that now. There'd been many opportunities to consummate their love, but Daniel had always been the one to put a stop to it. She'd respected and loved him for that. He'd refused the ring when she'd tried to return it, which was how she'd come to wear it around her neck, keeping it close to her heart, no matter how many miles stood between them. Or how much pain.

Early the next morning Julie arrived at work intent on checking the list of occupants in her office complex. The Inland Empire Building housed fifteen floors of offices. As she studied the directory in the foyer, the listing for Daniel Van Deen, Attorney, seemed to leap off the board. Only one floor separated her from Daniel. For five of the six days she'd been in Wichita, they'd been this close without even knowing it.

A shiver ran down her spine and she slowly turned to see Daniel approaching the elevator, a newspaper wedged under his arm. He pushed the button and the wide doors opened. He stepped inside and turned around, his eyes locking with hers from across the foyer.

She watched as frustration swept over his features. His dark eyes narrowed as he stared back at her—and then the elevator doors glided shut.

Julie released a deep breath. Daniel hadn't forgiven her. The seething look he'd just sent her confirmed that.

Her legs felt unsteady as she took the next elevator up to the office of Cheney Trust and Mortgage Company. Grateful that she was the first one in that morning, she sat at her desk, trying to calm her nerves. Her hand trembled as she opened the bottom drawer of her desk and set her purse inside.

Sherry Adams, Julie's pretty blonde coworker, strolled in about fifteen minutes late. Their employer, Jack Barrett, had arrived before Sherry and had pointedly frowned at the empty desk, silently noting her absence. Julie had only been working at the office a few days and she didn't know Sherry well, but she could see that, despite her faults, the young divorcee was a valuable asset to the company.

"Morning," Julie said. "You seem to be in a good mood."

"I am." Sherry gave a brilliant imitation of a fashion model, her skirt flaring as she whirled around.

"I take it you want me to guess?" Julie asked.

Sherry shrugged playfully. "Not really. I just thought you'd be interested to know that I was asked out by the most eligible man in town."

"Congratulations."

"Thank you." Sherry smiled. "Actually, this is the culmination of five weeks of plotting and fine-tuning my womanly charms. I must admit, this guy's been one tough fish to catch."

"Well, double congratulations then," Julie said with a laugh.

Sherry sat and rolled her chair over to Julie's desk. "I don't suppose . . . you-know-who . . . is in yet?" Sherry inclined her head toward the closed door of Jack Barrett's office.

"'Fraid so," Julie said. "About fifteen minutes ago."

"Did he say anything about me being late?" Sherry asked, not looking the least bit concerned.

"Not to me he didn't."

"One of these days, old Barrett's going to fire me—and with good reason."

"I doubt that," Julie assured her. "Now tell me about your hot date."

"It's with Danny Van Deen."

Julie bit back a gasp and lowered her gaze, hoping to hide her surprise.

"He's a lawyer in the building," Sherry continued. "I've had my eye on him for a while. He's only taken a nibble so far, but it won't be long before I reel him in."

Julie forced her voice to maintain the same level of cheerfulness. "Good luck."

"Of course, I can't let him know how interested I am. That would be the kiss of death with a guy like Danny. But keeping my cool shouldn't be too difficult. By the time we're standing at the altar, he'll think it was his idea."

"I thought you didn't believe in wedded bliss anymore."

"Sure I do. It just didn't work out with Andy. I feel bad

about that, but we fell out of love with each other. Not much either of us could do about it, really."

"And . . . this Van Deen . . . has he ever been married?"

"Nope. I can't understand it. He's perfect husband material—handsome, intelligent and sensitive under that cool exterior of his. He dates often enough, but nothing ever comes of it. Until now." She laughed softly. "I'll have him at the altar before he knows what hit him."

"Good luck," Julie murmured.

"I'm going to need all the luck I can get," Sherry added, straightening her desk. "Are you taking the first lunch today?"

"If you'd like," Julie replied absently as she flipped through the pages of a report on her desk.

"Would you mind cutting it short so I can get out of here by twelve-thirty? I'll make it up to you later, I promise." Sherry's brilliant blue eyes held a pleading look. "There's a dress I saw this morning and I want to try it on. That's actually the reason I was late. Wait until Danny Van Deen sees me in that."

"Sure," Julie agreed. "I can be back early."

The remainder of the morning was quiet. The two women took turns answering the phone. Because she wasn't fully accustomed to the office, Julie relied on Sherry for help, which she willingly supplied. Sherry was a generous person, who seemed to harbor no ill against anyone. That was what made her divorce so hard to understand. Julie couldn't imagine a woman like Sherry giving up on something as important as a marriage.

Shortly after noon, Sherry reminded Julie of their agreement. Julie removed her purse from the desk drawer and stood, ready to leave for her lunch break when Jack Barrett strolled out of his office.

“Are you going for lunch?” the balding man asked.

“Yes,” Julie replied. “Would you like me to get you something?”

“Not today, thanks.” He handed her a large manila envelope. “But would you mind dropping this off at Daniel Van Deen’s office?”

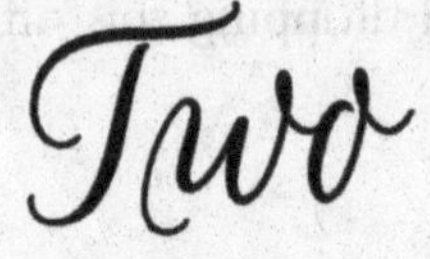

Panic filled Julie's eyes as she cast a pleading glance at Sherry.

"Go on. You might catch a glimpse of him and then you'll know what I mean!" Sherry seemed oblivious to the real reason behind Julie's reluctance.

Jack Barrett looked suspiciously from one to the other. "Is there a problem?"

"No problem," Sherry said.

Julie nodded her agreement, hoping to bow gracefully out of the situation.

"His office is one floor down. Number 919, I think." Sherry wrinkled her nose. "His name should be on the door."

Julie managed a smile and walked out of the office. By the time she reached Daniel's floor, the envelope felt as if it weighed fifty pounds.

Her hand was clammy as she turned the knob and entered the office.

A round-faced secretary glanced up and smiled. "Can I help you?"

The first thing Julie noticed was the woman's ring. She was married. But why should it matter that Daniel's secretary was married?

"I . . . have a package," she stammered. "For Mr. Van Deen. From Jack Barrett."

"Agnes, did you find—" Abruptly, Daniel had appeared, his words cut short as he caught sight of Julie. For a moment there was a hard look in his eyes, but then they softened and an expression Julie couldn't define came over his features.

"Mr. Barrett's sent the papers you asked about this morning," Agnes said, and although Julie heard her speak, it somehow felt as if she and Daniel were alone in the room.

"You did ask about the Macmillan papers?" The woman's words sounded distant.

"Yes," said Daniel, his words breaking the spell as he continued to stare at Julie.

The secretary took the envelope from Julie's limp hand, her sharp gaze shifting from one to the other. "Was that all?"

Julie snapped to attention. "Pardon?"

"Was there something else?"

"No," she mumbled. "Thank you."

A puzzled look appeared on the woman's face. "Thank you for dropping this off."

Julie smiled and turned, walking out of the office with her head held high.

The rest of the day passed in a blur and by the time she got home that night, Julie felt physically and mentally drained.

As she entered her apartment, Julie discovered her new phone had been installed. She decided to call her mother.

"Hi, Mom," she said, trying to sound cheerful.

"Julie. How are you?" Her mother sounded concerned. Margaret Houser lived in San Diego, where she'd moved when she was widowed. With Julie's older brother, Joe, in Montana, none of her family lived in Wichita anymore.

"Fine, Mom. Everything's fine."

"I'm so glad you called. I've been worried. Have you looked up any of your old high school friends?"

"Not yet," said Julie, though truthfully, she doubted she would. The only real friends she'd had in Wichita had gone elsewhere. "Mom." She took in a deep breath. "I've seen Daniel."

The concern in her mother's voice returned. "How is he?"

"We . . . we haven't talked. But I can tell he's changed. I feel like I hardly know him. He never understood why I left. He's not likely to understand why I came back."

"Don't be so sure, sweetheart." Her mother's voice was reassuring. "He's been hurt, and it makes sense that he's changed over the years."

"Mom, I don't think he'll talk to me."

"I've never known you to be a defeatist," her mother said in a supportive tone. "But I do worry about Daniel's mother. Be careful if you have to deal with her."

"I will." Julie's fingers flipped through the white pages of the telephone directory. Clara Van Deen's number was unlisted, but Daniel's was there. As her mother continued, Julie ran her finger back and forth over his name. The movement had a strange, calming effect on her, as if she were reaching out to him.

"Did you hear me, Julie?"

The question pulled Julie back into the conversation. "I'll be careful around Mrs. Van Deen, I promise."

"That woman can be completely unreasonable," her mother went on. "Don't forget, I was the one who had to deal with her after you left."

"I know and I'm sorry about that."

"I still think you did the right thing, honey."

Even after three years, Julie wasn't certain. She'd been so naive. There'd been many times she should have objected more strongly, should have forced a stop to the outrageous wedding plans. But like Daniel, she'd been overwhelmed by his mother's dominant personality. Even when Julie had tried to tell Mrs. Van Deen how she felt, her wishes were quickly pushed aside.

"Julie, are you still there?" her mother asked.

"Yes, I'm here. Sorry, Mom, it's been a long day. I'll talk to you next week."

"I'll be thinking about you."

"Thanks, Mom." Her mother's support had gotten her through some difficult times in the past and she was grateful to have it now.

Julie replaced the receiver, then slumped forward on the couch, burying her face in her hands. A tightness was building in her throat. It felt as though no time had passed. Her anxiety was as keen now as it had been three years ago.

Julie had been aware right from the start that Daniel's mother wanted her son to marry a more socially prominent girl. To her credit, Clara Van Deen had accepted Julie as Daniel's choice, but then she immediately set to work making Julie into something she'd never be. First came the makeover. Julie's hair was cut and styled to meet Clara's standards. Clara then purchased an entire wardrobe of what she claimed were outfits better suited for her new role as Daniel's wife.

Julie had found herself swallowing her pride a hundred times over. She tried to do exactly as Mrs. Van Deen asked. She wanted to make Daniel proud. He was climbing the corporate ladder and Julie didn't want to do anything that might jeopardize his success.

The out-of-control wedding plans were what had finally caused Julie to run. All she'd wanted was a simple ceremony with only their immediate families, but before she knew it, Daniel's mother had issued invitations to four hundred supposedly close and intimate friends she couldn't possibly insult by not including.

"But, Daniel," Julie had protested, "I don't know any of these people."

"Don't worry about it," Daniel had said, kissing the tip of her nose. He'd never fully understood the depth of her anxiety. "They'll love you as much as I do."

Daniel had negated any further protests with a kiss that left Julie unable to argue.

As the date drew closer, Julie's marriage to Daniel became the talk of the town, making Julie herself the reluctant focus of many a social gathering.

After each event, Mrs. Van Deen would run through a list of things that Julie had done wrong. No matter how hard Julie tried, there was always something worth criticizing.

"I can't take it anymore," Julie cried to her mother one night.

"You need to speak up," her mother advised. "Tell her how you feel."

"Don't you think I've tried?" Julie hid her face in her hands. "This isn't a wedding anymore, it's a Hollywood production."

Every day the pressure mounted. The wedding plans grew until what had started out as a simple ceremony was now a monster that threatened to devour Julie whole. Everything was beyond her control—the caterers, musicians, flower girl, bridesmaids and dresses. Even their honeymoon had been arranged by Mrs. Van Deen.

"Daniel, please listen to me," Julie had begged a week before the wedding. "I don't want any of this."

"Honey, I know you're nervous," he'd said soothingly. "But it's only one day and then we can go ahead with the rest of our lives."

But Julie had doubted they could. Every incident with his mother just reinforced her belief that the wedding was only the beginning. Eventually, Mrs. Van Deen would take over every aspect of their marriage, and when Daniel's mother made a large down payment on a house for them, Julie's suspicions were confirmed.

"It's her wedding gift to us," Daniel had explained. But the house was just a short distance from his mother's and the writing on the freshly painted walls was clear. His mother had insisted on helping Julie decorate. Such important details couldn't be left in the hands of an immature twenty-one-year-old, she'd implied.

"Doesn't it bother you that she's taken over our lives?" Julie had asked plaintively.

She could see that Daniel did care, but would do nothing.

"For the first time since Dad died, my mother has a purpose. Can't you see how much happier she is now?"

But Julie couldn't see anything other than a growing case of claustrophobia.

That night she couldn't sleep, and by the time the sun rose the next morning, Julie had packed her bags.

"You can't do this," her mother protested when she realized her daughter's plans.

"I've got to," Julie said, her eyes red from crying. "I wouldn't be marrying Daniel. I'd be marrying his mother."

"But the wedding's in five days!"

"There isn't going to be a wedding," Julie said adamantly. "What should have been a simple and beautiful ceremony has turned into a three-ring circus and I won't be part of it."

"But Julie—"

"I know what you're going to say," she interrupted. "But this isn't just pre-wedding jitters. Daniel and I are never alone anymore. His mother's taken over every aspect of our relationship."

"Talk to him, sweetheart. Explain how you feel," Margaret advised. "At least do that much. This is a serious step you're considering."

Julie took her mother's advice and went to Daniel's office. They met as he was on his way out the door.

"Julie." He seemed surprised to see her.

"I need to talk to you," said Julie, her hands tightly clenched.

Daniel glanced at his watch. "Can it wait? I'm short on time."

She shook her head forcefully. "No. It can't wait."

Daniel seemed to notice her agitated manner. He pressed a hand to the small of her back and led her into his office. "Honey, I know things have been hectic lately, but it's bound to improve once we're married. We'll have lots of time together then, I promise."

"That's just it, Daniel," Julie said. "We aren't going to be married."

Daniel inhaled sharply. "What do you mean? What's this all about?"

With a trembling finger, she removed the diamond ring and held it out to him. "I can't marry you, Daniel."

"Julie!" He was completely stunned. "Put that ring back where it belongs!"

"I can't."

He slumped onto the arm of his office chair. "I don't understand."

"I didn't expect you would." Julie bowed her head. "Do you remember last week when I suggested we drive across the border and elope? You laughed." Her voice wavered. "But I was serious, Daniel. Dead serious."

"My mother would never forgive us if we did something like that."

Julie sighed. "That's the problem, Daniel. You wouldn't dream of crossing your mother, but you don't seem to care what all of this is doing to me."

"My mother loves you."

"She loves the woman she's created. Haven't you noticed? Look at me, Daniel. Am I the same woman you proposed to three months ago?"

Daniel averted his eyes. "I don't know what you're talking about."

"Look at me," she repeated. "My hair is different, my nails are manicured, and my . . . my clothes . . ." Tears welled up in her eyes as her voice broke. "Do you realize she expects me to call her every morning to ask what I should wear? I haven't worn a pair of jeans in weeks," she exclaimed. "I'm slowly being molded into what she thinks your ideal woman should be. I can't take it anymore."

Daniel stood, threading his fingers through his hair. "Why didn't you refuse?"

"Don't you think I've tried? No one listens to me—not

even you, Daniel. What I think or feel doesn't seem to matter anymore. I'm . . . not sure how I feel about you anymore."

"Is that so?" he demanded.

"It is," Julie said defensively. "I want out. Here." Again, she tried to return the ring.

Daniel stared at her for a long moment before dropping his gaze to the diamond in her hand. He turned and stalked to the window on the far side of the room, his back to her. "Keep it."

"But, Daniel," she began. "I'm—"

"I said keep it," he broke in. He turned to face her, his mouth a rigid line. His dark eyes were clouded with hurt and pain. "Now get out of my life and stay out."

Tears ran down her face as she drove straight to her mother's. The clothes, the wedding dress—she left everything Mrs. Van Deen had purchased strewn across her bed. Julie then loaded her suitcases into the back of her car and drove to her aunt's in California.

That had been three years ago and every night since she'd wondered if she'd done the right thing. She straightened on the sofa. The guilt had been weighing on her, but her love for Daniel had never died. She'd hurt him and his mother. Right or wrong, there were better ways to handle the situation.

Now, she'd come back to ask for Daniel's and Mrs. Van Deen's forgiveness.

Three

The next morning, Julie waited in the Inland Empire foyer for Daniel to enter the building. She needed to talk to him. She'd dreamed of it for months, praying that a heartfelt apology would wipe out the pain she'd caused him. Then—and only then—could they start to rebuild their relationship.

She spotted him the moment he pushed past the double glass doors.

Julie watched him approach the elevator. Without a sound, she moved closer so that when the doors opened, she could enter behind him.

Frustration knotted her stomach as two other people boarded the elevator.

If Daniel was aware of her, he didn't let on. But Julie had never been more aware of anyone or anything in her life. She felt his presence beside her. The years had been good to him. He'd been boyishly attractive three years ago; even though he'd lost the relaxed, carefree quality he'd had then, he was still devastatingly handsome. No wonder Sherry had set her sights on him.

A long moment passed and Julie yearned to reach out and touch him, anything to force him to acknowledge that she was there. He couldn't ignore her forever. Sooner or later, they'd have to talk.

He stared straight ahead as the creases around his mouth hardened. Julie's stomach tightened. She couldn't take her eyes off him. His features were so achingly familiar, but on closer inspection, the changes in his appearance were even more prominent. Streaks of gray mingled with the sandy-colored hair at the side of his head and Julie had to restrain herself from brushing her hand across his temple. She leaned against the back wall for support.

The two strangers exited on the fifth floor, leaving Julie alone with Daniel. This was exactly what she'd hoped for, and yet her tongue was suddenly uncooperative. There was so much she wanted to say, and she'd practiced exactly how to begin so many times. But now that the opportunity was there, she found herself incapable of uttering a single word.

"Hello, Daniel," she managed after an awkward silence. The air between them felt charged, adding to Julie's discomfort.

Daniel ignored her, staring straight ahead.

"We need to talk," she continued, her voice barely above a whisper.

Silence.

"Daniel, please."

The thin line of his lips tightened as he directed his attention away from her.

She laid her hand gently on his forearm and sighed. The hopelessness of the situation overwhelmed her. The man who stood beside her became a watery blur as tears filled her eyes.

Julie dropped her hand. The elevator stopped and she watched him leave.

Julie was grateful to be the first one in the office again. She collapsed into her chair, fighting off waves of nausea. Pain pounded at her temples. It was too soon. She'd been expecting too much. Daniel needed more time; she had to be patient. When he was ready, she'd be waiting.

Sherry strolled into the office five minutes early, a wide grin on her face. "Morning," she said.

Julie pretended to be absorbed in reading a paper on her desk.

"Aren't you going to ask how my hot date went?"

Julie didn't want to hear it, but knew she should play along. "Sure." She swallowed hard and banished the mental image of Daniel holding Sherry in his arms.

"Awful," Sherry admitted with a wry grin. "Talk about disappointing! I could've had two heads for all the attention he paid to me and my new dress."

"Maybe he was worried about a case or something." Julie couldn't repress her delight. If Sherry became involved with Daniel, things would become unpleasant.

"Or something is right," Sherry shot back.

"If last night was such a disaster, how come you're so cheerful this morning?"

"Because Danny apologized and asked me out again this weekend," Sherry said. "And when he takes a woman out, he spares no expense. We went to the best restaurant in town—what a waste. Danny barely touched his dinner."

Danny! Julie shuddered at the casual use of his name. Daniel used to hate it. No one called him Danny.

Julie smiled stiffly. "I hope everything works out better next time."

"It will," Sherry said confidently. "Next time, he won't be able to take his eyes off me." She laughed lightly. "I won't let him." She smiled and hung her jacket in the closet.

"Are you doing anything special this weekend?" Sherry asked a while later.

"Painting my living room," Julie said. Such distractions were vital at the moment. Anything to keep her mind from the thought of Sherry and Daniel falling in love. Throughout the morning, Julie debated whether or not she should say something to Sherry. But what? She had no claim to Daniel now.

When Julie woke on Saturday morning, the sun was shining. It was far too beautiful a day to spend indoors. She recalled how Daniel's mother loved to garden; Clara Van Deen grew the most gorgeous irises.

When Julie climbed into her car, her destination had been the paint store, but as she drove, she found herself on the street that led to Clara's house instead.

She pulled to a stop across from the lovely two-story home with the meticulously landscaped front yard. A fancy sports car was parked in the driveway. Julie doubted that Mrs. Van Deen would ever drive something like that.

The long circular driveway was bordered on both sides by flowering red azaleas. Julie stared at the house for a long time, undecided about whether or not she should approach Daniel's mother, having had no luck with Daniel himself. She wondered what had become of Clara Van Deen, realizing that she could be a greater challenge than her son.

No. Julie shook her head. Now wasn't the time. Not when she was dressed in jeans and a sweatshirt. She'd need to look and feel her best when she faced Mrs. Van Deen. Her desire to get the confrontation over with as quickly as possible would benefit neither of them. Before she could change her mind, she pulled away from the curb and headed toward the closest shopping center.

The paint she chose for the living room was an antique white that would brighten the place up. Her spirits lifted as she returned to the apartment. She was actually looking forward to a quiet afternoon painting.

She unhooked the drapes and carefully laid them across the back of the sofa. As she began to spread out newspapers, a knock at the door caught her off guard. She rushed to answer, stumbling over the ottoman on her way.

Stooping to rub her injured shin, she opened the door.

Daniel stood there, and he did not look amused.

"Leave my mother alone," he said.

Julie stared back at him, completely speechless.

"Did you hear what I said?" he demanded, his expression cold.

She nodded.

"I saw you parked in front of her house this morning. Stay away from her, Julie. I'm warning you."

Julie jutted her chin out defiantly. "The time will come when I'll have to talk to her." She retreated into the living room.

Daniel entered and followed, closing the door behind him. "Not if I can help it."

Julie turned to face him. "You can't."

"Don't bet on it," he snarled.

"Daniel, I've come a thousand miles to talk to you and your mother."

"Then you wasted your time because neither of us cares to see you."

Julie met his gaze. "I didn't come back to hurt either of you. I've come to make amends."

"Amends?" He threw the word back at her as he paced the carpet, his hands buried deep in his pockets. "Do you really think you could ever undo the humiliation I suffered when you walked out?"

"I'm sure I can't, but I'd like to try. I was young and stupid. Don't you understand? A thousand times I've regretted what I did—"

"Regretted," he repeated sarcastically. "I used to dream you'd say that to me. Now that you have, it means nothing. Nothing," he muttered. "I look at you and I don't feel a thing. You came back to apologize? Fine. You've made your peace. But don't go to my mother, bringing up the past. She has no desire to see you. Whatever you and I shared is over and done with."

Julie closed her eyes, warding off the sting in his voice. She wouldn't be so easily swayed from her goal. "You don't mean that," she whispered.

"I've blocked you from my mind," he continued. "But unfortunately, my mother has never been the same. I can't forgive you for what you've done to her."

"But that's the reason I've come back," Julie said, trying to stay calm although her stomach churned uncomfortably. "I want to make it up to you both. Can't you see how sorry I am? I never stopped thinking about you. Not for a day. Not for a minute. You've haunted me all this time."

"Do you expect me to pat you on the head and tell you everything's just fine? That we can pick up where we left off?" His eyes narrowed. "It's not that easy."

Julie struggled to keep her composure. "You've changed so much." She raised her hand to his mouth, her touch light against his lips. Daniel abruptly jerked his head away and took a step back.

"I don't want to hurt you or your mother," she said again.

"Then leave before you do."

"I can't. This is too important to me. I've got to make things right."

"You'll never be able to do that. Sometimes it's best for the past to remain buried."

"Believe me, I've tried to put this behind me. I can't."

Daniel looked exhausted. "Leave, Julie. You'll only make everything worse."

"I won't go," she insisted. "Not until I've talked to your mother. Not until I pay her back every penny."

"Why now?" He sank onto the sofa and leaned forward until his elbows rested on his knees.

"You're not the only one who's changed, Daniel. I'm not a naive twenty-one-year-old anymore. I'm an adult willing to admit I made a terrible mistake. I was wrong to have run away instead of confronting the problems we faced. I regret what I did, but more than that, I've realized there isn't anyone I could ever feel as strongly about as you. Whenever another man held me, I found myself wishing he was you. It's you I came back for, Daniel."

He stared at her disbelievingly. "You mean to tell me what? That your conscience hasn't quit bothering you?"

"Yes, but it's so much more than that. I want to make everything up to you."

"Well, that's fine and dandy, Julie. You've come here, we've talked and now you can go. I absolve you of everything. Just stay out of my life—understand?"

Pain flashed across his face, and for a fleeting moment, Julie saw a glimmer of the old Daniel. Something was troubling him, something deep beneath the surface.

"Daniel." She moved to sit beside him, wishing she could comfort the man she loved. She weighed her words carefully. "Something's wrong. Won't you tell me what it is?"

He looked right through her and Julie knew his thoughts were elsewhere.

He stood, impatiently shaking off his mood. "Leave my mother alone," he said again. "Do you understand?"

"I'm so sorry." Julie hung her head in defeat. Everything she'd tried to explain had meant nothing.

As he started to go, she stood and faced him. "I promise not to do anything to hurt her. Will you trust me?"

"I shouldn't." A nerve moved in his jaw and again Julie was aware of some internal struggle. Without another word, he walked out of the apartment.

Julie remained exactly where he'd left her, numb and completely unaware of how much time passed. Finally forcing herself into action, she finished covering the floor with newspapers and opened the first gallon of paint.

She worked until well past midnight. By the time she finished, the room was barely recognizable. The sense of accomplishment helped lift her spirits.

Her hand skimmed the ring dangling from her neck. Her body ached as she cleaned the paintbrushes under the kitchen faucet, but her mind raced.

Maybe Daniel was right. Maybe contacting Clara Van Deen would do more harm than good.

Later that night, as she lay in bed, staring at the darkened ceiling, Julie couldn't let the thought go. She'd come this far. The clock dial illuminated the time—2:00 a.m. Although she was exhausted, she hadn't been able to sleep. Julie pounded her pillow and rolled over to face the wall.

Write to her.

The idea suddenly flashed through her mind. She threw back the covers and sat up, eager to search for a pen and pad.

Sitting on the bed, Julie drafted the letter:

Dear Mrs. Van Deen:

I know this letter will come as a shock to you. My hope is that you're willing to hear what I have to say.

I wonder if you've ever done anything in your life that you've regretted. Something that's haunted you over the years. Something you'd give anything to do over again. I have. For three years I've carried the guilt of what I did to you and Daniel. I know there's nothing I can say that would ever undo the embarrassment or hurt I caused, but I do beg your forgiveness, and ask that you allow me to make this up to you in some way. I'd do anything for that opportunity.

You'll find my address above, along with my phone number. Please contact me if you're willing to talk.

Julie read the letter again the following morning and typed it into her computer, printed it and mailed it off. The next move would be Mrs. Van Deen's.

A week passed before Julie received a response, but she saw Daniel almost every day in between. Not once did he speak to her, but his eyes held an unspoken warning that made Julie wonder if his mother had told him about the letter.

The scented envelope addressed in delicate handwriting caught her attention the minute she picked up her mail on Saturday afternoon. Julie's heart soared.

She'd hardly got inside her apartment before she ripped

open the envelope. Her fingers shook as she removed the single sheet of stationery.

It read simply: *Saturday at four.*

"That's today," Julie said aloud. Frantically, she glanced at the kitchen clock. It was just after one—only three hours to prepare. Surely, Mrs. Van Deen had done that deliberately, hoping to catch her off guard. But she'd be disappointed. Julie was ready. She knew what she had to say and she was eager to finally say it.

After carefully surveying her wardrobe, Julie decided on a simple blue business suit. It was the same one she'd worn to her job interview with Mr. Barrett six weeks earlier. She wanted to show Mrs. Van Deen that she wasn't an awkward young girl anymore.

At precisely four o'clock, Julie pulled into the curved driveway. Mrs. Batten, the elderly cook who'd been with the family for years, answered the door. She didn't appear to recognize Julie.

"Yes?" The woman's tone wasn't particularly civil.

"Good afternoon. I'm here to see Mrs. Van Deen."

Mrs. Batten hesitated.

"We have an appointment today at four," Julie added.

Again the woman paused, but then stepped aside, allowing Julie to enter the foyer.

The interior of the house was exactly as she remembered it. The same mahogany table and vase sat beside the carpeted stairway that led to the second floor. To her left was the salon, as Mrs. Van Deen called it; at one time Julie had regarded it as a torture chamber. To her right was the massive dining room.

"This way," Mrs. Batten instructed, her voice only slightly less frosty.

Like an errant student being led to the principal's office, Julie followed two steps behind the elderly woman. She was escorted through the house to the back garden Mrs. Van Deen prized so highly.

"You may wait here." Mrs. Batten pointed to a pair of cast-iron chairs separated by a small table.

Julie did as she was told.

"Would you like something to drink while you wait?" the woman asked, refusing to look at Julie.

"No. Thank you," she mumbled, clasping her hands in her lap.

Fifteen minutes passed and still Julie waited. Daniel's mother was doing this deliberately. Testing her. But Julie was determined to sit there until midnight if necessary.

She tensed at the sound of footsteps behind her.

"Hello, Julie." The words were said in a low and trembling voice.

Julie stood and turned to see Daniel's mother—frail and obviously weak. She leaned heavily on a cane, her back hunched, and yet she was elegant as ever. Her hair was completely white now and she was thin, far thinner than Julie remembered.

"Sit down." Mrs. Van Deen motioned with her hand and Julie perched on the hard metal chair, grateful for its support.

Daniel's mother took the seat beside her, both hands resting on her wooden cane. "To say I was surprised to receive your letter would be an understatement."

Julie's grip on her purse tightened. "I'd imagine so."

"Does Daniel know you're back?"

Julie nodded. "We work in the same building."

Mrs. Van Deen didn't comment, but smiled weakly.

The changes Julie had noticed in Daniel were nothing compared to those she saw in his mother.

"You have a Wichita address?"

"Yes." Julie's voice quavered slightly. "I moved back here."

"Why?"

"Because—" Julie swallowed "—because I hope to make amends and I didn't think I could do that if I flew in for a weekend."

Mrs. Van Deen smiled knowingly. "That was wise, dear."

"I came because I deeply regret my actions—"

"Do you still love my son?"

Julie focused on her hands, which were tightly coiled around the small leather purse. The question was one she'd avoided since her return, afraid of the answer. "Yes," she admitted. "Yes, I do, but I . . ."

"But you hate me?"

"Oh, no." Julie met her gaze. "The only person I've hated over the years was myself."

The old woman's smile was thin. "There comes a time in a woman's life when she can look at things more clearly. In my life, it comes as I face death. As you've probably guessed, I'm not well."

Julie's vision blurred with sudden tears. She hadn't expected Daniel's mother to be so kind or understanding.

"There's no need to cry. I've lived a full life, but my heart is weak and I can't do much of anything these days. Ill health gives one an opportunity to gain perspective."

"Then you forgive me?" Julie whispered, her voice close to cracking.

The frail hand tightened around the cane. "No."

Julie closed her eyes. An apology would have been too easy; she should have realized that. Daniel's mother would want so much more. "What can I do?" Julie asked softly.

"I want you to forgive me." Mrs. Van Deen's voice was gentle.

She reached across the space that separated them and patted Julie's hand. "I was the reason you did what you did. I've buried that guilt deep in my heart. I behaved like an interfering old woman."

Julie noticed several tears sliding down Mrs. Van Deen's weathered cheek, and knew that her own face was wet, too.

"We've both been fools," Julie said.

"But there's no fool like an old one." Mrs. Van Deen wiped her tears with the back of her hand. She looked pale and tired, but her eyes held an unmistakable radiance.

As if on cue, Mrs. Batten carried in a silver tray with a coffeepot and two china cups. Mrs. Van Deen waited until the woman left before asking Julie to do the honors.

Julie poured the coffee with a smile, stirring sugar into Mrs. Van Deen's before presenting it to her.

Mrs. Van Deen nodded approvingly. "Very good."

Julie laughed, perhaps her first real laugh in three years. "I had a marvelous teacher." She sat back and crossed her legs, her own cup and saucer in one hand.

"Tell me what you've done with yourself all this time." Mrs. Van Deen looked genuinely interested.

"I went to school in California for a while and lived with my aunt. My mother joined me later on and I got a job as a bank teller before working my way into the loan department. From there, I got a job in a trust company. Nothing too exciting."

"What about men?"

The abrupt question flustered Julie. "I . . . dated some."

"Anyone serious?"

Julie shook her head. "No one—did Daniel find anyone . . . serious?"

The former radiance dimmed. "He never tells me."

"He's changed."

"Yes, he has," his mother admitted. "And not for the better, I fear. He's an intense young man. Some days he reminds me of . . ." She paused.

"Mrs. Van Deen, are you okay?"

"I'm fine, Julie. You sound like Daniel. He's always worried about me. And please, I'd prefer it if you called me Clara."

Even when she was engaged to Daniel, Julie had never been granted the privilege of using Mrs. Van Deen's first name. Permission to do so now confirmed their new understanding.

"All right then. Clara." The name felt awkward on Julie's tongue.

"I do have regrets." The older woman looked as if she were someplace far away. "I would so have liked to hold a grandchild."

Julie took a sip of her coffee, hoping the warm liquid would ease the tightness in her throat.

"I know what it's cost you to come here," Mrs. Van Deen continued. "You have far more character than I gave you credit—" The woman paused to take several deep, labored breaths. "I'm sorry, Julie, but I'm suddenly not feeling very well." Mrs. Van Deen raised her hand to cover her heart.

A wave of panic swept through Julie. Daniel's mother wasn't just weak, she was on the verge of collapse. "I'm calling for help," Julie said.

She retrieved her cell phone from her purse and dialed 911, trying to remain calm as she relayed the address to the operator.

After being told that an ambulance was on its way, Julie struggled to recall the lessons she'd taken in CPR. She moved to kneel next to Daniel's mother, taking one weathered hand in hers.

"Don't worry, child," Clara assured her. Her voice was weak.

Julie began loosening the older woman's clothes, words of reassurance tumbling from her lips. Clara was slowly losing consciousness. How soon would help arrive? Julie eased her onto the ground. Sirens could be heard in the distance and Julie breathed a little easier.

The ambulance pulled up and Julie stumbled aside as two men approached and set to work on the now-unconscious woman. They lifted her onto a stretcher, then transported her to the waiting vehicle.

Julie's heart pounded wildly as she followed close behind. Mrs. Batten joined her on the front lawn and the pair watched as the EMTs loaded Daniel's mother into the ambulance.

"What happened?" Mrs. Batten asked. Her face was pale.

"We were just talking," Julie explained. "And then she suddenly had trouble breathing. She just . . . collapsed."

Mrs. Batten raised her hand to her chest in silent prayer.

"I'm going to the hospital," Julie said. She knew she'd go crazy waiting around here.

The hospital was a whirlwind of activity when she got there. She almost collided with Daniel as she hurried down the wide corridor. He stopped and glared at her accusingly, as though he blamed her for his mother's poor health. He entered the waiting room, leaving Julie alone in the hall.

Daniel didn't want her there, but she couldn't leave without knowing how Clara was.

The hospital's chapel offered her the solitude she sought. She sat in the back pew and covered her face with her hands. An eternity seemed to pass before she felt strong enough to stand.

Daniel was pacing the small waiting area when she returned. He swiveled to face her as she walked into the room.

"Don't ask me to leave," she said.

He ran his fingers through his already rumpled hair. "The EMT told me you're the one who called in time to save her life."

Julie didn't answer. Her arms cradled her stomach as she paced alongside him. They didn't speak. They didn't touch. But Julie couldn't remember a closer communication with anyone. It was as if they were emotionally connected, offering each other hope.

The universe seemed to come to a stop as soon as the doctor stepped into the room. "She's resting comfortably," he announced.

"Thank God," Daniel said. He released a shuddering breath.

"Your mother's a stubborn woman. She insists on seeing both of you. But, please, take only a minute. Is that clear?"

Julie glanced at Daniel. "You go."

"She asked for both," the doctor repeated. "She was very specific about that."

Clara Van Deen looked as pale as the sheets she was lying against when Julie and Daniel entered her room in the intensive care unit.

She opened her eyes and attempted to smile when she saw them. "My dears," she said, "I'm so sorry to cause you all this trouble."

"Don't worry about that," Daniel whispered. "You need to rest."

"Not yet," she murmured. "Julie, you said you'd do anything to gain my forgiveness?"

"Yes," Julie said, her voice hardly sounding like her own.

"And Daniel, will you do one last thing for me?"

"Anything. You know that."

Clara Van Deen's tired eyes closed and opened again as if she was on the brink of slipping away. "I would like the two of you to marry—for my sake."

Four

Julie woke in the gray light of early morning. She hadn't slept well and imagined Daniel hadn't either. They'd hardly spoken as they left the hospital; they'd scarcely even looked at each other. The tight clenching of Daniel's jaw said plenty about his feelings on the matter of any marriage between them.

When she'd arrived home Julie changed into something comfortable and made herself a cup of strong coffee. She sat in the living room, bracing her feet against the coffee table as she slouched on the sofa. Daniel's mother was so different from what Julie had been expecting. She'd been so sure that Clara would lash out at her, but instead she'd discovered a sick, gentle woman who suffered many regrets. Julie longed to ease Clara's mind, knowing that as she lay weak in a hospital bed, facing death, she needed the assurance that her son would be happy.

But, Julie also knew that she and Daniel could never grant her request, not when Daniel resented Julie so much.

Later that evening, as she lay awake in bed, a calm came over her. She loved Daniel, had never stopped—and, if possible, found she loved him even more now. Every time she looked at him, she felt it. As she closed her eyes, Julie reminded herself of the reasons she'd returned to Wichita.

When she got to the hospital the next morning, the parking lot was full. Although she hadn't reached a decision, Julie felt a sense of peace. She'd talk to Daniel—really talk—and together they'd decide what to do.

A faint antiseptic odor greeted her as she pushed through the glass doors that led to the hospital foyer.

Daniel was in the waiting area outside the intensive care unit. He glanced up as Julie approached, his eyes heavy from lack of sleep.

"Good morning," she said. "How's Clara?"

"My mother," he returned stiffly, "is resting comfortably."

Julie took the seat across from him. "Can we talk?" Sitting on the edge of the cushion, she leaned toward him, clasping her hands together.

Daniel shrugged.

"Did you sleep at all?" she asked.

A quick shake of his head confirmed her suspicions. "I couldn't. What about you?"

"Some." She noticed that Daniel wouldn't look at her, not directly. Even when she'd entered the room his gaze had met hers only briefly before shifting to something behind her.

"The doctor's with her now," he said.

"Daniel." Julie found it difficult to speak. "What are we going to do?"

His laughter was mirthless, chilling. "What do you mean,

do? My mother didn't know what she was saying. They gave her so many drugs yesterday she wasn't thinking straight. Today she won't remember a word."

Julie didn't believe that any more than she thought Daniel did, but if he wished to avoid the issue there was little she could say.

They sat in silence, his eyes still refusing to meet hers, which allowed Julie the opportunity to study him. The lines on his face were more pronounced now, deeply etched with his concern. His brow was furrowed. Julie knew that Clara was all the family he had.

The coffee machine across the hall caught her attention and Julie walked over to it, retrieving enough change from her purse for two cups. She added sugar to each and cream to Daniel's. He glanced up briefly as he accepted the paper cup. He looked surprised that she remembered how he liked his coffee.

They both set their cups aside and stood when the doctor came into the room.

"How is she?" Daniel asked.

"She's very weak, but better than we'd expected. The fact that she survived the night is nothing short of a miracle." The doctor paused to study them both. "Your mother seems to be a fighter. And since she's come this far, the chances of her making a complete recovery are good."

Julie felt as though a weight had been lifted from her shoulders.

"She's resting now, and both of you should do the same."

Daniel nodded. "I didn't want to leave until I was sure she'd be all right."

The doctor shook his head. "I don't know what you talked about last night, but it's certainly made a world of difference in her attitude. She's been improving ever since."

Julie's eyes met Daniel's. All the color had drained from his face.

"Go home and get some rest. There's nothing you can do here. I'll call you the minute there's any change."

"Thank you, Doctor," Daniel said.

They remained standing even after the doctor left. Daniel closed his eyes and released a long sigh.

"Can I give you a lift?" Julie asked quietly. Daniel didn't look as if he was in any condition to drive.

He shook his head. "No."

"You'll call me if you hear anything?"

Daniel nodded that he would.

"Everything's going to work out for the best," Julie whispered. She turned and walked away, ready to head home to her apartment.

Julie didn't mean to fall asleep, but after calling her mother to tell her about Clara Van Deen's attack, she decided to stretch out on the sofa and rest her eyes for a few minutes. The next thing she knew, someone was knocking on the door.

Julie glanced at her wristwatch and was shocked to see that it was after two.

"Just a minute," she called and hurriedly slid her feet back into her shoes as she ran her fingers through her tangled hair. "Who is it?" she asked before releasing the lock.

"It's Daniel."

Julie immediately threw open the door. "Is she all right? I mean, she's not worse, is she?"

"No, she's doing remarkably well."

"Thank God," Julie whispered as she stepped aside to let Daniel in.

"Did I wake you?" he asked.

With a wry smile, Julie nodded. "It's a good thing you did or I wouldn't be able to sleep tonight."

"They let me see her for a few minutes," Daniel said. He stood uneasily in the center of the living room.

"And?"

"And—" he paused and ran a hand through his hair "—she asked when we were planning to have the wedding."

Julie sat down on the sofa. "I was afraid of that."

Daniel remained standing. "Apparently, she's been talking to the nurses about us. The head nurse told me she firmly believes that the fact you and I are going to be married was what kept my mother alive last night."

"And," Julie finished for him, "you're afraid that telling her otherwise could kill her."

Daniel moved to the far side of the room and spoke with his back to Julie. "I talked to the doctor again. He explained that if my mother can grow strong enough in the next few months, there's a possibility that heart surgery could correct her condition."

"That's wonderful news!"

He turned to her with a hard look in his eyes. "Yes, in some ways it's given me reason to hope. But in others . . ." He shook his head and let the rest of his words fade away. "Why did you come back, Julie? Why couldn't you have left well enough alone?"

"I already explained," she answered. "I want—no," she amended, "I need your forgiveness."

"My forgiveness," he repeated and lifted his head so she could read the conflict in his eyes. "I wish to God I'd never seen you again."

The pain of his words slammed into her and she struggled to remain composed. "But I am here and I won't leave until I've accomplished what I came to do."

He muttered a curse under his breath. "I don't know what to do. I can't see us getting married. Not with the way I feel about you now."

"No," she agreed. "I can't see adding that complication to our relationship."

"We don't have a relationship," he reminded her. Then he left the apartment, slamming the door behind him.

On her way home from work on Monday, Julie dropped by the hospital with a flower arrangement. Mrs. Van Deen remained in intensive care. Julie doubted she'd be able to see her, but when she reached the nurses' station, she was informed that special permission had been granted for her to visit. The same five-minute limitation applied.

Clara Van Deen opened her eyes and gave Julie a feeble smile as she entered the room.

"I'm so pleased you came," Clara whispered, reaching out to squeeze Julie's hand.

"I can only stay a few minutes," Julie told her in a soft voice.

"I know."

"How are you feeling?"

"Much better now that I know Daniel will be happy."

A strangling sensation gripped Julie's throat. She couldn't think of any way to tell Clara that she and Daniel weren't going to be married.

"It was all my fault," Clara said. "With you and Daniel married, I can undo some of the harm I did."

"But . . ." Julie groaned inwardly. "Marriage isn't something to rush into. I'm still very much in love with Daniel, but he's been badly hurt and needs time to forget the past."

Clara closed her eyes. "Daniel loves you. He always has. His pride's been hurt, but he'll come around. I know he will."

So much for that argument, Julie mused, recalling her conversation with him the day before.

"Trust me, Julie," Clara said, opening her eyes once more. "The reason he's hurting so much is because he loves you."

The nurse came into the room. "I'm sorry, but I'm going to have to ask you to leave now."

Julie leaned down and gently kissed Clara on the cheek. "You rest now. I'll stop in tomorrow afternoon."

"Tell Daniel you love him," she whispered, her voice barely audible. "He needs to know that."

Julie didn't answer one way or the other. How could she admit that to a man who fought her every chance he got? Julie couldn't set herself up for that kind of pain.

Daniel was in the waiting room when she entered. He stood and looked at her expectantly.

"She seems much better today," Julie said.

He nodded. "Can we go someplace to talk?" he asked.

The hospital cafeteria was almost empty, with only a few people sitting at tables near the window.

"Go ahead and sit. I'll bring us something. Iced tea?" he suggested, arching a questioning brow.

The day had been warm for early spring and Julie smiled her thanks.

He carried the two glasses on an orange tray, setting them down before taking a seat himself.

"I talked to Dr. Givens," he said, staring into his tea.

Julie's hand curled around the icy glass, the cold seeping up her arm.

"He seems to feel that if we . . . if I . . . were to disappoint my mother over this marriage it could be detrimental to her recovery."

The cool sensation stopped at Julie's heart. "Does this mean you want to go ahead with the wedding?" she asked softly.

"No." He sighed. "A marriage between us would never work. Any possibility of finding happiness together ended when you left. But my mother's health—"

"Daniel," she said, her voice gaining strength, "I know you may find this hard to believe, but I never stopped loving you."

His gaze hardened. "If you'd loved me, you'd never have walked out. I don't think you know what it is to love, Julie."

Her mouth trembled with the effort to restrain an angry retort. She'd done what Daniel's mother suggested; she'd humbled herself. Daniel had to know how difficult it was for her to say those words and yet he threw her declaration of love back in her face. "If you honestly believe that, there's no point in having this discussion." She stood and hurried from the room. Tears blurred her vision as she made her way to the parking lot.

Before she could reach her vehicle, a hand gripped her upper arm, spinning her around.

"Running away again?" he said coldly. "Not this time. I need you to marry me, Julie. As soon as I can make the arrangements."

"I'd have to be crazy to marry a man like you!"

"Do you want to carry the guilt of my mother's death on your shoulders? If you leave now, that's what'll happen. It'll kill her. Are you ready to face that, Julie? Or don't you care?"

Julie pulled herself free of his grip. "Daniel," she said, "marriage is sacred."

"Not always," he insisted. "This'll be one of convenience."

"Will it stay that way?" Her questioning eyes sought his.

"Yes." His gaze was steady. "I couldn't touch you."

Biting her inner cheek, Julie refused to reveal the hurt he'd inflicted. It shouldn't matter. Considering how he felt, Julie didn't want Daniel to make love to her. "And after your mother . . ." She couldn't bring herself to mention the possibility of Clara Van Deen's death.

"You'll be free to go—no strings attached. An annulment should be fairly simple."

"I don't know." Julie smoothed a hand across her forehead. "I need time to think."

"No," Daniel shot back. "I need to know now."

What choice did she have? Slowly, deliberately, Julie nodded. "All right, Daniel, I'll marry you. But only for your mother's sake."

His lip curled sardonically. "Do you think I'd marry you otherwise?"

"No, I don't suppose you would." Unfastening the chain from around her neck, Julie handed him her original engagement ring.

"You kept it?" Shock rang through his voice.

Julie stared into his dark eyes. "I couldn't bear to part with it. I wore it all these years. Close to my heart. That must tell you something."

He laughed shortly. "It must have given you a sense of triumph to have kept that all this time. To be honest, I'm surprised there's only one. In three years I would have expected you to add at least that many more."

"No," Julie answered, lowering her gaze, "there was never anyone but you."

"You don't honestly expect me to believe that, do you?"

"It doesn't matter what you believe."

"Keep it around your neck. That ring represented feelings I don't have anymore. I'll buy another one later."

"If that's what you want," Julie whispered.

"I'll make the arrangements and get back to you."

Julie didn't have to wait long. Daniel called the following afternoon with more information. The wedding would be in one week. Daniel picked her up after work Tuesday night so they could apply for the marriage license. After the required three-day wait, they'd have a wedding—of sorts. Everything was cut-and-dried. Even as he relayed the details, Daniel had remained emotionless.

Julie's mother was shocked but pleased, and planned to fly in for the wedding. Unfortunately, she'd have to get back to her volunteer job the next day and Julie was relieved that her mother's stay would be cut short. She wasn't sure how long she could act the role of a happy bride.

The night before the wedding, with her mother sleeping in her bed, Julie tossed restlessly on the sofa. Just before six, she decided to give up and moved from the couch. She doubted she'd slept more than a couple of hours.

Standing at the window, she stared into the night, watching the dawn begin to overtake the darkness.

She bit her lip nervously. Today was her wedding day and in these last hours before the ceremony, she felt her freedom slipping through her fingers. Even now, Julie wasn't sure she was doing the right thing. Of one thing she was sure; right or wrong, she wouldn't walk out on Daniel a second time.

Several hours later, long after the last stars had faded with the morning sun, a car came to take Julie and her mother to the church. Clara Van Deen had insisted that her minister marry them. Neither Julie nor Daniel had any objections.

Daniel met them at the church. His eyes roamed over the long white dress Julie had chosen and something unreadable flickered across his face.

"Are you ready?" he asked casually, stirring her fear that she was making a terrible mistake. Julie swallowed hard and decided to ignore it.

The ceremony was short. Daniel responded methodically to the minister's instructions as if the words held no meaning for him. In contrast, Julie's voice wavered as she recited her vows.

Daniel glanced at her when she pledged her love, a glint of challenge in his gaze.

Julie's fingers trembled as he slipped a plain gold band on her finger. The simplicity of the ring suited her, but she was sure Daniel had chosen it in contrast to the beautiful diamond he'd given her the first time. Julie was confident the difference didn't stop there.

After the ceremony, Julie's mother hugged them both, her eyes shining with happiness. They rode to the hospital together and were allowed a short visit with Daniel's mother.

Clara Van Deen smiled as a joyful tear escaped from the corner of her eye.

"Trust me, Julie," she whispered. "Things will work out."

Julie nodded, smiling feebly as she kissed Clara's wrinkled brow.

From the hospital, Daniel and Julie drove her mother to the airport. Margaret Houser insisted on paying for everyone's lunch. If she noticed the stilted silence between the bride and groom, she said nothing.

Julie suddenly wished for a longer visit with her mother, but Daniel was obviously in a hurry and after an abrupt goodbye, he ushered her back to the car.

Watching him as he drove, Julie clutched the small bouquet of flowers her mother had given her. The unfamiliar gold band felt strange against her finger and she found herself toying with it.

At a red light, Daniel caught her staring at her hand. "Don't be so anxious to remove that wedding ring. It's not going anywhere anytime soon."

Julie glared at him. "Of course. You've made your feelings perfectly clear."

Neither spoke again until Daniel had parked at his condominium in Wichita's most prestigious downtown area. The doorman smiled as he held the door open for Julie.

"Good afternoon, Mr. Van Deen," he said, eyeing Julie and the two suitcases Daniel carried.

Daniel nodded and placed his hand under Julie's elbow, hurrying her toward the elevator. The doors parted at the press of the button and Julie was ushered inside. The strained silence continued as he unlocked the door of the condo, swinging it wide to allow Julie to enter first.

Julie hesitated, wondering what lay before her.

"You don't expect me to carry you over the threshold, do you?"

"Of course not," she replied shortly. She took a deep breath and entered her new home.

The condo was surprisingly spacious. The tiled entry led to a sunken living room carpeted in plush brown pile. Two picture windows overlooked the downtown area and Julie paused to admire the view from fifteen floors up.

Daniel moved around her and carried her suitcases to one of the bedrooms. He stopped outside the door. "This is your room," he said, interrupting her search for city landmarks.

Julie moved away from the window and followed the sound of his voice.

A glance inside the room confirmed her belief that this had been a guest room. Fitting, Julie thought, since she was little more than an unwelcome guest in Daniel's life.

"The rest of your things will be delivered sometime this afternoon," he informed her. "I have to get back to the office for a couple of hours."

Back to the office! Julie couldn't believe it. They'd barely been married three hours. She'd taken the day off work. He could've done the same.

"What am I supposed to do?" she asked. "Make myself at home in a strange house—alone?"

"Unpack," he replied flippantly.

"That'll take all of five minutes. Then what?"

"Don't tell me I have to stay home and babysit you for the next twenty years."

"Go ahead and leave," Julie said. "No need to hurry back on my account."

Daniel laughed mirthlessly as he headed out the door. "Don't worry, I won't."

As she'd told him, five minutes later, both suitcases were empty. After a quick tour of the condo, Julie returned to her room. She yawned, and her neck hurt from a sleepless night on the sofa, so she decided to take a nap. The bed was soft and welcoming; within minutes she fell into a deep, comfortable slumber.

She woke around four, feeling refreshed. Daniel had been gone, and she considered going out for dinner, letting him come home to an empty apartment. It would serve him right. But no, being antagonistic wouldn't help their situation. She'd prepare dinner and try to make the best of things.

The kitchen was beautifully organized and well stocked—either Daniel enjoyed cooking or he had someone come in to cook for him. Julie's hand tightened against the counter. She couldn't deny that the thought of Daniel bringing another woman into this kitchen made her feel jealous.

She quickly prepared a fresh salad and dessert, and then thawed two large steaks in the microwave until they were ready to grill.

After a moment's deliberation, she chose to set the dining room table rather than the small one in the kitchen. This was, after all, their wedding day—although Daniel seemed to be doing his best to forget that.

Another suitcase and several boxes from her apartment were delivered shortly after five and Julie spent the next hour unpacking and arranging her things among Daniel's. She wasn't surprised to find that they shared similar tastes in literature and art. As she placed each book on the shelf, she frequently discovered that Daniel already owned a copy.

Julie didn't know why this astonished her. They'd discovered a number of similarities since their first meeting. Julie wondered if Daniel still played tennis. That was how they'd first met. The attraction had been immediate and intense. They'd fallen so deeply in love.

As dusk fell over the city, Julie lit the candles, creating a warm, romantic mood. She regretted the harsh parting words she'd exchanged with Daniel that afternoon. Maybe this dinner would show him that she was willing to work things out. She'd taken the first step. But the next one had to come from Daniel.

Minutes ticked into hours and at eleven Julie finally accepted that Daniel wouldn't be coming home for dinner. She wasn't sure if he'd be home at all.

After blowing out the candles and turning on the lights, she began to clear the table piece by piece, returning the china place settings to the rosewood cabinet.

When half the dishes were cleared, the door opened. Julie paused, clutching the expensive plate tightly to her stomach, her heart pounding wildly.

From across the room, Daniel's eyes met hers.

Julie smiled nervously and resumed her task, praying he wouldn't comment. She should have known better.

"A romantic dinner complete with candlelight? What's this, Julie? An invitation to your bed?"

Five

"No," she said, hoping her voice sounded light and carefree. "It wasn't that at all."

"Pity," he mumbled under his breath.

Julie had to bite her tongue to keep from asking where he'd been. That was exactly what he wanted her to do, but she refused to play his games.

"If you'll excuse me, I think I'll go to bed."

Daniel continued to stare at her from the tiled entryway. "I didn't know if you'd eaten or not."

Julie shook her head. "No, I thought I'd wait for you."

"I'm surprised you did."

She moved past him and down the hall to her room. Daniel had made it clear they'd make no pretense of a honeymoon and Julie was going back to work in the morning. As she undressed, she could hear Daniel's movements in the kitchen.

Tying the belt on her housecoat, Julie moved across the hall to the bathroom to brush her teeth. The appealing aroma of broiling steak reminded her that she hadn't eaten since lunch. She tried to focus on brushing. Not for anything would she go back into that kitchen.

In her room, she sat on the bed and opened the novel she'd been reading. The light tap at the door startled her.

"Your steak is ready." Daniel stuck his head in and smiled. "Medium rare, as I recall."

Julie opened her mouth to tell him exactly what he could do with the steak, then stopped herself. It had been a tiring day for both of them and the last thing they needed was an argument.

"I'll be there in a minute." Strangely pleased with this turn of events, Julie put on her slippers and joined him in the kitchen.

The table was set for two. Their steaks were served with grilled tomatoes and melted cheddar.

Julie opened the refrigerator and brought out the salad she'd made.

As she set the bowl on the table, Daniel said, "There were some briefs I needed to review for a court case in the morning."

Julie paused as she sat at the table, fork in hand. Daniel was telling her why he was late. She hadn't expected it, sure he'd wanted her to fret.

"Perhaps it would be best to let the other person know if one of us is going to be late," she said as her knife cut into the steak.

"Sounds fair," Daniel commented.

Julie smiled. The evening had gotten off to an uneasy start, but they were working things out.

"We should probably decide on some house rules," she suggested casually.

"Such as?"

"Since you did the cooking, I'll do the dishes."

"That seems reasonable." Daniel grinned approvingly. He hadn't smiled at her—really smiled—since she'd returned. She'd almost forgotten how wonderful it felt.

Julie laid her knife on the plate and looked up. "That was wonderful. I don't remember you being such an excellent cook."

"I've managed to pick up a few skills," he said dryly.

Julie stood and carried their plates to the sink while Daniel poured them each a cup of coffee.

"Shall we drink this in the living room?" he asked.

"I'll be there in a minute. I want to get these in the dishwasher."

When Julie joined him, Daniel was standing at the window looking out at the sparkling lights of the city.

"My mother seemed better today, didn't she?"

Julie took her coffee cup from the end table and sat down. "Yes, she did. There was some color in her cheeks for the first time since she collapsed."

"It's going to be an uphill battle for her in the coming months."

"I know. I'll do anything I can to help her," Julie said, taking a sip of her coffee. Daniel remained at the window with his back to her.

"I think we should agree that no matter what happens between us, we won't take our squabbles to my mother."

"Of course not." Julie blinked. She was surprised that Daniel would think otherwise. "If we need to talk something over, the person I'll come to is you."

"Good." He moved to sit in the wing-back chair beside her. "Don't worry about the housework. The cleaning lady comes twice a week."

"What about the cooking?" She focused on the mug in her hands. "I hate to admit it, but I'm not much good in the kitchen. You're probably more adept—do you want to take turns?"

"If you'd like."

"It might be the easiest thing." She shrugged. How could they sit beside each another—husband and wife—and talk of trivialities? Julie didn't want her marriage to begin this way. Twice before the wedding, she'd tried to discuss their past and both times Daniel had cut her off. He obviously wanted to leave that period in their relationship behind them. Julie realized they'd have no future until they faced the hurts and misunderstandings of the past. But tonight wasn't the time.

"You look tired," Daniel commented.

"Sorry." Julie shook her head to clear her thoughts. "I guess I am."

"Let's turn in."

Together they carried their cups into the kitchen. Julie put them in the dishwasher and Daniel showed her how to start it. The soft hum of running water followed them into the hallway.

Daniel flipped off the light switch and the condo went dark. Julie's eyes adjusted to the moonlit room.

"Can you find your way?" Daniel asked.

"Sure," Julie said. Their eyes met in the darkness and everything went still. She couldn't see his expression well enough to know what he was thinking, but time seemed to slow.

When his hand reached out to caress her cheek, a warm sensation spread down her neck. She sighed, closed her eyes and placed her hand over his.

"Good night, Julie," he said tenderly, removing his hand. He walked her to her room, but then hesitated in the open doorway.

For a fleeting moment, the hurt that had driven them apart faded. Julie took a wishful step in his direction. This man was her husband. They were meant to be together.

"If you'd like, I'll cook breakfast in the morning," she offered, wanting an excuse to linger with him in the darkness.

He didn't answer, and Julie wondered if he'd heard her. "I thought you said you weren't much of a cook," he finally said.

"I can manage breakfast."

"Did you eat out often? Is the reason you can't cook because you dated so much?"

"No," she answered simply. "Not much at all."

Silvery moonlight filled the narrow hallway as Julie studied her husband, waiting for a reaction.

"I wish I could believe that," he said with a sigh, "but you're much too beautiful not to have men fawning over you." And with that, he abruptly walked away.

Julie's clock radio went off at six, filling the silent room with music. She lay in bed for several minutes, listening to a couple of songs before throwing back the covers and climbing out of bed.

Slipping into her housecoat, she hurried into the kitchen to put on a pot of coffee. The morning was glorious. The sun was shining and Julie stood at the window looking down on the city as it stirred to life.

When she turned around, she found Daniel waiting by the coffeepot, clutching a large mug.

"Good morning," she greeted him with a warm smile.

Daniel mumbled something unintelligible under his breath.

"What did you say?" she asked as she took his empty mug out of his hand, and poured in what little coffee had drained through.

"Nothing," he said.

"No one told me you were such a grouch in the mornings," she teased. "I'll go get dressed and stay out of your way until you've had your coffee."

"That's probably a good idea."

Julie returned to her bedroom and dressed, choosing a new outfit—a gray-and-blue striped dress with a wide V neckline. Putting on a pair of pumps, she did her makeup and brushed her hair before re-entering the kitchen.

The bacon was sizzling in the pan when Daniel came in to pour himself a second cup of coffee.

"How do you want your eggs? Over easy?" She was surprised to see the scowl on his face. "Is something wrong?"

"That dress."

"It's new. Don't you like it?" She swallowed uncomfortably.

"It's a little revealing, don't you think?"

"Revealing?" Julie gasped. "In what way?"

Daniel grabbed the paper and sat down to read it. "The neckline."

"The neckline?" Julie's hand flew to the V-shaped front. She hadn't found it to be too low. "There's nothing wrong with this dress," she insisted.

"That's a matter of opinion," he said from behind the paper.

"How do you want your eggs?" Julie repeated, choosing to ignore his reaction to her dress.

The newspaper was a barrier between them. "I've lost my appetite," he muttered.

"So have I," she whispered, turning off the burner.

The office was only a few minutes away. Neither spoke on the drive over. Julie kept her hands folded in her lap, her head rigid as she focused straight ahead. She hadn't changed her outfit, nor would she. Daniel was being unreasonable. A wry smile touched her mouth. And she'd expected him to like the new dress.

He pulled into the parking garage across the street and into his allotted space.

"I may be late tonight," he said.

Julie nodded without looking at him. "I thought I'd go to the hospital after work."

"Then I'll meet you there."

They sounded like robots, their voices clipped and emotionless.

Julie did a double take when she entered the office—Sherry was already at her desk.

"Are my eyes deceiving me?" Julie teased. "Sherry early? That's impossible."

Sherry's smile was weak. "Morning." She lowered her head and blew her nose in a tissue. "I guess it's a bit of a shock, isn't it?"

"What's wrong?" Julie asked.

"Wrong?" Sherry laughed. "What makes you think something's wrong?"

"Maybe it's the mountain of wet tissues, or perhaps the red eyes. But then I've always had a reputation for being a good sleuth."

Sherry made a gallant effort to smile.

"I guess I should've said something the first time you mentioned Daniel," Julie explained, realizing what this was probably about. "I didn't want to hurt you, Sherry. Not for anything. Daniel and I have known each other for several years."

Sherry glanced up tearfully. "It's not that. I was surprised to hear about you two, but that's not the problem."

Julie was confused. "Then why are you crying?"

"It's Andy." Sherry said, her voice wavering.

"Your ex-husband?"

Sherry tugged another tissue from the brightly colored box and nodded. "The divorce isn't final until the end of the month."

"And you're having second thoughts?" Julie's knowledge of Sherry's marriage was limited to the bits of information her friend had shared. As far as Julie could tell, they didn't have any one specific reason to separate. Both had been too involved in their jobs and they'd grown apart. The trial separation had led to the decision to file for the divorce. In the short time Julie had known Sherry, it had been obvious that Sherry wanted to prove how much fun she could have without her husband.

"I . . . I saw Andy last night."

"Did you two talk?" Julie asked. She didn't want to pry, but figured Sherry would feel better if she confided in someone.

"Talk!" Sherry hiccuped loudly. "There was a voluptuous blonde draped all over him."

"But Sherry, that shouldn't bother you. For heaven's sake, you've been out with a dozen different men just since I've known you."

"Yes, but that was different," Sherry said.

"How?"

"Andy didn't care if I saw someone else."

"How can you be so sure?" Julie asked. "Maybe he did care. But maybe he's decided the time has come for him to start dating again, too."

"Not Andy. He's always hated blondes."

"You're blonde," Julie pointed out.

"I know, but the woman he was with last night isn't like his usual type."

Julie couldn't question her further because Mr. Barrett entered the room just then, nodding a brief greeting as he hung his coat in the closet. He seemed about to say something when he noticed Sherry's red face. Swiftly, he retreated into his office, closing the door.

"Why don't we see if we can take our lunch hour together and talk some more," Julie suggested.

"I'd like that," Sherry said, dabbing at the last of her tears. "I meant to tell you earlier how nice you look today. Is that a new outfit?"

"Yes." Julie smiled. "Do you like it?"

"It's perfect on you."

"What about the neckline?" Julie tilted her head back and arched her shoulders.

"What about it?" Sherry asked.

"It's not too revealing?"

"Revealing?" Sherry echoed. "No way."

"That's what I thought."

Clara Van Deen was looking much improved when Julie arrived at the intensive care unit that afternoon. She took Julie's hand in hers as Julie approached the bed.

"How's my new daughter?"

"How's my new mother?"

Clara closed her eyes and when she opened them again, they were glistening with tears. "Better now that I've made up for some of the pain I caused you and Daniel."

"I'm glad to hear that," Julie said. "I love him, Clara."

"And Daniel loves you. Don't ever doubt that, Julie. I don't know much about his life anymore—I understand he saw lots of women—but, Julie, there was never anyone he truly loved. No one but you."

Julie squeezed the old woman's hand gently. "I'll be a good wife to him."

"I don't doubt that for a minute." Clara's smile was weak, but infinitely happy.

When Daniel got there thirty minutes later, Julie was in the waiting room leafing through a dog-eared magazine she'd already read twice. She glanced up to see that his gaze had fallen on her neckline and the fullness of her breasts, but his expression was unreadable.

"Your mother seems better," Julie said.

Daniel nodded. "I'm looking forward to visiting with her."

Julie's eyes were drawn to her husband. His rugged appeal gave the impression that he worked outside. His face was quite tanned for early spring and Julie suspected he was exercising regularly. She wondered if he still played tennis.

"I talked to the doctor this afternoon," Daniel said as he rubbed his hand along the back of his neck.

"And?" Julie uncrossed her legs, setting the magazine aside.

"He said she's improved enough for him to consider open-heart surgery."

"When?" Julie breathed.

"A month from now."

"That's wonderful!" If the surgery was a success, the possibility of Daniel's mother returning to a normal life would be greatly increased.

"Is it?" Daniel responded almost flippantly. "Even if she gains enough strength for the surgery, her chances of survival are only fifty-fifty."

"But what would they be without it?"

Daniel wandered to the far side of the room, then pivoted sharply. "Far less than that."

Julie understood and shared his concern, but she felt that the chance of a longer, healthier life for his mother was worth the risk. "Everything's going to be fine," she assured him.

"How do you know that?"

"I don't," Julie admitted. "But your mother's content. Her spirits are high and she has the will to live. A positive attitude is bound to help." It was on the tip of her tongue to reveal that on the day Clara had collapsed, she'd mentioned how much she longed for grandchildren. Julie believed sheer willpower would see her mother-in-law through this surgery.

Daniel's expression tightened as he studied her.

The nurse arrived and told Daniel he could go in to see his mother.

Later, when they'd driven home, Julie noticed a spark of amusement in Daniel's eyes, an expression that was still there as she set the table for dinner.

"What's so funny?" she finally asked.

"What makes you think anything's funny?"

Julie pretended an interest in the green salad she was tossing. "Every time I look up, you're trying to keep from laughing."

"Something my mother said, that's all," Daniel told her.

"About me?" Julie asked stiffly, hoping she wasn't the brunt of some joke.

"Indirectly."

They ate in near silence. Not an intentional silence, at least not on Julie's part, but there was very little to talk about, since Daniel hadn't allowed her into his life. Julie was confident that he'd open up in time, but the one thing they desperately needed to talk about, Daniel refused to discuss.

"Are you still playing tennis?" Julie asked as she cleared the table.

"Often enough."

Julie noted that he didn't ask if she still played. They'd met on the courts and had regularly played as a doubles team. Julie still enjoyed the game, but didn't know how to volunteer that fact without making it look as if she was seeking an invitation—which, of course, she was.

"I'll do the dishes later." Daniel broke into her unhappy thoughts. "There are a few papers I want to go over tonight."

"Do you bring work home a lot?" Julie hadn't meant to sound so accusatory.

"Hardly at all," Daniel replied defensively.

She offered to do the dishes for him so he could work, but Daniel turned her down. "When I say I'm going to do something, I do it," he said pointedly.

Julie gripped the edge of the oak table. "In other words, you don't walk out five days before a wedding. That's what you're saying—isn't it, Daniel?"

"That's exactly what I'm saying," he snapped.

Julie stood and pushed her chair back from the table. Without a word, she left the kitchen, reached for her jacket and headed for the door.

"Where are you going?" Daniel demanded.

"Out," she replied and closed the door behind her. Half hoping Daniel would come after her, Julie lingered in the hall, but he didn't follow. She should have known.

Without her purse and nowhere to go, Julie was back in an hour after taking a brisk walk.

When she returned, Daniel was in his office, or so she assumed. The two pans from their meal were washed and stacked on the kitchen counter. Julie dried them and put them away. When she'd finished she glanced up to see that Daniel was standing in the doorway of the office, watching her.

"You came back."

"What's the matter?" she asked. "Were you hoping I wouldn't?"

A muscle twitched in his jaw as he broke the pencil he was holding. He pivoted and returned to his office.

Julie closed her eyes and took several calming breaths. This tension between them was taking its toll. She couldn't live like this. When she was younger, she'd avoided confrontation and had paid dearly for it, but she wasn't the same Julie now as she'd been then. She didn't avoid conflict these days, but she didn't instigate it either.

Daniel remained in his office with the door shut, while Julie sat alone in the living room reading. She felt drowsy, but shook herself awake, determined to be up when Daniel came out. She wasn't going to run away, not anymore. It was important that he recognize that.

But as her eyelids became heavier, she was afraid she couldn't fight off sleep anymore. She closed her book, switched the light to its lowest setting and leaned her head against the back of the chair, finally surrendering.

"Julie." Daniel's whisper woke her. "You'll get a crick in your neck."

She opened her eyes and stretched. The soft glow from the lamp was the only light in the house. Daniel stood above her, his shirt open. He studied her carefully and Julie yearned to reach out to him, slide her arms around his neck and gently place her mouth on his. He hadn't kissed her, had avoided touching her, but Julie felt that if he walked away from her now, she couldn't bear it.

"Julie," he whispered.

Surely, he could see the hunger she was feeling for his touch, her need to be loved, forgiven and trusted by him again.

He helped her to her feet, his manner impersonal.

"Daniel," she pleaded softly.

Without a word, he wrapped his arms around her, his gaze drawn to her lips as he slowly closed the distance between them.

Julie sighed as she slid her hands over his shoulders and linked her fingers at the base of his neck. "Oh, Daniel," she whispered, "it's been so long."

He held her against him, his mouth moving sweetly over hers as he brought her closer.

Julie thrilled to the urgency of his mouth as he kissed her. He buried his face in the curve of her neck as Julie drove her hands through his thick hair.

Daniel pulled away and looked into her eyes. Julie smiled and brushed her mouth over his, kissing the tiny cleft in his chin. That was something he'd always loved and she wanted him to know she hadn't forgotten.

His body stiffened against hers as he tugged his arms free. "Good night, Julie," he murmured before turning and walking away. He hadn't forgotten anything, either.

How many times would he walk away from her before they were even, before she'd been punished enough for the way she'd left him? Standing alone in the darkened room, Julie had no answer. Defeated, she retired to her room, hoping to find some peace in sleep.

The next day, they continued their new routine. They rode to work together in silence, and from there they went to the hospital, taking turns visiting his mother. Daniel cooked dinner while Julie changed out of her work clothes.

"I'm going to the library," she announced as she set their plates in the dishwasher.

"How long will you be?" Daniel asked without looking up from the mail he was sorting through.

"About an hour." Anything was better than sitting in a silent house again while Daniel closed himself off in his office.

He shrugged, but said nothing.

"Would . . ." Julie hesitated. "Would you like to come?"

"I've got things to do around here," he replied.

Julie let herself out the front door, her heart aching. The first night, she'd accused Daniel of playing games. Now she was the one escaping, hoping that he'd somehow show that he wanted her to stay. He didn't.

Six

Saturday morning, Daniel left the condo before Julie climbed out of bed. Lying awake with her bedroom door partially open, Julie listened to his movements as he walked down the hall. She expected him to go into the kitchen but was surprised to hear the front door click a few moments later.

Julie slipped out of bed and found a pot of coffee on the kitchen counter along with a note. The message read: *Playing tennis all day.*

All day, Julie mused resentfully. They'd talked about tennis earlier in the week. There'd been ample opportunity for him to include her in today's outing had he wished to.

After brewing a fresh pot of coffee, Julie sat at the round oak table, mug in hand. She'd known when she agreed to marry Daniel that there were several factors working against them. Some days, Julie was convinced that he'd never forgive her for leaving. But at other times, she could feel him studying her, apparently still interested. He hadn't touched her since the other night. Julie could tell he regretted that one slip and was taking measures to ensure that it wouldn't happen again.

She cooked a light breakfast, then dressed in jeans and a sweatshirt. The last of her things had arrived from the apartment. Only a few of her everyday items were necessary, since Daniel's condo was fully furnished.

Stacking the cardboard boxes in the bottom of her closet, Julie located the one full of mementos from her relationship with Daniel. Now that they were married, she could set them out freely. If she left their engagement photo out in the open, it might prompt him to discuss the things he chose to ignore.

Encouraged by the thought, she set the gold-framed picture on top of the television and stepped back to examine it. As always, she was struck by how happy they looked and vowed that one day they'd be that happy again.

She placed a few other things around the room and then stood back to admire her efforts. The condo now reflected who they'd been as a loving, happy couple. Daniel couldn't help being affected by it. Undoubtedly, he'd be surprised that she'd kept all these things, but she wanted him to understand that although she'd left, she'd never stopped loving him.

After a shower, Julie had lunch and decided to drop in at the hospital to visit Clara.

"Good afternoon," Julie said, leaning over to lightly kiss Clara's cheek. "How are you feeling today?"

"Much better."

She looked well, and Julie felt encouraged.

"Where's Daniel?" Clara asked.

"He's playing tennis." Julie hoped that her mother-in-law wouldn't ask for details because Julie wouldn't know what to say. She hoped to paint an optimistic picture of their marriage, but she wasn't willing to lie.

"That's right," Clara said. "Daniel mentioned something about playing in a tournament this weekend. I'm surprised you aren't at the club with him. As I recall, you two made an excellent team."

So he'd told his mother but hadn't bothered to say anything to her. Maybe he had another partner and didn't want Julie interfering with his plans. The thought made her jealous, but she squashed the feeling before her mother-in-law could read her expression.

"You still play, don't you?" Clara asked.

"I'm a bit rusty," Julie admitted. The Country Club—Julie could vividly recall how uncomfortable she'd been around those people. Daniel had taken her there several times for dinner or tennis, but Julie hadn't been able to overcome her insecurity.

"I thought you'd want to be with him," Clara continued, studying Julie carefully.

"I'm meeting him later," Julie said. It wasn't exactly a lie. She would show up at the Country Club. The time had come for her to face some of the other ghosts of her past.

"There was no need to disrupt your day to come and visit me," Clara said. "I already know how much you care. Whether I live or die is of no consequence to me. All I want before I go is the assurance that the two of you are happy." The white-haired woman regarded Julie seriously. "I wouldn't, however, mind a grandchild or two." She smiled. "Daniel seemed quite amused when I mentioned how much I was looking forward to grandchildren."

So that was what he'd been so smug about the other night. "I think he feels we should wait," Julie improvised.

"His words exactly. But try to convince him, Julie. I don't have all the time in the world. And he's at the age when he should be thinking of starting a family."

"I'll bring it up," Julie promised. "But remember we've only been married a little while."

Clara closed her eyes. "It seems so much longer. In my muddled mind, it's difficult to remember you were gone all those years."

"My heart was here," Julie said softly.

"Would you read to me, dear?" Clara asked, handing over a book from her nightstand.

"I'd be happy to."

Julie read until she was certain Clara was asleep, then she slipped quietly from the room. She was set on facing Daniel at the Country Club, but her determination began to waver. Her unexpected arrival could be uncomfortable for everyone involved. No, she reasoned. As his wife she had a right to see her husband. Resolutely, she left the hospital, got into her car and headed for the outskirts of town.

Julie was lucky to find a parking space in the crowded lot. The tennis courts and surrounding areas were jammed with spectators. Julie signed in as Daniel's wife and was grateful no one questioned her.

It only took her a few minutes to find him. He was on the courts in what she learned was the men's singles semi-final. She sat in the bleachers, silently engrossed in the competition, proud when Daniel won. The championship game followed fifteen minutes later. It was a tense match and Daniel's composure astonished her. He lost the title, but shook hands with his opponent, smiling as he exited the court.

The crowd gathered around the winner as the stands emptied. Julie made her way to her husband.

Daniel was wiping his face with a hand towel.

"Nice game," she said from behind him.

He didn't pause or give any indication that he was surprised as he turned toward her. "How'd you know where to find me?"

"Well, your note. And then your mother mentioned the tournament, so I thought I'd stop by to cheer you on."

"I saw you in the stands," he said.

She noticed that he didn't indicate one way or the other how he felt about her being there. "You were good. Your game's improved."

"I've played better," he said, packing away his racket.

"Good game, Van Deen" a deep baritone voice said from behind them.

Daniel's posture stiffened. "Thanks." He slung the towel around his neck.

Julie didn't recognize the tall, athletic man who'd joined them.

"I see you brought your own cheering section," the man said.

Daniel wrapped an arm around Julie's waist, bringing her to his side. "Patterson, meet my wife, Julie. Julie, this is my friend and associate, Jim Patterson."

"Your wife!" Jim exclaimed. "When did that happen?"

"Recently," Daniel said.

Jim chuckled and rubbed the side of his jaw, bemused. "It must've been recent. Does Kali know?"

At the mention of another woman's name, Julie eyed her husband speculatively. She'd briefly wondered if there was anyone Daniel was seeing seriously, but figured Sherry would have known if he'd been involved with someone else. Clearly, Jim knew more than her coworker.

"I haven't talked to Kali yet," Daniel replied.

"This calls for a celebration," Jim said, obviously trying to cover the awkward moment. "Let me buy you two a drink."

"Not today," Daniel answered. "Unfortunately, Julie has an appointment she needs to get to." His arm slid from around her waist to her lower back. "I'll see you to your car, honey." He steered her toward the parking area.

Julie looked back over her shoulder. "It's a pleasure to have met you . . . Mr. Patterson."

"We'll have that drink another time," Jim promised with a brief salute.

Once they were alone, Julie shook Daniel's hand loose. "What was that all about? And who's Kali?"

He clenched his jaw. "No one you need to concern yourself with."

"And why couldn't we stay for a drink?" she sputtered. "It's time I met your friends. I'm your wife."

"Don't remind me."

She looked away, refusing to let him see how badly his words had hurt her.

Daniel jammed his hands into his pockets. He looked as if he was about to say something more, but Julie didn't wait to find out. She turned and walked briskly to her car. She couldn't get out of that parking lot fast enough.

Unwilling to return to the empty condo, she drove around until the hurt and anger had faded. So there'd been another woman. She could accept that as long as this Kali remained in the past. She'd need to be told, of course, that Daniel had married or there'd be trouble down the road.

Julie wasn't so naive as to think that Daniel had lived like a monk during the time she was gone. But it still hurt more than she thought possible. What worried her most was his reluctance to tell her anything about Kali.

When she got home two hours later, Daniel was sitting the living room.

"Julie." He jumped up and approached her, running a hand through his hair. "Where were you?"

"I went for a drive. I needed time to think."

He scowled and nodded.

She glanced at her watch. "I didn't realize it was so late. It's my turn to cook, isn't it? I'll start something right away. You must be starving."

The sound of his voice followed her as she headed for the kitchen. "I thought I'd take you out tonight."

Julie froze. "Take me out?"

"As you said earlier, it's time you and I were seen together."

Julie breathed a sigh of relief. This dinner invitation was his way of telling her he was sorry for what had happened that afternoon. It wasn't an eloquent apology, but it was encouraging.

"Well?" Hands deep in his pockets, he studied her.

She replied with a slow, sensual smile. "I'd like that."

"Wear something elegant."

Her smile faltered. "I'm afraid I may not have anything appropriate. Would you mind if we went somewhere less formal?"

"As I recall, you liked fancy places."

"I was twenty-one," she explained. "I never really liked it, but I couldn't tell you that. I was afraid if you knew how shy I really was . . ."

A flicker of surprise touched Daniel's features. "Our relationship was riddled with misunderstandings, wasn't it? Why didn't you tell me how you felt?"

"I was so crazy about you, I was ready to be anything you wanted."

"Everything but my wife," he said, his expression impassive.

"I couldn't," she said. "Not then." She left the kitchen and moved into her bedroom. Leaning against the door, she closed her eyes. Surely, Daniel must realize that if they'd gone through with the wedding three years ago their marriage would have been doomed. Julie knew that it wasn't any more secure now and the thought saddened her.

She changed into a pale blue dress and a white jacket. A glance in the mirror confirmed that even the most critical eye would find no fault with the neckline. She completed the outfit with white high-heeled sandals and a single strand of pearls which Daniel had given her. She doubted he'd remember, though. He'd given her so many beautiful things.

She went into the living room, where Daniel was waiting. He wore dark slacks with a blue shirt under a sports coat.

"I made a phone call and was able to get last-minute tickets for the dinner theater," he said as he pulled out of the parking garage.

Julie nodded. "That sounds wonderful. Thank you. What's playing?"

"Never Too Late," he said, casting an amused glance at Julie.

"Seems appropriate," she said, returning his smile. She prayed it wasn't too late for them.

When his hand reached for hers, Julie felt a warm sensation radiate up her arm from his touch. It had always been like that. Daniel was capable of stirring emotions in her that she'd only dreamed existed.

Dinner was delicious and the comedy had both of them

laughing. For those few hours, they managed to set aside their difficulties and were husband and wife without the past intruding.

"Would you like to go someplace for a drink?" Daniel asked on their way out of the dinner theater.

"We could if you like," she said. "But I think I'd prefer a cup of coffee in our own kitchen so I can prop up my feet. I shouldn't have worn these shoes."

"If you promise to wear a more sensible pair the next time I take you to dinner, then I'll give you a foot rub," Daniel admonished with a lazy smile.

"You're on." It felt good to joke with him. Tonight it had been so easy to pretend they were a loving husband and wife enjoying an evening out together.

Back at the condo, Julie made them cappuccinos, while Daniel put on a CD. Mellow music filled the space, a beautiful love ballad.

She carried the cups into the living room and sat on the opposite end of the sofa from Daniel. "Here." She swung her feet onto his lap. "Work your magic."

While she sipped from the cup of creamy coffee, Daniel gently massaged her feet.

"Why do you wear those silly things?" he asked. "You've got a blister on your heel."

"I know," Julie said, "but they're the only decent pair of dress shoes I have."

"Is that a hint for me to hand over my credit card?"

Julie swung her feet onto the floor. "No," she answered evenly. It was difficult to tell if he was teasing or not. She studied his face, but he hid his emotions well.

"A husband enjoys buying his wife gifts. You certainly had

no difficulty accepting things from me in the past. You kept them, too, if the pearls are any indication."

"I kept every reminder of you I could," she whispered. She looked at the television and stiffened when she saw that the framed engagement photograph was missing.

"What happened to the picture?" She got to her feet. "I put it here this morning and now it's gone."

"I put it away," Daniel said.

"Away?" she echoed in disbelief. "What do you mean, *away?*"

Daniel stood up and moved to the opposite side of the living room. "It's in your bedroom."

"But why?" she asked, watching his reaction.

"Because I was angry and I took it out on the photo."

Julie went pale. "You . . . didn't destroy it, did you?"

"No, but I was tempted. I don't want reminders of that time in my life."

"I see," Julie said, trying to remain calm. She refused to give in to the tears. For a minute she thought he would explain further, but he just walked into his office and closed the door.

Julie was shaking so badly the cappuccino sloshed over the rim of her cup and into the saucer as she carried it to the kitchen. After rinsing everything in the sink, she returned to the living room and removed the other mementos she'd placed there. Those items, however small, meant a great deal to her. She couldn't bear to have Daniel reject them as he had the photograph.

That night, she woke from a fitful slumber around three. Just when it looked like she was making progress with Daniel, something would happen and she'd realize how far they still had to go.

She got out of bed and wandered to the kitchen for a glass of milk. She stood at the picture window, looking down on the silent, sleeping city below. She sensed more than heard Daniel coming up behind her. Julie remained where she was.

"You couldn't sleep?"

"No." The word tumbled from her mouth as tears filled her eyes.

His hand clasped her shoulder and he pressed his face into her hair. "Julie, I'm sorry about the picture. The minute I saw how much it meant to you, I regretted taking it down. To be honest, I wasn't sure why'd you put it out. I thought you wanted to torment me."

"Torment you?" She turned, her gaze seeking his in the moonlight.

He took the glass of milk from her, set it aside and brought her into the warm circle of his arms. His chin rested on her head as his hands roamed soothingly up and down her back.

It felt so right to be in his arms again, almost as if she'd never left.

With one finger under her chin, he lifted her mouth to his. Julie stood on tiptoe and fit her body to his, feeling Daniel resist momentarily as she melted against him.

"I'm sorry, Julie," he whispered against her lips.

"I know," she said, kissing him once more. Daniel moaned and hungrily kissed her back, holding her so close it was difficult to breathe.

"I won't make you cry again," he promised.

Julie sighed longingly and pressed her face to his shoulder. Nestled in the comfort of his embrace, she tried to stifle a yawn.

"Come on, sleepyhead," he whispered and kissed her temple. "I'll tuck you in."

Daniel led her back to the bedroom, his arm around her waist. Julie's heart was pounding as he helped her into the bed.

He wanted her, Julie was sure of it. She was his wife and he longed to take her in his arms and love her as a husband should. Yet he kept his distance, his face revealing the conflict he felt.

"Good night," he whispered, finally turning away.

"Good night," she repeated, suppressing her own frustration.

Daniel lingered in the doorway and Julie leaned up on her elbows. "Daniel?"

"Yes?" He turned back eagerly.

"Thank you for tonight. I enjoyed the show."

"I did, too," he said softly. "We'll do it again soon. Next time I'll take you to Gatsby's."

"Really?"

"If you'd like, we could take up tennis again," he suggested.

"I would like that," she responded happily. "Very much."

"Tomorrow?"

"That would be lovely."

To his credit, Daniel did play a set of tennis with her the following morning. But he glanced repeatedly at his watch, distracted from their game. He beat her easily, but then it'd been a long time since Julie had played anyone who challenged her the way Daniel did. He seemed out of sorts by the time they finished. Julie couldn't understand his attitude. And she'd been hoping to meet more of his friends, but Daniel introduced her to no one.

"Half the morning's gone," he commented as they left the court. Again, he glanced at his watch impatiently. "I've got several things I need to do this afternoon."

Julie remained tight-lipped as they returned to the condo. Daniel had been the one to suggest the game, not her. Almost immediately, he closed himself in his office. When lunch was ready half an hour later, Julie entered to find him poring over papers and checking the internet. He barely noticed she was there.

"Would you prefer to eat in here or the kitchen?"

Daniel looked up. "Here," he said.

Julie brought in a tray with tomato soup and two grilled cheese sandwiches.

"Thanks," he muttered.

Julie ate silently while leafing through the Sunday paper. Later in the afternoon, she did the weekly shopping and ran a few other errands. On her way back home, she dropped by the hospital. Clara was being transferred out of intensive care the next morning and Julie promised to stop in for a visit the following evening on her way home from work.

After leaving the hospital, Julie picked up some hamburgers at a drive-thru for dinner. To her surprise, Daniel was still in his office when she returned. "You're still at it?" she asked as she entered the room.

He looked up and nodded. "This case is more involved than I thought."

"I brought you some dinner."

"Thanks," he said. "I could use a break. What've you made?"

Julie glanced at him guiltily. "Well, I didn't exactly cook . . ." She held up the paper take-out bag.

"Julie," Daniel groaned. "Sometime in the next twenty years, you're going to have to learn to cook."

That meant they'd still be together in twenty years, she mused contentedly.

Seven

"Married life doesn't seem to agree with you," Sherry commented as she watched Julie work.

"What do you mean?" Julie asked. Another week had passed and just when she thought the tension was lessening between her and Daniel, something would happen to set them back. They hardly spoke in the mornings—not even on their drive to work. In the evenings they visited his mother, came home and ate dinner. Immediately afterward, he'd hole himself up in his office, and sometimes Julie wondered if he forgot she was there. He treated her more like a roommate than a wife.

"Maybe I should keep my mouth shut," Sherry continued, "but you don't have the look of a happy bride."

Julie bit her lip as she opened a file and stared blankly at the pages inside. "I don't feel much like a bride."

"Why not?"

A tear traced its way down Julie's cheek. "Daniel's so busy right now. I hardly ever see him."

Sherry rolled her chair close to Julie's desk and handed her a tissue. "Believe me," she said sympathetically, "I know the feeling. That's how all of my problems with Andy started. He worked such long hours that we didn't have time to be a couple anymore. He was so involved with his job that eventually we drifted apart. It reached the point where I'd be gone a week before he even knew I was missing."

Julie felt comforted to know she wasn't alone.

Ten minutes later, Mr. Barrett came out of his office. "I was wondering . . ." he started. "Would you two like to take an extra half hour for lunch today? It's been a hectic week."

Julie and Sherry exchanged surprised glances. "Thank you," Sherry said. "We'd love to."

The long lunch with Sherry proved to be just what Julie needed to raise her spirits.

"You know," Sherry said between bites of her chicken and cashew salad, "if I had it to do all over, I'd make it so Andy never wanted to leave the house again."

Julie stirred her clam chowder without much interest. Her appetite had been nonexistent lately. "What do you mean?"

"Think about it." Sherry leaned against the table, her eyes shining mischievously. "There are ways for a woman to keep her husband home at night."

Julie simply nodded, her thoughts spinning.

As the day progressed, Julie gave more thought to Daniel's actions. In the beginning he'd been bitter, but as the weeks progressed, his hostility was fading. He'd promised after taking down their engagement photo that he wouldn't hurt her again.

And he hadn't. If anything, he was all the more gentle—and the other night, she'd found him holding the photo, studying their young, happy faces. Julie had held her breath, worried he'd look at the picture and remember the pain and embarrassment she'd caused. Instead his gaze had held an odd tenderness. She'd been puzzled when he then retreated into his office. If he'd forgiven her, if he loved her and wanted her, wouldn't he come to her? Julie was beginning to hate that guest bedroom. She didn't belong there; she was his wife, and she longed to fill that role completely.

In the weeks since their wedding, physical contact between them had been brief, but she'd seen the desire in his eyes. He wanted her. He spent the evenings avoiding her for fear of what would happen otherwise. His pride was punishing them both.

A smile touched Julie's lips as she recalled a pearly-white satin nightgown she'd recently admired in a department store window. Perhaps she should do as Sherry suggested and lure her husband to bed without involving pride or egos. The more she thought about it, the more confident she became.

That evening, Julie and Daniel drove to visit Mrs. Van Deen in the hospital.

"It's so good to see you," she murmured in a cheerful tone.

"Hi, Mom." Daniel kissed her cheek and held Julie close by his side.

"Julie, you're looking lovely. That color agrees with you."

Daniel looked at his wife as if seeing her for the first time that day. His eyes softened as he noted the way the pink dress accented her figure. "It certainly does," he agreed.

"How are you feeling?" Julie asked, still blushing from Daniel playing the role of the loving husband.

"Better," Clara said with a sigh. "The doctor said he'd never seen anyone make a swifter recovery. I told him I have something to live for now. My son has the wife he's always wanted and I'll soon have the grandchildren I've dreamed of."

Daniel's grip tightened around Julie's middle and she had to suck in a breath to keep from crying out. Her hand moved over his to silently let him know he was hurting her. Immediately, his grip slackened.

"My grandchild will have the bluest eyes," Clara continued, oblivious to the tension in the room. "My husband's eyes were blue. Deeper than the sea. I wish you'd known him, Julie. He would have loved you just as I do. He was a good man."

"I'm sure he was," Julie said.

"A lot like Daniel." Clara gestured toward her son.

Julie glanced up at him as Daniel's mother continued reminiscing about the late August Van Deen.

When Julie and Daniel returned home that evening, Julie breathed a long sigh.

"What was that about?" Daniel asked.

"It's nothing," Julie said. "I was just hoping that our lives will be as rich and rewarding as your parents' were."

Daniel smiled. "They did have a wonderful life together."

Daniel went to drop his briefcase in his office. It was nearly seven and they hadn't eaten dinner.

Julie put some noodles on to cook then headed for her room to change clothes, donning a pair of navy-blue cords and a thin sweater that clung to her curves. She refreshed her makeup and dabbed on Daniel's favorite perfume for good measure, then returned to finish preparing dinner.

Daniel looked surprised as he joined her in the kitchen. He studied her for a moment, noting the change in outfit.

"I didn't want to spill anything on my dress," Julie told him, hiding a smile.

He answered with a short nod, but couldn't seem to keep his eyes off her as she deftly moved around the tiny kitchen.

He didn't talk much during dinner, but that wasn't unusual. Perhaps Julie was reading too much into his actions. After so many years of living alone, he was probably used to keeping his thoughts to himself.

With seduction plots brewing in her head, every bite of her meal seemed to stick in her throat. After a few minutes, she stood and scraped half her dinner down the garbage disposal before placing her plate in the dishwasher.

"I thought I was doing dishes," Daniel said, looking up from the table.

"There aren't many," Julie said dismissively.

"Hey, we made a deal. When you cook, I wash the dishes," he said. "Now scoot."

Having been ousted from the kitchen, Julie sat to watch some TV, but her mind wasn't focused.

Daniel worked away in the kitchen, but Julie felt his eyes occasionally rest on her. A few times she'd glanced up and smiled at him.

"A penny for your thoughts," he said, handing her a hot cup of coffee.

Julie swallowed a laugh. "You wouldn't want to know," she teased. "You'd run in the opposite direction."

"That sounds interesting."

"I promise you it is."

Daniel surprised her by sitting in the wing-backed chair beside her. "Julie." He took the remote control and muted the television. "Can we talk a minute?"

"Sure." She turned toward him expectantly.

"I haven't been the best of company lately," he started.

"There's no need to apologize," Julie told him. "I understand."

"You do?"

"You must be exhausted. Heaven only knows when you sleep. You've been working yourself half to death this last month." Crossing her legs, Julie leaned back into the couch. "And then this evening your mother started talking about grandchildren and neither one of us has the courage to tell her we aren't sharing a bed." Nervously, she glanced down at the steaming coffee. It was on the tip of her tongue to admit how much she wanted that to change, how much she longed to be with him and start a family together.

"Julie, listen."

Just then, the phone rang, distracting them both.

"Hold that thought," Julie said, reaching for the receiver. Whoever it was, she'd get rid of him in a hurry. For the first time, Julie felt like they were making strides in their marriage. "Hello," she answered.

There was silence on the other end.

"Hello?" Julie repeated.

"Who's this?" a husky female voice replied.

"Julie Van Deen," she answered. "Who's this?"

"So it's true," the woman said, clearly shocked.

"Who am I speaking to?" Julie asked, already certain it had to be the woman Jim Patterson had mentioned at the club the other day. Julie had bitten back many questions about her, but now they were resurfacing.

"Kali Morgan," the woman answered.

A chill raced up Julie's spine. "Would you like to talk to Daniel?"

Kali paused. "No. Just . . . just give him my best . . . to you both."

"Thank you," Julie murmured. Confused, she hung up the phone.

Daniel was looking at her expectantly. "Who was it?"

"An old friend of yours," she said weakly.

"Who?"

"Someone who clearly didn't know you had a wife."

"Kali." The word was a statement, not a question.

"You didn't tell her about us, did you?"

Daniel stood, putting some distance between them. His voice was unsure, worried. "What did Kali say?"

Julie searched his expression. The man who stared back had become a stranger. Daniel didn't seem to find it necessary to tell Kali that he got married. Maybe he believed that he'd go back to his old life eventually, keep his options open in case his mother didn't survive. He could quickly annul their marriage. Or maybe he was just looking for ways to hurt her as she'd hurt him. If so, he'd succeeded.

Daniel took a slow step toward her. "Julie, please don't look at me like that."

She felt her chest tighten as she got up and moved down the hall to her room. The bag containing the nightgown she'd bought rested on her bed. She stared at it in disbelief. Only minutes before she'd intended to seduce her husband.

Daniel appeared in the doorway. "Julie, be reasonable. Surely, you didn't think I've lived the last few years like a priest."

Everything went incredibly still. "For three years, my heart grieved for you until I couldn't take it anymore . . . and I came back because . . . because facing your bitterness was easier than trying to forget you."

"Julie." His voice took on a soft, pleading quality. He paused as if desperately searching for the right words. "Kali and I had been dating for several months," he explained. "But that's in the past. I haven't touched her since the day I saw you in the elevator."

"Touched her," Julie repeated shakily. "Is that supposed to reassure me? You haven't touched me either!" She felt her stomach heave and she rushed into the bathroom.

Daniel followed her. Julie stood in front of the sink and pressed a cool rag to her face.

"What did you expect me to do?" he shouted. "You walked out on me!"

Julie turned sharply to face him. "You didn't tell her we were married!" She hiccuped on a sob. "And . . . and all these years I've loved you."

"Don't tell me there hasn't been anyone in—"

"No," she shouted. "I seldom dated. You were the only man I ever loved. The only man I ever could love." She wept into the washcloth.

"Julie." He moved to stand behind her, a hand on each shoulder.

"Don't touch me," she commanded and shrugged her upper torso to shake him off. "Your tastes have changed, haven't they, Daniel? You must find me incredibly stupid to think you still care."

She started to leave but he pulled her into his arms. "You're going to listen to me, Julie. Perhaps for the first time since we met, we're going to have an honest discussion."

Julie was in no mood to be reasonable. "No," she cried, pushing past him to get back to her room. Grabbing the package from her bed, she shoved it in his arms. "Here. Once I'm gone, you can give this to one of your other women." With that she slammed the bedroom door.

Sherry was at her desk when Julie got to work the following day.

"Morning," Julie greeted her, doing her best to disguise her misery. She knew she looked terrible. Makeup had been unable to camouflage the effects of her sleepless night. For the first time since getting married, Daniel had left for work without Julie.

"Morning," Sherry replied without looking up. It was obvious she'd been crying again.

"Did something happen?" Julie pried.

Wiping her face with the back of her hand, Sherry sat up and sniffled. "After our talk yesterday, I got to thinking about how much I miss Andy . . . so I saw him last night."

"Was he with another woman again?"

"No, this time he was with me," Sherry said. "I . . . I told him I wasn't positive I wanted the divorce and that I thought we should talk things over more thoroughly before we take such a serious step."

"I think that's wise." Julie recognized how difficult it must have been for Sherry to contact her husband and suggest that they meet. She and Daniel weren't the only ones with an overabundance of pride.

"We sat and talked for ages and, well, Andy ended up spending the night." Sherry continued, her fingers nervously toying with a tissue. "Then this morning when I woke up, Andy was gone. No note. Nothing. He regrets everything—I know he does. I feel so cheap and used and . . ." She paused and blew into the tissue.

"Sherry." Julie moved to gently pat her on the back. Julie

definitely felt her friend's pain. Like a pair of idealistic fools, they'd hoped everything would work out because they loved their husbands. "I'm sure there's a perfectly logical explanation for why Andy left." Julie tried to sound optimistic.

"I feel like a one-night stand."

"But you are married," Julie said.

"Yes, but not for very much longer."

"Things have a way of working out for the best," Julie assured her, hoping it was true.

Sherry attempted a smile. "How did everything go for you?"

"Fine," Julie lied but, at Sherry's narrowed look, amended, "Terrible."

The office door opened and Julie and Sherry lowered their heads, pretending to be absorbed in their work. Mr. Barrett passed through the room with his usual morning greeting.

"He must think we've gone off the deep end," Sherry whispered once he was in his office with the door closed.

"Maybe we have."

They worked companionably, taking turns answering the phone. When she had a free moment, Sherry placed her purse on the desk and took out her makeup case. "Count your blessings, Julie. You're much too levelheaded to do some of the dumb things I've done."

"Maybe you should reach out to him?" Julie suggested.

"I couldn't . . . not after what happened."

"I'm sure he'd be willing to talk, especially after last night," Julie insisted.

"I wish that was true," Sherry said. "But somehow, I doubt it."

Daniel was already in his office when Julie got home that evening. At their usual visit, Clara had mentioned that her son had been by earlier. Her mother-in-law had noticeably studied the dark shadows under Julie's eyes, but didn't comment. Julie was grateful. Answering Clara's questions would have been her undoing.

Hanging up her jacket in the closet, Julie headed for the kitchen. A package of veal cutlets rested on the countertop. Julie sighed as she reached for the frying pan.

"I thought it was my turn to cook," Daniel said from behind her.

"All right," she muttered. "But I'm not very hungry. In fact, I think I'll lie down for a while."

He took so long to answer that Julie feared another confrontation.

"Okay," he said at last. "I'll call you when dinner's ready."

"Fine." They were treating each other like strangers.

Julie moved into the room and sat dejectedly on the side of her mattress. A month into their marriage and she was little more than an unwelcome guest in Daniel's life. She leaned back and closed her eyes.

It seemed only minutes later when Daniel knocked lightly against the open door. "Dinner's ready."

Julie toyed with the idea of telling him she wasn't feeling well. But Daniel would easily see through that excuse. It was better to face him. Things couldn't possibly get much worse.

The table was already set when Julie pulled out a chair to join Daniel.

"Your mother looked better tonight," she said.

Daniel deposited a spoonful of wild rice on his plate before answering. "She asked about you. I didn't know if you'd be stopping in to see her or not."

"I did," she told him.

"So I surmised."

Five minutes passed and neither spoke. Julie looked out the window and noted the thick gray clouds rolling in.

Daniel noticed them, too. "It looks like rain."

Julie nodded. Another awkward silence filled the kitchen until Julie stood and started to load the dishwasher.

"I'll do that," Daniel volunteered.

"It's my turn."

"You're beat."

"No more than you," Julie countered, stubbornly filling the sink with hot tap water.

The dishes took all of ten minutes. The hum of the dishwasher followed her into the hallway. The thought of spending another night in front of the television was intolerable. But going out was equally unappealing. Daniel had disappeared inside his office and Julie doubted she'd be seeing him again that evening, which was just as well.

Deciding to read, she returned to her room. Once she was settled on her bed, a flash of satin caught her attention. Setting her book aside, she discovered that the nightgown she'd shoved at Daniel was hanging in her closet. She ran her fingers over the silky smoothness, suddenly feeling emotional. She'd so wanted things to be different.

"Julie," Daniel called through the closed door. "Are you all right?"

"I'm wonderful," she said sarcastically. "Just leave me alone."

For a moment, nothing happened. Then the door was shoved open.

Julie gasped as Daniel marched into her room and hoisted her in his arms.

"Put me down," she cried.

"You're my wife, Julie Van Deen. And I'm tired of these games." He marched down the hallway to his bedroom and slammed the door closed with his foot.

"You didn't even tell Kali you were married!" she shouted.

"I couldn't," he shouted right back. "She was in England on a business trip."

Julie's anger died a swift and sudden death. She went completely still.

"I don't know what's going on in that head of yours," Daniel continued. "For heaven's sake—we're married. What's Kali got to do with us now?"

"Nothing," Julie whispered, laughing softly. "Nothing at all."

"What's so amusing?" he barked. He sank onto the edge of his bed, his hold on her loosening as she rested in his lap.

"You wouldn't understand," she murmured, linking her arms around his neck. "I thought you were planning . . . Never mind." Gently, she kissed him.

"Julie," he breathed, his arms tightening around her.

"Are you really tired of playing games?" she asked, teasing him with a series of short, playful kisses along his jaw.

"Yes," he said, gripping the back of her head and directing her lips to his. "Oh, yes."

His hands began undoing the tiny buttons of her blouse. Frustrated with the small pearl-shaped fastenings, he abandoned the effort and broke the kiss long enough to try to pull the blouse over her head.

Winded, Julie stopped him. "We've waited a whole month. Another thirty seconds shouldn't matter."

As she freed her blouse, Daniel softly cupped her breasts and buried his face in the hollow of her throat. "I couldn't live another month like that," he told her. "I couldn't sleep knowing you were just down the hall. Every time I closed my eyes, all I could see was you."

"I've wanted you so badly," she said, sliding her hands up and down his shoulders.

Hungrily, he kissed her again. "You're my wife, Julie, the way you were always meant to be."

"Wake up, sleepyhead," Daniel whispered lovingly in her ear. "It's morning."

"Already?" Julie groaned, resting her head in the crook of his arm. Her eyes refused to open.

"How are you this morning?" Daniel asked, kissing the crown of her head.

"Very happy." Julie smiled.

"Me, too. I never stopped loving you, Julie. I tried. Believe me, I tried every way I could to forget you. For a time I convinced myself I hated you. But the day I saw you in the elevator, I knew I'd been fooling myself. One look and I realized I'd never love another woman the way I love you."

Raising her head, Julie rolled onto her stomach and kissed him.

The hunger of his response surprised her. Quickly, he spun them sideways so that Julie was on her back, looking up at him.

"Daniel," she protested lightly. "We'll be late for work."

"Yes, we will," he agreed. "Very late."

An hour later, while Julie dressed, Daniel cooked breakfast, humming as he worked.

"You're in a good mood this morning," she teased, sliding her arms around his middle.

Daniel chuckled. "And with good reason." He pulled her into his arms, kissing her soundly. "I love you."

She smiled. "I know."

"I think it's time we took that diamond ring hanging around your neck and put it on your finger, where it belongs," he said. He helped her remove the chain and slid the solitaire diamond onto her finger with a solemnness that told her how seriously he took his vows. "I wanted you the minute the minister pronounced us husband and wife," he admitted sheepishly. "I had to get out of the house that day because I knew what would happen if I stayed."

"And I thought—"

"I know what you thought," he said. "It was exactly what I needed you to believe. My ego had suffered enough for one day. I couldn't tolerate it if you knew how badly I wanted you."

The workdays flew by and after a wonderful weekend together, Julie and Daniel spent a quiet Sunday with his mother at the hospital. Clara Van Deen's heart surgery was scheduled for the following Tuesday and both Julie and Daniel wanted to spend as much time with her as possible.

"Have you told Julie about her surprise yet?" Clara asked as Daniel wheeled his mother into the sunny hospital courtyard.

"Surprise?" Julie's face lit up. "What surprise?"

"Oh, dear." Mrs. Van Deen glanced over her shoulder at her son. "I didn't let the cat out of the bag, did I?"

Leaning forward, Daniel kissed his mother's cheek. "Only a little," he whispered reassuringly. "I was waiting until later."

"Later?" Julie spoke again. "What's happening later? Daniel, you know how much I hate secrets."

"This one you'll enjoy," he promised. He laughed at her puzzled expression and slid a hand around her waist. "I won't make you wait any longer than this afternoon," he said. The mischievous look in his eyes was enough to make her feel light-headed.

After an hour in the fresh air, Clara Van Deen announced that it was time for her to go back inside.

Daniel stood and started to wheel her inside. "We shouldn't have kept you out so long."

"Nonsense," Clara protested. "I've been wanting to feel the sun for days."

Within half an hour Clara was fast asleep. Standing on opposite sides of the hospital bed with the railing raised, Daniel whispered, "Are you ready for your surprise now?"

Julie nodded eagerly. Now that she thought about it, he had been acting suspicious. Several times he'd looked as if he wanted to tell her something, but then stopped himself.

Holding hands, they strolled out to the parking lot. Daniel opened the car door for her and stole a lingering kiss when no one was looking.

"Are you going to give me any hints?" Julie asked excitedly.

"Not a one," he teased. "You'll just have to be patient."

Daniel took the freeway that led past the densely populated suburbs and out of town. Finally, he exited, turning down a winding road in the countryside.

"For heaven's sake, Daniel, where are you taking me? Timbuktu?"

He chuckled. "Wait and see."

Julie felt so lucky to be with him. Finally. Everything was so perfect. So right.

When he pulled the car into the long driveway of a newly built two-story house, Julie was awestruck.

"What do you think?" he asked, one brow raised inquisitively.

"What do I think?" she repeated. "You mean this . . . house . . . is my surprise?"

"We're signing the final papers on Monday morning. There are several things you'll have to decide. The builder needs to know what color you want for the kitchen counters, and you need to pick the design of the tile for the bathrooms. From what I understand, there are several swatches of carpet for you to look at while we're here."

Julie nodded, not knowing what to say. She couldn't understand why Daniel wanted a place so far from the city. It would mean a long daily drive both ways in heavy traffic. Julie loved the city. Daniel knew that.

"Come inside and I'll give you the grand tour." He climbed out of the car, walked around to her side and extended his hand. "You're going to love this place."

Julie wasn't convinced. Why would he pick out something as important as a house without consulting her? Daniel took out the key and opened the front door, pushing it aside so she could enter before him. At first, she was overwhelmed by the magnificence of the home. The sunken living room contained a massive floor-to-ceiling brick fireplace. The crystal chandelier in the formal dining room looked like something out of a Hollywood movie. No expense had been spared. But the kitchen was compact and the only real eating space was in the formal dining room. It also didn't appear to have a family room.

"What do you think?" Daniel asked eagerly.

"Nice." Julie couldn't think of anything else to say. It was a beautiful home, that she couldn't deny, but it wasn't something she would have chosen. In many ways, it was exactly what she wouldn't want.

"The swimming pool is this way." He led her through the sliding glass doors off the kitchen to a deck. A kidney-shaped pool was just beyond. Although the cement structure was empty, Julie could picture aqua-blue water gently lapping against the tiled side.

"Nice," she repeated when he glanced expectantly toward her.

"If you think this is impressive, wait until you see the master bedroom." Daniel took her hand and pulled her through the hallway.

The room was so large that Julie blinked twice. Fireplace, walk-in closets, soaker tub in the private bath. It was perfect. Just not for Julie.

"What about the other bedrooms?" she asked.

"Upstairs."

Like a robot Julie followed him up the open stairway. The first bedroom they came to was a decent size and had a bath. The second room was smaller. Julie assumed it would be Daniel's office. The third room looked as if it could be an art room with huge glass windows that overlooked the front of the house.

Julie made the appropriate comments, but felt as if she was being suffocated. She didn't know how much more of this she could take. Abruptly, she turned and walked down the stairs.

"Julie." Daniel followed her out the front door. "What's the matter?"

Shaking her head, Julie tried to control what she was feeling. That Daniel would look for and buy a house without consulting her felt all too familiar—and not in a good way. She wasn't a naive young girl anymore. His mother had picked out their first home as a wedding present without consulting Julie. And now Daniel was doing the same.

"You don't like it, do you?" A hint of challenge was evident in his voice.

"That's not it," she admitted. She was angry with Daniel, but equally upset with herself. Most women would love a home like this. Unfortunately, she wasn't one of them.

"All right," Daniel breathed, scrutinizing her. "What don't you like? I'm sure whatever it is can be changed."

"Changed?" she flared back. "Can you change the location? I love Wichita. I want to live in the city. I thought you did, too. What suddenly made the country so appealing?"

"Peace, solitude—"

"What about the hour's commute in traffic every day?"

"I'll get used to it," he said, attempting to reason.

She crossed her arms. "Sure you will."

Frustrated, he mirrored her closed off pose. "Is there anything else?"

Julie swallowed hard. "Three years ago I didn't say anything when your mother bought us a house. I let everything build up inside until it exploded and I fled. I can't do that anymore. This is a beautiful house, but it's not for us. Someday I'd like to have children. This isn't a family home. It's for a retired couple, or a family with teenagers."

Daniel frowned; his forehead was lined with disappointment.

"I . . . I appreciate what you're trying to do, but—"

"Be honest, Julie. You don't appreciate anything about this." He held the car door open for her and shut it once she was inside.

She waited until he was in the driver's seat. "Daniel." His name rushed out in a low breath. "I'm sorry I seem so ungrateful. But something as important as a home should be chosen by both of us. I realize you were saving this as a surprise and I'm sorry if I ruined that."

Either he didn't hear her or he chose to ignore her. The tires squealed as he pulled out of the driveway and onto the road.

On the drive home, Julie sat in miserable silence. Moving into that house feeling the way she did wouldn't have been right. She'd come too far to allow something like this to happen a second time.

When they arrived back at the condo, Daniel went directly into his office to make a series of phone calls while Julie tried to understand what had motivated him. Only that afternoon, Julie had doubted that anything could destroy their utopia. Now she saw how fleeting their happiness was.

Julie was cooking dinner when Daniel joined her. She kept her back to him, needlessly turning the slices of beef every few seconds. "I wish you hadn't closed yourself off in your office," she began. "I thought we were beyond that. It's important that we talk this out."

He didn't answer.

She turned to find him sitting at the table, reading the newspaper. "Are you giving me the silent treatment?"

He lowered the page. "No."

"Then let's talk," she continued, but his attention had returned to the paper. "If . . . if that house means so much to you then I'll adjust." Making a concession like this was one of the most difficult things Julie had ever done. But her marriage was worth more than her pride.

Apparently engrossed in his paper, Daniel didn't speak for several long minutes. "You're right. I should have consulted you first."

"Then why are you so angry?" she asked.

He set the paper aside. "I don't know," he admitted honestly. "When you left, my mother claimed you were ungrateful for everything we'd done for you. I'm beginning to understand what she meant. I bought that house for you, Julie, and for our life together."

"What a horrible thing to drag up now. You're being completely unfair."

"Was it fair when you walked out on me three years ago? Don't talk to me about fair."

Julie couldn't believe what she was hearing. Clearly unconcerned about the damage he was causing, Daniel raised the newspaper and continued reading.

A full minute passed before Julie could move. She turned off the stove and walked out of the kitchen.

Daniel claimed to have forgiven her, but he hadn't. Not in his heart.

"Julie." He followed her into the living room. "I didn't mean that."

"I doubt that," she said. "I believe you meant every word."

"Maybe I did," he said.

The next thing Julie heard was the front door closing softly.

Julie left early the following morning, not waiting for Daniel. She was already at her desk when Sherry arrived.

"You're so punctual," Sherry commented as she sat in her rollback chair and stowed her purse in the bottom drawer.

"I try to be," Julie said, not looking up from her paperwork.

"I'm going to run down and grab a maple bar for breakfast. Do you want one?"

"Sure," Julie agreed rather than explain why she wasn't hungry. She was handing over enough money to cover it when the office door opened.

Standing on the other side was Daniel. A muscle twitched in his jaw as he glared at Julie. She could see his anger and the effort he made to control it.

Sherry looked from one to the other. "If you'll excuse me, I'll run downstairs."

Julie smiled a silent thank-you. Sherry winked and edged her way past Daniel.

"Don't do that to me again," he commanded.

"I needed some time alone," Julie explained. "I thought you'd understand . . . You felt the same way yesterday."

"That was different," he snapped.

"If you can disappear until the wee hours of the morning then I have a right to leave for work unannounced."

The phone rang and she swiveled around to answer it, presenting Daniel with a clear view of her back. Halfway through the call, she sensed he'd left and the tension in her shoulders relaxed.

Sherry returned by the time Julie was off the phone. Julie could tell she was full of questions, but Julie didn't feel up to explaining and thankfully, Sherry seemed to pick up on that fact.

"You have tomorrow off, don't you?" Sherry asked, changing the subject.

Julie had nearly forgotten. "Yes. Daniel's mother is going in for heart surgery."

With Daniel under so much stress, he didn't need a war between them. Tonight, she'd insist they put an end to this.

The day dragged by but her visit with Clara that evening went well. Although Julie stopped by immediately after work, she learned that Daniel had already come and gone and they'd only missed each other by a matter of minutes.

Julie stayed for a longer visit than usual. They chatted together, and talked about gardening, which Clara enjoyed. The nurse arrived and gave the older woman a shot to help her relax. Julie waited until she was confident Clara was sleeping comfortably.

Daniel wasn't home when she came through the front door. Julie felt as if she were carrying the weight of the world on her shoulders. Briefly, she wondered if he'd gone to Kali. No. He wouldn't. She couldn't believe he'd do something like that.

She forced herself to cook dinner, but had no appetite and only picked at the cutlet and salad. After washing her dishes, she turned on the television. Every five minutes, her eyes drifted to the wall clock. Where was Daniel? His mother was having major heart surgery in the morning. This was a time when they needed each other more than ever. Julie turned off the television and went to bed.

Shadows flickered against the dark bedroom walls as Julie lay staring at the ceiling. The front door clicked softly and Julie sat upright. A quick look at the clock confirmed it was after midnight.

Daniel paused in the open doorway of their room. He loosened his tie as his eyes locked with hers. He took off his coat and carelessly tossed it over the back of a chair. The space between them seemed impossibly wide.

Frantically, her mind searched for the right words. She should have been rehearsing what to say.

She reached out to him and for one heart-stopping moment, thought he might reject her. She watched as he stiffened, hesitant. With a low groan he crossed the room and fell into her arms.

"I'm sorry," she whispered. "Oh, Daniel, I'm so sorry. We need each other now more than ever. Let's forget the house." She hugged him tightly, wanting to laugh away the hurt they'd each foolishly inflicted.

"Julie," he said in a husky voice. The anger was gone. He buried his face in her neck and inhaled deeply. "I need you."

"Yes," she breathed, weaving her hands through his hair. "I love you." She drew his mouth to hers.

An hour later, her head lay nestled against the cushion of his chest, and Julie lovingly ran her fingers over his bare skin. "We can't settle all our arguments this way."

Daniel chuckled and ran his hand down the length of her spine. "I think it has its advantages."

"I feel terrible about our fight. The way I handled everything was wrong. You wanted to surprise me and—"

"No." He gave her a squeeze. "You were right. Anything as important as a house should be a mutual decision. When I got over being angry, I saw how unreasonable I'd been."

"It reminded me too much of what had happened before." She shrugged, unsure of dragging the past into this moment. "Do you really want to live in the country?"

The pause was long enough that she raised her head.

"Not if you don't," he answered.

"My home is with you." She snuggled closer to his warm body. She could still sense that something was troubling Daniel, something more than his mother's pending surgery. Whatever it was had to do with their marriage. Julie didn't know what, but she had a feeling she would soon.

Daniel paced the waiting room as Julie sat in a vinyl-cushioned chair, attempting to read. Repeatedly, her concentration wandered from the magazine to her wristwatch.

"What time is it?" Daniel inquired with a worried frown.

What he was really asking, Julie knew, was how much longer it would be. The doctor had informed them the surgery would take at least five hours—possibly longer.

"I'm sure it'll be anytime now," Julie said. They'd been in the waiting room most of the day. A nurse came at noon and suggested they break for lunch, but Julie couldn't have forced anything down and apparently Daniel felt the same way.

Her husband took the seat beside her and reached for her hand. "Have I told you how much I love you?"

Before Julie could answer, the doctor, clad in a green surgical gown, walked into the room. His brow was moist and he looked as exhausted as she felt.

Julie and Daniel stood, Daniel holding on to her hand with such force that her diamond cut into her fingers.

"Your mother did amazingly well," the doctor announced. "Her chances at a full recovery are excellent."

Julie smiled brightly at her husband as relief washed over her.

"Can we see her?" Daniel asked.

Julie knew him well enough to know that he wanted visual confirmation of his mother's condition.

"Yes, but only for a few minutes. You can both go in. She'll be in intensive care for a few days, then, if everything goes well, she'll be moved to a room on the surgical floor."

Julie appreciated the support the doctors and staff had given throughout this whole ordeal.

"Thank you, Doctor." Julie stepped forward to shake his hand. "Thank you very much."

Julie and Daniel were led into the intensive care area. When Julie saw Clara, her appearance came as a shock. She was deathly pale and surrounded by tubes and machines.

"How are you feeling?" Daniel leaned forward to hug her.

"I'm fine," she assured him. She tried to lift one hand, but it was taped to a board to hold the IV in place.

Daniel laid his hand over his mother's and gave it a squeeze.

"I'm afraid I'm going to have to ask you to leave," a nurse requested a few minutes later. "You're welcome to come back tomorrow, but for now, Mrs. Van Deen needs to rest."

Julie thanked the nurse and they said their goodbyes, promising to return the next day.

The air outside the hospital smelled fresh and clean. Julie paused to take several deep breaths before getting in the car. She was exhausted. With her head resting against the back of the seat, she closed her eyes as Daniel drove them home.

"Julie." A voice spoke softly in her ear. "Wake up."

She yawned and opened her eyes. "I didn't realize I was so tired."

"We didn't get much sleep last night," he reminded her. "And the way I feel right now, we may not tonight, either."

Daniel led her directly into the bedroom and pulled back the covers. "I want you to take a nice long nap and when you're rested, my mother has ordered us to have a night on the town."

"A night on the town?" She didn't think she'd have the energy.

"Mom and I had a long talk yesterday and she feels that we deserve a night out."

Julie opened her mouth to protest.

"No arguing," Daniel said sternly. "She insisted."

Daniel tucked her in and kissed her lightly on the forehead.

"Aren't you going to rest?" Julie asked.

"Honey, if I crawl in that bed with you, it won't be to sleep." He laughed and brushed the hair from her temple. "Actually, I've got some work to do. That should take an hour or two. Just enough time for you to catch up on some sleep."

Julie relaxed against the fluffy pillow and pulled the blanket over her shoulder. Her mind drifted easily into happy, serene thoughts as sleep overcame her.

The next thing Julie knew, Daniel was beside her, holding her close.

"Is it time to get ready for dinner?" she muttered, reveling in the warmth of the bed.

"I think breakfast is more in order."

"Breakfast?" She sat up. "I couldn't have slept through the night." She looked around, confused.

"I could have paraded a marching band through here yesterday evening and you wouldn't have budged."

Julie leaned back against the oak headboard. "I can't believe I slept like that. I was dead to the world for fifteen hours or more."

"I imagine you're starved."

Strangely, she didn't feel hungry, but once she ate some breakfast, she realized how famished she'd actually been.

"I'm sorry I ruined your night," she said, swallowing the last of her toast.

Daniel looked up from his plate and smiled. He reached over to trace the delicate line of her jaw. "You didn't ruin anything," he said. "Do you know how incredibly beautiful you are when you're sleeping? I could have watched you for hours. In fact I kinda did."

Somewhat embarrassed, Julie shook her head.

"I lay awake last night, and I realized I'm the luckiest man in the world."

"Yesterday was a good day to think that. Your mother survived the surgery, and we've been given a second chance."

"Yes, we have," Daniel agreed, his mouth seeking hers.

"What did you and Daniel decide on regarding this house business?" Sherry asked later that week over lunch.

Julie shrugged, setting aside her turkey sandwich. "It's on hold. We've more or less decided to wait until we have a reason to move."

"Do you want to start a family right away?"

"Yes." And no. Things weren't perfect. The incident with the house had proven that. Daniel loved her, but Julie was convinced he didn't completely trust her. It was almost as if he was waiting for her to pack her bags and walk out on him again. Julie realized that only time would persuade him otherwise. She wanted a secure marriage before they had children.

After lunch, the two women returned to work. The phone was ringing when they entered the office.

"I'll get it," Sherry volunteered, reaching for the receiver.

Julie didn't pay much attention to the ensuing conversation until Sherry laughed and handed the phone to her. "It's for you. Personal."

"Daniel?"

"Nope. Jim Patterson."

Julie hadn't encountered Jim since the day of the tennis match. "Hello, Jim," she greeted him, curious as to why he'd be contacting her.

"Julie. Sorry to call you at the office, but I didn't want Daniel to answer and I didn't have your cell number."

"It's no problem. What can I do for you?"

"The Country Club has voted Daniel Man of the Year. We'd like to keep it a secret until the big night so don't let on that you know."

"I won't breathe a word," she promised. "Daniel will be so pleased."

"Each year we do a skit that tells the life story of the recipient. You know, *This Is Your Life* type of thing. Of course we tend to ham it up a bit."

Julie giggled, imagining the types of jokes they must come up with.

"I was wondering if you and I could get together and go over some of the details of Daniel's life. I'd ask his mother, but apparently, she's in the hospital."

"I'd be happy to do that," Julie said.

They agreed on a time and Julie was beaming with pride when she hung up the phone.

Daniel turned up at her office at quitting time. Usually, she walked down the one flight of stairs to his suite and waited for him. But she was running behind, having stayed late to sign final escrow papers with a young couple. Julie was still with the Daleys when Daniel walked through the door.

Julie smiled at her husband and gestured for him to take a seat. "I'll be done in a minute," she told him.

"I didn't realize it was so late," Mrs. Daley said, glancing up from her wristwatch. "We've got to pick up our son from day care. Is there much else to sign?"

Julie scanned the documents. "No, you're both free to go as soon as you hand over the certified check."

"I've got that here." Mr. Daley reached into his jacket pocket.

Once everything was settled, Mr. Daley shook Julie's hand and thanked her again for her help. This was the best part of her job. The Daleys were buying their first home—a dream they'd saved toward for years.

After they were gone, Julie quickly sorted through the remaining paperwork.

"Why couldn't Sherry have stayed?" Daniel asked stiffly.

"Because I volunteered," she answered on the tail end of a yawn. She lightly shook her head from side to side. "I don't know what's the matter with me lately. I've been so tired."

Daniel set his briefcase down and claimed the chair recently vacated by Mr. Daley. "I don't understand why you continue to work. There's no need. I make a decent living."

"I'd be bored if I didn't work." Julie immediately shelved the idea, surprised he'd even suggest it.

"You might have time to learn how to cook."

"Are you complaining about my meals?" she joked, knowing

he had every right to. As long as she stuck to the basics, she was fine, but their menu was limited to only a handful of dishes and Daniel wasn't too fond of the lack of variety.

"I'm not actually complaining," he began, treading carefully. "But I want you to give some serious thought to quitting your job. I don't like you having to work so hard."

"It's not hard," she protested. "Besides, I enjoy it. Sherry and I make a great team."

"Whatever you want." Daniel clearly wasn't pleased and Julie couldn't understand why.

Only a week after surgery, Clara Van Deen was sitting up in bed looking healthier than Julie could remember since returning to Wichita.

"I can't tell you how grateful I'll be to go home," she said. "Everyone's been wonderful here. I can't complain, but I do so miss my garden."

"And your garden misses you," Julie said with a wink to her husband.

"That's right." Daniel shook his head. "Weeds up to my knees."

Clara grimaced. "I can't bear to think what weeks of neglect have done to my precious yard."

Unable to continue the game any longer, Julie patted her mother-in-law's hand reassuringly. "Your garden looks lovely. Now, don't you fret."

"Thanks to Julie," Daniel inserted. "She spent a good portion of the weekend in that garden on her hands and knees."

"I should have been thinking of ways to keep my husband's mouth shut," Julie said with a sigh. "It was supposed to be a surprise."

Clara looked touched. "Did you really?"

"She has the blisters to prove it," Daniel said.

Clara smiled her thanks. "Say, Julie, isn't today the day you were meeting with—"

"No," Julie interjected before her mother-in-law could say anything more. After Jim had contacted her about Daniel's award, Julie had shared the good news with Clara. Apparently, she'd forgotten it was supposed to be a surprise.

"What's this about Julie meeting someone?" Daniel asked.

"Nothing," Julie replied.

"It's a surprise," Clara explained. "I nearly let the cat out of the bag the second time. Forgive me, Julie."

"There's nothing to forgive."

"Will someone tell me what's going on?"

"My lips are sealed," Julie teased.

"Mine, too." Clara shared a conspiratorial wink with her daughter-in-law.

"At least let me know whom you're meeting with," Daniel pleaded as they walked to the car.

"Never."

"I could torture it out of you," he whispered seductively.

"I'll look forward to that." She slid an arm around his waist and smiled up at him. He looked so handsome that she couldn't resist stealing a kiss.

"What was that for?"

"Because I love you."

A brief look of doubt passed over his features. One so fleeting that Julie was almost sure she'd imagined it. But she hadn't. After everything that had transpired between them, her husband didn't fully believe she loved him. Time, she told herself, he only needed time. As the years passed, he'd learn.

On the ride home, Julie thought about how they'd traveled

this same route so many times over the past six weeks that sights along the way began to blend into one another.

She sat upright. "Daniel?"

"Hmm?"

"Take a right here," she directed.

"Why?"

"There's a house on the corner that's for sale." They must have passed the place a thousand times. Julie had noted the Realtor's sign, but hadn't given it a second thought. Now something about the house reached out to her.

Daniel made a sharp right-hand turn and eased to a stop in front of the two-story Colonial home. The paint was peeling from the white exterior and several of the green shutters were hanging by a single hinge. "Julie," he groaned, "it doesn't even look like anyone lives there."

Julie glanced around and noticed the other homes in the neighborhood. They looked well maintained. "All this place needs is a bit of tender loving care."

"It's the neighborhood eyesore," Daniel said impatiently.

"I'd like to see the inside. Can we contact the Realtor?" Already she was writing down the phone number.

"Julie, you can't be serious."

"But I am."

That evening they met the Realtor, Ryan Derek. "I'm afraid this place has been vacant for several months," he told them.

"What did I tell you?" Daniel whispered in her ear. "This isn't what we're looking for—"

"No," Julie interrupted as she climbed out of the car. "But I still like it. I like it very much."

"Julie," Daniel moaned as he joined her on the cracked walkway that led to the neglected house.

Ryan Derek hesitated and Julie sensed that his opinion of the place was similar to Daniel's.

"Can we go inside?" Julie asked.

"Yes, of course."

The moment Julie walked through the door she knew. "Daniel," she breathed, her hand reaching for her husband. "This is it. This is the house."

"But, Julie, you haven't even looked around."

"I don't need to. I can feel it."

The entryway was small and led to an open staircase with a mahogany banister that rounded at the top of the steps. To her right was a huge living room and to her left, a smaller room that would make a great library or office. Dust covered everything and a musty smell permeated the house. The hardwood floors were dented and badly in need of repair.

The formal dining room had built-in china cabinets and a window seat. The kitchen was huge with a large eating area. The main level had two bedrooms and the upstairs held three more. The full basement had plenty of room for storage.

"It doesn't have a family room," Daniel commented after their tour. "That's something you insisted on with the other house."

"This house doesn't need one," Julie insisted. She hoped that Daniel could see the potential of this house. "It's perfect. Right down to the fenced backyard, patio and tree house."

"Perhaps you'd see a few more houses before you decide," Ryan interjected.

Julie shook her head. "That won't be necessary."

She understood Daniel's doubts. This house would require some expensive repairs, but the asking price was reasonable.

"I feel you should be aware of several things." Ryan Derek's voice seemed to fade into the background as Julie moved from one room to the next, imagining how she would decorate. Two bedrooms downstairs were ideal. She could use one as a sewing area. The only problem she could foresee was having the washer and dryer in the basement. But the back porch was large enough to move the appliances out there. Of course, that would require some minor remodeling.

"Julie." Daniel caught up to her. "I think we should go home and think this over before we make our final decision."

"What's there to decide? If we don't go for it now, someone else will."

"That's not likely, Mrs. Van Deen," Ryan interrupted. "This place has been on the market for six months."

On the drive back to the Realtor's office it was all Julie could do to keep her mouth shut. Before she and Daniel climbed into their own car, Daniel and Ryan Derek scheduled another time for them to look at other houses.

"Why'd you do that?" she demanded when Daniel climbed into the driver's seat.

"Do what?"

"Set up another appointment."

"To look at houses—"

"But I've found the one I want," she declared. "Daniel, I love that house. We could look for another ten years and we wouldn't find anything more perfect."

"That house would be a nightmare. The repair costs alone would be more than the value. The roof needs to be replaced. There's dry rot in the basement."

"I don't care," Julie stated emphatically.

"I'm not going to fight with you about it. If we're going to buy a house then it has to be one we both agree on."

Julie had no argument. That house was everything Julie wanted. Hot tears blurred her vision. Something was definitely off with her lately. She couldn't believe she'd cry over something as silly as a house.

With Mrs. Batten's help, Julie ensured that Clara Van Deen's house was spotless the day she arrived home from the hospital. The smile on her mother-in-law's face was reward enough for the long hours Julie'd spent caring for her much-loved garden.

Mrs. Batten cooked a dinner of roast, potatoes and fresh strawberry shortcake, which had long been a family favorite.

"Is everything all right with you, dear?" Clara asked as they sat on the patio together in the late-afternoon sun.

The question surprised Julie. "Of course. What could possibly be wrong?"

Clara took a sip of tea. "I'm not sure, but you haven't been yourself the last couple of weeks. Has the house hunt got you down?"

"Not really." Julie straightened in the wrought-iron chair. "Daniel and I have more or less agreed to wait. There's no rush."

"But there was one house you liked?"

"We agreed to disagree." Julie changed the subject as quickly as possible. "Have you noticed how pink the camellias are?"

Deep in thought, Clara didn't answer. Daniel's expression was similar when he arrived at the condo an hour later.

Julie could tell something was wrong. "Is everything all right?"

"I thought we agreed not to take our disagreements to my mother."

Julie immediately understood. Clara had spoken to Daniel about the house. "We did," she admitted stiffly.

"My mother had a talk with me earlier."

"I know what it sounds like," Julie cut in, "but please believe me when I tell you that I only mentioned it. I tried to change the subject."

Julie watched as her husband's mouth thinned with impatience.

"I think I should have a talk with your mother," she continued. "She's going to have to learn that although we love her dearly, she can't get involved in our lives to the point where she takes sides on an issue. Okay?"

"Definitely."

Julie crossed the room, her arms cradling her middle protectively. They were walking on thin ice. Each desperately wished to maintain the fragile balance of their relationship.

Daniel cleared his throat and moved to stand behind her. "I can see that this house issue could grow into a major problem."

Julie shook her head. "I won't let it. It doesn't matter where we live, as long as we're together."

He gathered her in his arms. "I've been giving that house considerable thought."

"And?"

"I think we should be able to come up with a compromise."

"A compromise?"

"Yes." He pulled away slightly, his hands still linked at the small of her back. "We can buy that house if you agree to quit your job."

Ten

"Quit my job?" Julie repeated incredulously. "You've got to be joking."

"That house is going to need extensive remodeling. Someone has to be there to supervise the work."

"It isn't remodeling the house needs, it's repairs, most of which will have to be done before we move in." Julie walked to the far side of the room. "The house isn't the real reason you want me to quit—is it?"

"I want you to be my wife."

"And I'm not now?" she responded. "I enjoy my job. The problem is, you think I'm going to walk out on you again. It's almost as if you're waiting for it to happen."

"That's ridiculous."

"Is it?" she asked. "First you wanted a house that just happened to be an hour out of town. And now you want me to quit. Are you trying to close me off from the rest of the world?"

"I saw you with Jim Patterson last week," Daniel blurted out. "Will you tell me why you two found it necessary to have lunch together?"

"I can't," Julie replied defensively. "But I'm asking you to trust me. Surely, you don't believe Jim and I are involved in any way?"

"I've tried. A hundred times I've told myself that you must love me. You wouldn't have come back if you didn't."

"Of course I love you," she cried. "What makes you think I would even look at another man?"

Daniel lowered his gaze. "Sometimes I hate myself." The admission came with a bitter laugh.

"You don't trust me."

His expression confirmed her suspicions.

"I love you so much. I could never leave you," she said. "What will it take to convince you of that?"

Daniel couldn't meet her eyes. "I don't know. When I first saw you with Jim, I felt sick inside, then angry. Even though I'd heard you joke with my mother about some mystery meeting, I couldn't believe I'd see my wife and a good friend together. For two days I worried I'd wake up and find you gone."

"You actually thought I'd run away with Jim Patterson?"

"Why not? You ran away from me before."

"I haven't even thought about anyone else since I moved to Wichita."

"Why won't you tell me why you met him?" Daniel asked.

"I need you to trust me."

"I'm trying. Heaven knows I want to, but I don't know if I can."

"You don't look as if you slept at all last night," Sherry said when Julie walked into work the following morning.

"I didn't."

"Why not?"

When they'd gone to bed the night before, Daniel had stayed on his side of the mattress. He could have been on the other side of the world for all the warmth they shared.

"It's a long story," Julie answered. She got herself settled at her desk. "What would you say if I told you Daniel wants me to quit my job?"

"Does he?"

"Let's make this a hypothetical question." Julie wondered if, without knowing the background of her relationship with Daniel, Sherry would read the same meaning into his actions.

"Well, first he wanted to move to the boondocks," Sherry said thoughtfully, rolling her chair the short distance between their two desks. "And now he wants you home all day. My guess is that he's insecure about something. But I can't imagine why. It's obvious how much you love him."

"I wish Daniel realized that."

"You're not going to quit, are you? You've helped me so much with Andy. I'd really miss your friendship."

"No, I'm not quitting." Julie refused to give in to Daniel's insecurities. "Enough about my problems. How *is* everything between you and Andy?"

Sherry lowered her gaze. "Who would have thought wooing my husband would be so difficult?"

The phone rang and Sherry looked up. Suddenly pale, she motioned for Julie to answer as she rushed into the bathroom. Not for the first time in the past couple of weeks, Julie suspected her friend was pregnant.

Julie was off the phone by the time Sherry returned. "Are you going to tell me or are you going to make me ask?"

"How'd you know?"

"Never mind that. Does Andy know?"

She began to cry. "No." She sniffed. "If we do get back together, I want it to be because he loves me. Not because of the baby."

"The divorce proceedings were halted, weren't they?"

Sherry nodded. "But only because Andy and I felt we needed time to think things through. We're not living together."

"You won't be able to keep this secret for long," Julie advised.

"I know. That's why I've given him three weeks to decide what he wants. If I'm going to lose him, then I'd prefer to face that now and be done with it."

"How does Andy feel about having an ultimatum?"

Sherry looked ashamed. "Andy doesn't know."

"Oh, Sherry," Julie groaned.

A tear slid down her friend's cheek. "I realize that sounds crazy, but I firmly believe I'm doing the right thing. If Andy found out about the baby and we reconciled then I'd never be sure. This way I can be sure that Andy really loves me and wants to make this marriage work."

The phone rang again and the pair were quickly thrown into their work.

That night, Julie taught herself to cook Daniel's favorite dinner.

"Did I miss something?" he teased, smelling the air as he entered the kitchen.

"Miss something?"

"It's not my birthday, is it? I've got it! You overdrew the checking account. Right?"

"Just because I made Stroganoff doesn't mean I'm up to something," Julie said.

"In my short experience as a husband, my immediate reaction is . . . you are!"

"Well, you're wrong. I've taken all your complaints to heart and bought a cookbook. I can't have my husband fainting away from lack of proper nourishment."

"Would you like me to demonstrate how weak I am?" he asked, slipping his hands under her shirt.

"Daniel, not now."

"Why not?" he moaned against her neck.

"Dinner will burn."

"That's never bothered you before."

"I thought you were hungry."

"I am. Come to bed and I'll show you how hungry I am."

Julie switched off the stove and fell into her husband's arms; relishing in the urgency of his kiss.

Dusk had settled over the city as they lay in bed an hour later. Daniel's hand caressed her bare shoulder. "I'll be happy when you're pregnant," he whispered.

"Why?" Julie asked.

"I thought you wanted a family."

"I do." But not before they were more secure in their marriage.

"Then why ask?"

"I want to know why you want a baby." Her greatest fear was that Daniel would see a child as a means of binding her to him.

"For all the reasons a man usually wants to be a father." He tossed aside the blankets and sat on the edge of the mattress. "And as I recall, we agreed that when you were pregnant, you'd quit your job."

Julie reached for her robe at the foot of the bed. She didn't know why he'd start an argument after they'd just made love. "I think you should know I've made an appointment with the doctor."

Daniel eyed her carefully. "So you think you might be pregnant."

"No," Julie said. "I want to make darn sure that doesn't happen."

As the days passed, Daniel threw himself into his work and Julie did her best to give the outward appearance that everything was fine. With Daniel not around much, Julie spent more and more of her free time with her mother-in-law.

The two women worked at getting Clara's beloved yard into shape. Julie tried to disguise her unhappiness, but she was convinced that her mother-in-law knew something wasn't right.

"I was pleased to see that old engagement photo of you and Daniel on the television," Clara remarked, working the border of the flower bed. Clara had recently visited the condo for the first time since Julie had moved in.

"We both look so young," Julie said.

"It's strange to remember you like that."

Julie got the impression Clara wasn't referring to looks. "We've all changed."

"Something's bothering Daniel," Clara commented, studying her daughter-in-law closely.

"Oh?"

"I saw him briefly the other day and was shocked by how worn-out he looked."

"He's been working a lot of extra hours lately."

"Is that necessary?"

"I . . . I don't know." Julie moved on to the next section of the flower bed.

"You look a bit weary yourself," Clara continued. "Is everything all right with you two?"

Settling back on her heels, Julie sighed. "Clara, Daniel and I agreed—"

"I know. Daniel told me. But I can't help worrying. You love each other and yet you seem miserable. Whatever the problem is, it can't be worth all this torment. Believe me, I know how stubborn my son can be. Just be patient with him."

"I'm trying," Julie whispered.

Back at the condo, Julie soaked in a warm bubble bath. She had no idea where Daniel was. Although it was Saturday, he'd left early that morning, before she was awake.

Julie had hoped the bath would raise her spirits. She'd been so tired lately. It was ridiculous. It seemed she was going to bed earlier and earlier and often had trouble getting up in the morning. Her appointment with the doctor was coming up; she'd mention it to him. It was probably a reaction to all the stress. She'd had enough of that to last a lifetime.

Abruptly, Julie sat up in the tub, causing water to slosh over the sides. It seemed so clear. She was pregnant. So much had been happening that she'd completely lost track of time. Julie leaned back and placed a hand on her flat stomach. Daniel would be pleased, and despite her misgivings, Julie was, too. Tears flooded her eyes. She cried so easily these days and now she understood why.

Julie climbed out of the tub and wrapped a towel around her body.

Sitting on top of their bed, she reached for the phone and

dialed Daniel's cell. The phone rang twice before she hung up. What would she say?

Julie dialed a different number and waited several long rings. "Sherry," she said. "Congratulate me—we're both pregnant." With that she burst into sobs.

Eleven

"Here," Sherry said, handing Julie another tissue. "You're going to need this."

Julie glanced at the tissue, then back at her friend. "I'm through crying. It was a shock, that's all." Sherry had rushed over to the condo as soon as she'd hung up the phone.

"Discovering I was pregnant was a shock for me, too," Sherry said. "At first I was ecstatic, then I had so many doubts."

"A baby is exactly what Daniel wants."

"But for all the wrong reasons," Sherry assumed. "If Andy knew about me, I suspect he'd be thrilled. But again, for all the wrong reasons."

Julie nodded, feeling slightly ill. She hadn't eaten since breakfast, but the thought of food nauseated her.

"What did Daniel say?"

Julie winced. "He doesn't know yet."

"What are you going to do?"

"I don't know." Julie sighed. "He has to be told, but I don't know when. He's . . . hardly around these days."

"So he's pulling that trick again," Sherry huffed.

"He's working himself to death."

"That's what I thought about Andy. You aren't going to sit here and sulk. I won't let you."

"I'm not sulking."

"No, you're crying." She gave Julie another tissue. "Come on, I'm taking you out."

"Sherry, honestly, I appreciate your efforts, but the last thing in the world I want is to be seen in public looking like this."

Sherry giggled. "I'm going to let you in on one of life's important secrets."

"And what's that?" Julie asked.

"When the going gets tough, the tough go shopping."

"Sherry," Julie groaned. "I don't feel up to anything like—"

"Trust me, you'll feel a hundred percent better. And afterward, I'll treat you to dinner."

"But Daniel—"

"Did he bother to tell you he wouldn't be home for dinner the past three nights?"

"No."

"Then it's time you quit moping around and do something positive for yourself."

Julie realized her friend was right. "All right," Julie agreed, "I'll go."

It took the better part of an hour to make herself presentable, but Sherry was right, she felt better. Before they left, Julie wrote Daniel a short note, telling him her plans.

Sherry seemed intent on having a good time. First they hit

the outlet mall, scouting out baby items and trying on maternity clothes.

Next they took in a movie, followed by dinner at an Italian restaurant. On the way home, Sherry insisted they stop off at her house so Julie could see the baby blanket she was knitting.

"I think I'd better call Daniel," Julie said, sipping a cup of tea. The evening had passed so quickly. Already it was after eleven and although she'd left a note, he might be worried.

"Don't," Sherry chastised. "He hasn't called you lately, has he?"

"No," Julie admitted. They were like strangers who just happened to live together.

"I think I'll put on some music." Sherry reached for the stereo's remote.

The next thing Julie knew, she was lying on the sofa, wrapped in a thick comforter. Struggling to sit upright, she glanced at the clock. How was it light out?

"I was wondering what time you'd wake up," Sherry called from the kitchen. "How do you want your eggs?"

Julie was incredulous. "It's morning?"

"Right, and almost ten. You were tired, my friend."

"But . . ."

"I turned on the radio and within minutes you were fast asleep."

"Oh, no." Untangling the comforter from around her legs, she reached for her cell. "I'd better call Daniel."

As Julie dialed, Sherry handed her a small glass of milk and two soda crackers. Julie smiled her appreciation. Her stomach was queasy as it had been for several mornings. Julie had attributed it to nerves.

Several rings later, she hung up.

"No answer?" Sherry asked.

"No." Julie shrugged. "Maybe he was in the shower."

"Maybe," Sherry echoed. "Try again in five minutes."

"At least he knows I'm with you. If he was worried he would have called."

Sherry turned back to the stove. "He didn't know."

"I left a note."

"I stuck it in my pocket before we left. I'm sorry. I didn't know you were going to fall asleep. I thought if Daniel worried a little, it would be good for him."

"Oh, Sherry."

"It was a stupid thing to do. Are you mad?"

Julie shook her head. Sherry had no way of knowing that she'd walked out on Daniel once before or that he was worried she'd do it again.

"No," Julie said. "He doesn't appear to be concerned at any rate." For all she knew, he could've come home late, crawled into bed and not even noticed she was missing.

Fifteen minutes later, Julie was back home. The condo was dark so she walked across the living room to open the drapes.

"Julie?"

She swiveled around to find Daniel sitting on the edge of the chair, leaning forward, his elbows braced against his knees.

"Hello, Daniel." He looked as though he hadn't slept.

He stood, jamming his hands into his pockets. "I suppose you came back for your things."

"No." Somehow she managed to let the lone word escape. His clothes were badly wrinkled and his hair was askew. The dark stubble on his face was so unlike the neatly groomed man she'd lived with all these months.

"Well go ahead and get them," he said. "Don't let me stop you."

"You want me to leave?" she asked, her voice shaking in disbelief.

"I won't stop you."

"I see." Not knowing what to say, Julie took a step toward the hallway.

Daniel jerked his head up as she moved. His face was deathly pale.

"Julie," he called out.

She turned back expectantly. Tears filled her eyes and she wiped them aside with the back of her hand.

"I don't blame you for walking out on me," he spoke at last. "I drove you to it. I pushed you out of my life the first time and blamed you for it. I can't do that again." He took a tentative step toward her. "I lived for three long years without you and I won't go back to that. Julie—please—don't leave me. Let me make up for all the unhappiness I've caused you."

Julie flew into his arms and Daniel buried his face into her hair, taking in deep breaths as he refused to let her go.

"It doesn't matter why you saw Jim or any other man. I was a fool to think everything would be solved by having you quit your job."

"Daniel, listen—"

"Moving into the country was just as ridiculous," he interrupted. "I love you, Julie. You're the most important person in my life."

"Would you please listen for one minute? I'm not leaving and never was. I was with Sherry. And as for my job, I plan to work for another six months or so and then I'll think about quitting."

"Why six months?"

"Because by then the baby—"

"The baby?" Daniel repeated, completely stunned. "Julie, are you telling me you're pregnant? How? When?"

Julie laughed and lovingly ran her hand along his jaw. "You don't honestly need an answer to that, do you?"

"No," he said sheepishly. "All these weeks I'd hoped you would be. I wanted a child to bind you to me. I realize how wrong that was. You've always been with me."

When his mouth sought hers, Julie responded enthusiastically.

The doorbell chimed and Daniel glared at it irritably. "I'll get rid of them," he promised, kissing the corner of her mouth.

He opened the door to find a man Julie didn't recognize. "I'm looking for Julie Van Deen," the man said.

Julie looked at Daniel and shrugged. "That's me," she said, joining them in the front hall.

"Excuse me for intruding on you like this," the man continued. "I'm Andy Adams. Sherry's husband."

"Of course." Julie smiled. "I've heard a lot about you."

"Yes." He cleared his throat. "I'm sure you have. Sherry has mentioned you on several occasions, as well."

"Please come in. Can I get you something to drink?"

"No, thanks. If you don't mind, I'd like to ask you a few questions." He stepped inside, closing the door behind him.

"Is this about Sherry?" Julie didn't want to get caught in the middle of her friend's marital problems. That could get messy.

"Yes, it is," Andy said. "I hope that's okay."

"I know that she's decided to stop seeing you and—"

"But why?" he asked. "I don't understand. I love my wife. I always have. It wasn't me who wanted that stupid divorce. Sherry seemed to need space and I figured the best thing I could do was give it to her."

"But then you decided to taste a little of that freedom yourself," Julie supplied.

"It was all a game. I knew Sherry was going to be there that night. By that point, I was desperate. I thought a taste of her own medicine would help."

"It did," Julie confirmed, recalling her friend's reaction.

"A little too well," Andy admitted. "We were to the point of moving back in together when—whammo—Sherry announces it's over and she doesn't want to see me again."

"I thought you were the one who—"

"No," he said forcefully. "It's true I thought we should take things slow. I wanted Sherry to be sure of her feelings."

"Andy, I want you to think about something. When you and Sherry separated, she went off her birth control pills. Does that mean anything to you?"

Silence hung between them. "I'm going to be a father?"

Julie nodded happily.

"I'm going to be a father," he repeated as a smile lit up his face. "Why didn't she tell me?"

"I think that's something you're going to have to ask Sherry."

"I will."

"Good." Julie felt relieved.

"Thank you, thank you." Andy shook her hand then Daniel's. "I've got to talk to Sherry. I can't thank you enough." He opened the door and left, nearly tripping in his rush.

"I know exactly how he feels," Daniel said, taking his wife in his arms. "Like a fool who's been given a second chance at happiness. Believe me, this time I'm not going to blow it."

"We're home," Julie announced as her mother-in-law rocked her three-month-old son. Daniel had bought the house of her dreams and made extensive repairs. Most of the work they'd done together during Julie's pregnancy.

Clara had spent the evening with little Ted while Julie and Daniel attended a banquet at the Country Club.

"Was Jim surprised to be Man of the Year?" Clara asked, passing the baby to Julie.

"No more than I was last year," Daniel answered with a chuckle. "But then last year was a very good year."

"It was indeed." Clara smiled. "I was given a new lease on life."

"So was I." Daniel slipped an arm around his wife and leaned over to kiss his sleeping son.

"Was he good?" Julie asked.

"Not a peep. He's so sweet. So small. Theodore August Van Deen seems such a big name for such a tiny baby."

"He'll grow," Daniel said confidently. "And be joined by several more if his mother agrees."

"Oh, I'm in full agreement."

The baby let out a small cry.

"It isn't feeding time, is it?" Clara looked to Julie.

"Not yet," Julie assured her. "Don't worry, Grandma. Babies sometimes cry for no reason."

"Teddy-boy, Grandma's joy." Clara took the baby from Julie and placed him over her shoulder. Gently, she patted his tiny back.

Daniel wrapped Julie in his arms. "I love you, Julie Van Deen."

"And I love you," Julie said. She lifted her face to kiss him, perfectly happy to finally have the family she'd always hoped for.

★★★★★

Sugar and Spice

To the girls of Saint Joseph Academy—class of 1966

One

"You're going, aren't you?" Gloria Bailey asked for the third time.

And for the third time Jayne Gilbert stalled, taking a small bite of her egg-salad sandwich. She always ate egg salad on Tuesdays. "I don't know."

The invitation to her class reunion lay in the bottom of Jayne's purse, taunting her with memories she'd just as soon forget. The day was much too glorious to think about anything unpleasant. It was now mid-May, and the weather was finally warm enough to sit outside as they had lunch at a small café near the downtown Portland library.

"You'll regret it if you don't go," Gloria continued with a knowing look.

"You don't understand," Jayne said, pushing her glasses onto the bridge of her nose. She set aside the whole-wheat sandwich.

"I was probably the only girl to graduate from St. Mary's in a state of grace."

Gloria tried unsuccessfully to swallow a chuckle.

"My whole senior year I had to listen while my classmates told marvelous stories about their backseat adventures," she said wryly. "I never had any adventures like that."

"And ten years later you still have no tales to tell?"

She nodded. "What's worse, all those years have slipped by, and I've turned out exactly as my classmates predicted. I'm a librarian and living alone—*alone* being the operative word."

Jayne even looked the same. The frames of her glasses were more fashionable now, but her hair was the same shade of brown—the color of cedar chips, just a tad too dark to be termed mousy. She'd kept it the same length, too, although she preferred it clasped at the base of her neck these days. She no longer wore the school's uniform of red blazer jacket and navy pleated skirt, but she wore another one, of sorts. The straight black skirt or tailored pants, white silk blouse and business jacket were her daily attire.

Her romantic dreams had remained dreams, and the love in her heart was showered generously upon the children who visited her regularly in the library. Jayne was the head of the children's department, while Gloria was a reference librarian. Both of them enjoyed their jobs.

"That's easy to fix," Gloria returned with a confidence Jayne lacked. "Go to the reunion looking different. Go dressed to the teeth, and bring along a gorgeous male who'll make you the envy of every girl in your class."

"I can't be something I'm not." Jayne didn't bother to mention the man. If she hadn't found a suitable male in ten years, what made Gloria think she could come up with one in two months?

"For one night you can be anything you want."

"It's *not* that easy," Jayne felt obliged to argue.

Until yesterday, before she'd sorted through her mail, she'd been content with her matter-of-fact existence. She liked her apartment and was proud of her accomplishments, however minor. Her life was uncomplicated, and frankly, she liked it that way.

But the last thing Jayne wanted was to go back and prove to her classmates that they'd been right. The thought was too humiliating. When she was a teenager, they'd taunted her as the girl most likely to succeed—behind the pages of a book. All her life, Jayne had been teased about her love for reading. Books were everything to her. She was the only child of doting parents who'd given up the hope of ever having children. Although her parents had been thrilled at her late arrival, Jayne often wondered if they'd actually known what to do with her. Both were English professors at a Seattle college and it seemed natural to introduce her to their beloved world of literature at an early age. So Jayne had spent her childhood reading the classics when other girls were watching TV, playing outside and going to birthday parties. It wasn't until she reached her teens that she realized how much of a misfit she'd become. Oh, she had friends, lots of friends . . . Unfortunately the majority of them lived between the covers of well-loved books.

"You need a man like the one across the street," Gloria said.

"What man?" Jayne squinted.

"The one in the raincoat."

"Him?" The tall man resembled the mystery guy who lived in her apartment building. Jayne thought of him that way because he seemed to work the oddest hours. Twice she'd seen him in the apartment parking lot making some kind of transaction with another man. At the time she'd wondered if he was a drug dealer. She'd immediately discounted the idea as the result of an overactive imagination.

"*Look* at him, Jayne. He's a perfect male specimen. He's got that lean hardness women adore, and he walks as if he owns the street. A lot of women would go for him."

Watching the man her friend had pointed out, Jayne was even more convinced he was her neighbor. They'd met a few times in the elevator, but they'd just exchanged nods; they'd never spoken. He lived on the same floor, three apartments down from hers. Jayne had been living near him for months and never really noticed the blatantly masculine features Gloria was describing.

"His jaw has that chiseled quality that drives women wild," Gloria was saying.

"I suppose," Jayne concluded, losing interest. She forced her attention back to her lunch. There was something about that man she didn't trust.

"Well, you aren't going to find someone to take to your class reunion by sitting around your apartment," Gloria muttered.

"I haven't decided if I'm going yet." But deep down, Jayne wanted to attend. No doubt it was some deep-seated masochistic tendency she had yet to analyze.

"You should go. I think you'd be surprised to see how everyone's changed."

That was the problem; Jayne *hadn't* changed. She still loved her books, and her life was even more organized now than it had been when she was in high school. Ten years after her graduation, she'd still be the object of their ridicule. "I don't know what I'm going to do," she announced, hoping to put an end to the discussion.

Hours later, at her apartment, Jayne sat holding a cup of green tea while she fantasized walking into the class reunion with a tall, strikingly handsome man. He would gaze into her eyes and bathe her in the warm glow of his love. And the girls of St. Mary's would sigh with envy.

The problem was where to find such a man. Not any man, but that special one who'd turn women's heads and make their hearts pound wildly.

Stretching out her legs and crossing her bare feet at the ankle, Jayne released a steady breath and conjured up her image of the perfect male. She'd read so many romances in her life, from the great classics to contemporary titles, that the vision of the ideal man—nothing like the one Gloria found so fascinating—appeared instantly in her mind. He would be tall, with thick, curly black hair and eyes of piercing blue. A man with sensitivity, desires and goals. Someone who'd accept her as she was . . . who'd think she was a special person. She wanted a man who could look past her imperfections and discover the woman inside.

A troubled frown creased her brow. She knew that for too many years, she'd buried herself in books, living her life vicariously through the escapades of others. The time had come to abandon her sedentary life and form a plan of action. Gloria was right—she wasn't going to find a man like that while sitting in her apartment. Drastic needs demanded drastic measures.

Rising to her feet Jayne took off her glasses and pulled the clasp from her hair. The curls cascaded over her shoulder, and she shook her head, freeing them. Plowing her fingers through her hair, she vowed to change. Or at least to try. Yes, she felt content with her life, but she had to admit there was something—or rather *someone*—missing.

Not until Jayne had left her apartment and was inside the elevator did it occur to her that she hadn't the slightest idea of where to meet men. Mentally she eliminated the spots she knew they congregated—places like taverns, pool halls and sports arenas. Her hero wasn't any of those types. A singles bar? Did people even use that term anymore? She'd never gone to one, but it sounded like just the place for a woman on a man-finding mission. Gloria would approve.

Jayne walked out of her building and ten minutes later, she sat in the corner of a cocktail lounge several blocks away. It had the rather obscure name of Soft Sam's. An embarrassed flush heated her face as she wondered what had possessed her to enter this place. Each time an eligible-looking man sauntered her way, she slid farther down into her chair, until she was so low her eyes were practically level with the table. The men in this bar were not the ones of which dreams were made. Thank goodness the room was as dark as a theater, with candles flickering atop the small round tables. The pulsing music, surly bartender and raised voices made her uncomfortable. Repeatedly she berated herself for doing anything as naive as coming here. Her parents would be aghast if they knew their sweet little girl was sitting in what they'd probably call a den of iniquity.

Forcing herself to straighten, Jayne's fingers coiled around her icy drink, and the chill extended halfway up her arm. According to what everyone said, the internet and a bar were the best ways to meet men. She was wary of resorting to online dating services, but she might have to consider it. And as for the bars . . . What her friends hadn't told her was the *type* of man who frequented such places. A glance around her confirmed that this was not where she belonged. Still, her goal was important. When she returned to Seattle, she was going to hold her head up high. There would be an incredible man on her arm, and she'd be the envy of every girl in her high school class. But if she had to lower her standards to this level, she'd rather not go back at all.

Her shoulders sagged with defeat. She'd been a fool to listen to Gloria. In her enthusiasm, Jayne had gone about this all wrong. A bar wasn't the place to begin her search; she should've realized that. *Books* would tell her what she needed to know. They'd never failed her yet, and she was astonished now that she could've forgotten something so basic.

Jayne squinted as she studied the men lined up at the polished bar. Even without her glasses, she could see that there wasn't a single man she'd consider taking to her reunion. The various women all seemed overdressed and desperate. The atmosphere in the bar was artificial, the surface gaiety forced and frenetic.

Coming here tonight had been a mistake. She felt embarrassed about letting down her hair and hiding her glasses in her purse—acting like someone she wasn't. The best thing to do now was to stand up and walk out of this place before someone actually approached her. But if it had taken courage to walk in, Jayne discovered that it took nearly as much to leave.

Unexpectedly the door of the lounge opened, dispersing a shaft of late-afternoon sunlight into the dim interior. Jayne pursed her lips, determined to escape. Turning to look at the latest arrival, she couldn't help staring. The situation was going from bad to intolerable. This man, whose imposing height was framed by the doorway, was the very one Gloria had been so excited about this afternoon. He quickly surveyed the room, and Jayne recognized him; he was definitely her neighbor. The few times they'd met in the elevator, Jayne had sensed his disapproval. She didn't know what she'd done to offend him, but he seemed singularly unimpressed by her, and Jayne had no idea why. On second thought, Jayne told herself, he'd probably never given her a moment's notice. In fact, he'd probably paid as much attention to her as she had to him—almost none.

His large physique intimidated her, and the sharp glance he gave her was just short of unfriendly. He was more intriguing than good-looking. Though she knew that some women, like Gloria, found him attractive, his blunt features were far too rugged to classify as handsome. His hair was black and thick, and he was well over six feet tall. He walked with a hint of aggression in every stride. Jayne doubted he'd back down from a confrontation. She didn't know anything about him—not even his name—but she would've thought this was the last place he'd look for a date. But then, anyone who glanced at her would assume she didn't belong here, either. And she didn't.

Standing up, Jayne squared her shoulders and pushed back her chair while she studied the pattern on the carpet. Without raising her eyes, she fastened her raincoat and tucked her purse strap over her shoulder. The sooner she got out of this regrettable place, the better. She'd prefer to make her escape without attracting his attention, although with her hair down and without her glasses, it was unlikely that he'd recognize her.

Unfortunately her action caught his eye and he paused just inside the bar, watching her. Jayne hated the superior glare that burned straight through her. Blazing color moved up her neck and into her pale cheeks, but she refused to give him the satisfaction of lowering her gaze.

Jayne walked decisively toward the exit, which he was partially blocking. Something danced briefly in his dark blue eyes and she swallowed nervously. Slowly he stepped aside, but not enough to allow her to pass. The hard set of his mouth drew her attention. Her determined eyes met his. Brows as richly dark as his ebony hair rose slightly, and she saw a glimmer of arrogant amusement on his face.

"Well, well. If it isn't Miss Prim and Proper."

Jayne knew her expression must be horrified—he *had* recognized her—but she gritted her teeth, unwilling to acknowledge him. "If you'll excuse me, please."

"Of course," he murmured. He grinned as he gave her the necessary room. Jayne felt like running, her heart pounding as if she already had.

Humiliated, she hurried past him and stopped outside to hold her hand over her heart. As fast as her fingers would cooperate, she took her glasses from her purse. What on earth would he think of her being in a place like this? She didn't look like her normal self, but that hadn't fooled this sharp-eyed man. If he said something to her when they met again, she'd have an excuse planned.

She brushed the hair from her face and trekked down the sidewalk. He wouldn't say anything, she told herself. To imagine he'd even give her a second's thought would be overreacting. The only words he'd ever said to her had been that one taunting remark in the bar. It was unlikely that he'd strike up a conversation with her now. Especially since he so obviously found her laughable . . .

The following day at lunch, Jayne ordered Wednesday's roast-beef sandwich while Gloria chatted happily. "I've got the books on my desk."

"I only hope no one saw you take them."

"Not a soul," her friend said. "They look promising, particularly the one called *Eight Easy Steps to Meeting a Man.*"

"If you want, I'll pass it to you when I'm finished," Jayne offered.

"I just might take you up on that," Gloria surprised her by saying. Divorced for several years, she dated even less than Jayne did. "Don't act so shocked. I've been feeling the maternal urge lately. It would be nice to find a man and start a family."

The roast beef felt like a lead weight in the pit of Jayne's stomach. "Yes, it would," she agreed with a sigh. The worst thing about the lack of a husband was not having children. She always enjoyed them, and as the children's librarian she spent her days with other people's kids.

"I take it you've reconsidered my idea," Gloria continued.

"It might be worth a try." Jayne was much too embarrassed by her misadventure at the bar to say anything to her friend about it.

"You know, if that *was* your neighbor yesterday, you don't need to look too hard."

As far as Jayne was concerned, she never wanted to see *him* again.

"I suppose," she mumbled. "But I'd like to find a man with more . . . culture."

"Up to you," Gloria said, shaking her head.

The same afternoon, her arms loaded with borrowed books on meeting men, Jayne stepped onto the elevator—and came face-to-face with her neighbor. Her first instinct was to turn around and dash out again. His eyes darkened with challenge as they met hers, and she refused to give him the satisfaction of letting him know how much he unnerved her. With all the dignity she could muster, Jayne moved to the rear of the elevator, feeling unreasonably angry with Gloria.

His eyes flickered over her flushed face. Reaction more than need prompted her to push up her glasses, and she struggled to disguise her nervousness with deep breaths.

"Ninth floor, right?" he murmured.

"Yes." Her voice came out sounding like a frog with laryngitis. She'd been so flustered she hadn't even punched in her floor number. Hugging the books to her chest, she kept her eyes on the orange light that indicated the numbers above the elevator door.

"I have to admit it was a surprise seeing you last night," he said smoothly, clearly enjoying her discomfort.

Hot color flashed from her face like a neon light. "I beg your pardon?" If she could have gotten away with it, she would have given him a frown of utter bewilderment, as if to say she had no idea what he was talking about. But Jayne had never been a good liar. Her eye would twitch and her upper lip quiver. Fooling her parents had been impossible; she wouldn't dream of trying to deceive this way-too-perceptive man.

"I didn't know prim and proper little girls went into bars like that."

Clearing her throat, she sent him a look of practiced disdain usually reserved for teenagers she caught necking in the upstairs portion of the library. "Let me assure you, I am not the type of woman who frequents such places." She wished she didn't sound quite so stilted, and for the twentieth time in as many hours, she lamented her foolishness. Her back and shoulders ached with the effort to stand there rigidly. If he knew anything about body language, he'd get her message.

"You're telling me," he said and chuckled softly. Mischief glimmered in his eyes, and with an effort Jayne looked away.

"You must have mistaken me for someone else," she told

him sternly, disgusted with herself for lying. Immediately her right eye started to twitch, and her grip on the books tightened. The elevator had never made its ascent more slowly. She finally relaxed when it came to a grinding halt on her floor. The minute the door opened she rushed out. In her haste, her shoe snagged on the thick carpet and propelled her forward. With a cry of alarm she went staggering into the wide hallway, the books flying from her arms. The wall opposite the elevator halted her progress when she was catapulted into it, catching herself with open palms.

"Are you okay?" A gentle hand touched her shoulder. She turned and gave a convulsive jerk of her head as humiliation robbed her of speech. The dark eyes that had been probing hers were now filled with concern.

"I—I'm fine," she managed, wiping a shaking hand over her eyes, hoping to wake and find that this entire episode was a nightmare.

"Let me help you with your books."

"No!" she cried breathlessly and scrambled to gather up her collection. The last thing she wanted was his pity. He'd made his feelings known. He didn't think much of her, but he was entitled to his opinion—and his fun. "I'm fine. Just leave. Please. That's all I want." She was only getting what she deserved for behaving so irrationally and going into that stupid bar in the first place. Now she'd made everything worse. Never had she felt more embarrassed, and it was all her own fault.

Her hands shook as she fumbled with the clasp of her purse and took out her apartment key. She didn't turn around, but she could feel his eyes on her. Her whole body was trembling by the time she entered the apartment. She shut the door and leaned against it, closing her eyes.

Several minutes passed before she was able to remove her coat and pile the books on her kitchen table. She hung her coat in the hall closet, went into her bedroom and set her purse on the dresser. Organization gave guidance and balance to Jayne's life, and there was never a time she'd needed it more.

The teapot was filled and heating on the stove. Trying to put the unfortunate encounter in the elevator out of her mind, she looked through the books she'd brought home. *Finding a Man in Thirty Days or Less* was the first book in the stack. That one sounded helpful. She glanced at the next one, *How to Get a Man Interested in You.* These self-help books would provide all the advice she needed, Jayne mused. And if they worked for her, she'd pass them on to Gloria later. As always, Jayne would find the answer in books. The next title made her smile. *How to Convince a Man to Fall in Love with You Forever.* Nice thought, but all she really cared about right now was the one night of her class reunion.

She heard knocking and lifted her head abruptly, then slowly moved to the door, her legs weighted by reluctance. She was acquainted with only a few people in Portland. There was no one, other than Gloria, whom she'd call a good friend.

"Who is it?" she asked.

"Riley Chambers."

"Who?"

"Your neighbor."

Groaning inwardly, Jayne closed her eyes, dreading the thought of seeing him again for any reason. Hesitantly she turned the lock. "I'm perfectly fine," she said, opening the door.

"I thought you might be looking for this." He leaned against the doorjamb, leafing indolently through the pages of a hard-cover book.

Jayne's breath jammed in her throat as she struggled not to grab it from his hands. Noting the title, *How to Pick Up a Man,* she felt her face redden.

Brilliant little flecks of light showed in his eyes, which glinted with humor. "Listen, Ms. Gilbert, if you're so interested in finding yourself a man, I'd advise you to stay away from bars like Soft Sam's. They're not good places for little girls like you."

She frowned. "How do you know my name? Oh—the building directory."

He nodded.

"Well, *Mr. Chambers,* if you've come to make fun of me . . ."

"I haven't." The expression in his eyes hardened. "I don't want to ever see you there again."

"You have no business telling me where I can and cannot go." Her hands knotted at her sides in outrage. He was right, of course, but she had no intention of letting him know that. She jerked the book from his hand and when he stepped away, she slammed the door.

Two

Riley dropped his arms and grinned at the door that had closed in his face. So prim little Ms. Gilbert had a fiery temper. She might act like a shy country mouse, but his opinion of her went up several notches. With that well-tamed hair and those glasses, she hadn't left much of an impression the few times he'd seen her in the elevator. Her air of blind trust and hopeful expectation made her look as though she'd stepped out of the pages of a Victorian novel. She'd better watch out, or she'd be wolves' prey. He'd wanted to tell her to open her eyes and look around her. She was too vulnerable for this day and age. This was the twenty-first century, not some romantic daydream.

It'd surprised him to see her in Soft Sam's. Admittedly, she'd been a fish out of water. She was absolutely correct; it was none of his business where she went, but he felt oddly protective of her.

Ms. J. Gilbert—he didn't even know her first name—was as untouched and naive as they come. All sugar and spice and everything nice. Rubbing a hand over the back of his neck, Riley sighed impatiently. He didn't have time to think about a woman—any woman. But a smile formed as he recalled the fire that had flared in her eyes when she'd grabbed that book from his hands. She had spunk. Briefly he wondered what other treasures were waiting to be discovered in her. Riley gave himself a mental shake. Years of following his instincts told him that women like this could be trouble for men like him. Besides, his days were filled with enough conflict. He didn't need a woman distracting him from the problems at hand. Maybe when this business with Priestly was over, he'd have the time—No! The best thing he could do was forget Ms. Sugar and Spice.

If she was in the market for a husband—which she obviously was—there were better men. She was far too wide-eyed and innocent for him. In the end he'd only hurt her. She deserved someone who hadn't become cynical, who wasn't hardened by life.

Jayne stared out at the rain that rolled down the side of the grimy bus window. A low gray fog hovered over the street. After five years in Portland, she was accustomed to gloomy springs. The paper lay folded in her lap; the headlines were the same day after day, although the names and places changed. War, death, disease and destruction. She saw that a prominent state official had been questioned by the FBI about ties to the underworld. Jayne wondered if Senator Priestly was one of the officials who'd visited the library recently. She'd been impressed with the group on the tour; there had been a number of men

Gloria would have approved of. But then, that could mean neither Gloria nor Jayne was a good judge of character.

Riley Chambers was a perfect example of their poor judgment. He might not have been impressed with her, but from the first she'd thought he was . . . intriguing. A man of mystery. Despite the fact that they'd barely glanced at each other whenever they'd met in the elevator, she *might* have been interested in getting to know him. Her current opinion was decidedly different. He had a lot of nerve telling her not to go back to Soft Sam's! If it was such a terrible place, what was he doing there? The next time she saw him, she'd make a point of asking him exactly that.

Agitated, she pulled the cord to indicate that she wanted to get off at the next stop. She tucked the newspaper under her arm and hurried to the rear of the bus.

Avoiding a puddle, she leapt from the bottom step to the sidewalk and paused to open her umbrella. Riley Chambers didn't deserve another minute of her consideration. He'd made his views of her obvious. He'd called her a little girl. She had a good mind to inform him that at five-seven she could hardly be described as *little.* Even now his taunting comment rankled. Jayne had the feeling that he'd said it just to get a reaction out of her. Well, he'd succeeded, and that should please him.

Gloria was waiting for her when Jayne arrived at the library.

"Well, what did the books say?" her friend asked as soon as Jayne had put her bag inside her desk.

"Plenty. Did you know one of the best places to meet men is in the supermarket? Can you see me sauntering up to someone in the frozen-food section and suggesting we have children together?"

Gloria's laughter floated around the room. "That may be worth a try. What other place did they suggest?"

"The art gallery."

"That's perfect for you!"

Jayne sighed and tucked a stray curl into her tightly coiled chignon. "I suppose."

"You've got to show more enthusiasm than this, m'dear." Opening the paper on Jayne's desk, Gloria ran down a list of current city events.

"The Portland Art Gallery is showing work by one of your favorite artists—Delacroix. I bet you were planning on attending, anyway. Now all you need to do is keep your eyes peeled for any handsome, eligible men."

"I don't know, Gloria. I can't even catch a cold, let alone a man. Especially a handsome one."

"You can do it."

"Now you sound like a cheerleader," Jayne moaned, not sure she wanted any of this.

"You need me," Gloria insisted. "Look upon me as your own personal cheering section. All I ask is that you think of God, country and your best friend as you stroll through that gallery."

"What?"

"Well, if this works for you, then I may give it a try."

Jayne had her doubts. Over the past several years, she'd visited a variety of galleries and had yet to see a single attractive man. However, she hadn't actually been on the lookout.

"Well?" Gloria stared at her with her hands positioned challengingly on her hips. "Are you or are you not going to the Delacroix show?"

"Gloria . . ." Jayne said, hedging.

"Jayne!"

"Fine, I'll go."

"When?"

"Tomorrow afternoon."

Although she might have agreed to Gloria's suggestion, Jayne wasn't sure she was doing the right thing. All day she fretted about the coming art show. By five she was a nervous wreck. Feeling that she needed the confidence a new outfit would give her, Jayne decided to go shopping after work. This was no easy decision. She equated clothes-shopping with trauma. Nothing ever seemed to fit well, and she dreaded standing in front of those three-way mirrors that revealed every imperfection.

At the end of the day, Jayne walked down the library steps, balking at the thought of this expedition. Sheer force of will led her into The Galleria, the downtown shopping center, where she found a navy wool dress with side pockets and long sleeves. The dress didn't do much for her, but it was the first one that fit without looking like a burlap bag flung over her head. Feeling somewhat relieved, she paid the saleslady and headed for the escalator that would take her to the transit mall. On her way out Jayne noticed a young woman draped on the arm of a much older man. She batted her long lashes and paused at an expensive jeweler's window display.

"Last month's emerald is so, so lonely," Jayne heard the woman's soft voice purr.

"We can't have that, can we, darling," the older man murmured as he steered the blonde inside the store.

The episode left a bad taste in Jayne's mouth, and she wondered if the woman had met her sugar daddy in Safeway. It was beyond her imagination that men would be attracted to women so shallow. If this was the type of behavior men sought, Jayne simply couldn't do it.

* * *

Saturday afternoon, wearing her new dress, Jayne strolled bravely through the Portland Art Gallery. Wandering around, she saw a man standing against a wall; he seemed to be more interested in the patrons than the art. Gathering her nerve and her resolve, she stood in front of a Delacroix painting, *Horse Frightened by a Storm,* the most famous of the paintings on loan from the Seattle Art Museum. Jayne had long been an admirer of Delacroix's work and knew it well. He was, in her opinion, the greatest of the Romantic painters.

Again she studied the man, sizing him up without, she hoped, being too obvious. He was attractive, although it was difficult to tell for sure without her glasses. From what she could see, he looked approachable. Her hands felt clammy, and she resisted the urge to wipe them dry on the sides of her dress. Clearly she didn't know much about luring a man. But neither was she totally ignorant. She *had* dated before and had even felt the faint stirrings of desire. But her relationships usually died a natural death from lack of nourishment. Sad as it seemed, Jayne preferred her books.

She moved across the marble floor toward the man. Coming closer, she confirmed that he was attractive in a slender, refined way—not like Riley Chambers. Just the thought of *that* arrogant man brought a flash of hot color to her cheeks.

Trying to ignore the tension that knotted her stomach, Jayne mentally reviewed the books she'd read. Each had repeatedly stated that she couldn't wait for the man to take the initiative. One book had gone so far as to list ways of starting a conversation with a prospective love interest. Fumbling her purse clasp, Jayne pulled out the list of ideas she'd jotted down. She could ask for change for the parking meter, but she didn't own a car and lying would make her eye twitch. She discarded that plan. Next on the list was pretending not to notice the targeted male and accidentally-on-purpose walking straight into him. Too clichéd, Jayne decided. She wanted to be more original. The book had suggested asking him what time it was. Okay, she could try that.

Dropping the list in her purse, she took three strides toward the blonde man and did an abrupt about-face. She was wearing a watch! How could she ask the time when there was a watch on her wrist? She'd look like an idiot!

Jayne's heart felt as though it was pounding right out of her chest. Who would've supposed that anything this simple could be so difficult? Sighing, she remembered the look Gloria had given her as she hustled her out the door of the library. If she didn't make her move, Gloria would never let her live it down.

Eyes closed, she took slow, even breaths until calm reason returned. This whole idea was ludicrous. Dressing up and loitering around an art gallery hoping to meet men was so contrary to her painfully shy personality that she could hardly believe she was doing it. The girls of St. Mary's wouldn't be impressed by such desperate measures. Who did Jayne think she was going to fool? She'd turned out exactly as they'd predicted, and there was nothing she could do to change that.

"Excuse me." A male voice interrupted her thoughts. "Do you happen to have the time?"

Jayne's eyes flew open. "The time," she repeated.

The man Jayne had noticed came to stand beside her. Instantly her eyes went to her wrist. He must have read the same book!

"I'm afraid I forgot to replace the battery in my watch," he said with a sheepish smile, dispelling that notion.

"It's nearly three," she stammered, holding out her arm so he could examine her watch.

"I saw you were looking at the Delacroix painting of the horse."

"Yes," Jayne murmured. It'd worked! It had really worked. She smiled up at him brightly, remembering the adoring look on the young woman's face as she'd stared into the eyes of her sugar daddy.

"By the way, my name's Mark Bauer."

"Jayne Gilbert," she said and offered him her hand. Recalling "darling's" reactions, Jayne lowered her lashes alluringly so that they brushed the arch of her cheek.

"He's my favorite artist—Eugene Delacroix." Mark gestured at the painting with one hand.

Ferdinand Victor Eugene Delacroix, Jayne added mentally.

"When Delacroix died in 1863 he left behind a legacy of eight hundred oil paintings," Mark lectured.

And twice as many watercolors, Jayne said—but only to herself. "Is that a fact?" she simpered.

Warming to his subject, Mark continued by explaining the familiar painting, pointing out the colors chosen by the artist to establish mood. He went on to describe how particular lines in the work expressed certain feelings. Jayne batted her lashes at Mark and pretended to be impressed by his knowledge. She wished she had her glasses on so she could see more clearly what he looked like. From a distance he'd appeared attractive enough; close up he was a little blurry.

By the time Jayne was on the bus for the return trip to her apartment, she was thoroughly disgusted with herself. She wasn't any better than that syrupy blonde clinging to the arm of her generous benefactor. She was sure she knew much more about art than Mark did and yet she'd played dumb. He'd apparently done a quick search on Google to collect some basic facts, then spun them into the art history lecture she'd just heard. And she'd pretended to be awed. . . .

Something was definitely wrong with her. She'd always been such a sensible woman. It astonished her that Mark hadn't seen through her act. She wasn't convinced she even liked the man. He spoke for half an hour on a subject he obviously knew very little about while Jayne continued to play dumb and batted her lashes every ten seconds. She supposed he was hoping to impress her, but, in fact, had accomplished just the opposite. The whole production had been pointless—for both of them. He'd asked for her phone number, but she figured she'd never hear from him again.

A walk in the park helped her clear away the confusion that clouded her perspective. She'd thought she'd known what she wanted. Suddenly she was unsure. Knights riding around on white horses, looking for women to escort to class reunions, seemed to be few and far between these days. But then, she didn't know much about knights and even less about men. Quite possibly, each and every one of them would turn out to be like Riley Chambers. The thought caused a shiver of apprehension to race over her skin and she realized for the first time that a slow drizzling rain had begun to fall. Of course, she'd left her umbrella at home. And of course there were no cabs in sight.

Burying her hands deep in her pockets, she quickened her pace. She was three blocks from her building when the clouds burst open in sheets of rain that pelted the sidewalk relentlessly. Jayne was drenched within seconds. Rivulets of water ran down the back of her neck until her hair fell in limp strands. When she stepped into the lobby, her glasses fogged, and her new dress was plastered to her. She felt the overwhelming desire to sneeze. This had been the most miserable day of her life. Not only had she behaved like an idiot over the first man to fall in with her schemes, but she'd been foolish enough to get caught in a downpour. The only thing worse would be to run into Riley Chambers.

No sooner had the thought formed than the man materialized.

Jayne groaned inwardly and stepped into the open elevator, praying he'd take another. The way her luck was going, Jayne should have known better.

Riley followed her inside and stared blatantly at the half-drowned country mouse, a small puddle of water forming at her feet. He couldn't resist a tiny smile as he studied her. Ms. J. Gilbert was badly in need of someone to watch over her. He hadn't seen her in the past couple of days, and it hadn't taken long to realize she was avoiding him. That was fine. She brought out his protective instincts with those wide, innocent eyes, which was something he couldn't really afford. She disturbed him, and innumerable times in the past two days thoughts of her had flitted through his head. Casually he'd tossed them aside, chalking up his curiosity to concern that she might go back to Soft Sam's.

Jayne turned her head away. "Go ahead and laugh," she told him as they began their slow ascent. "I know you're dying to make fun of me."

Riley scowled briefly. Suddenly she reminded him of a cat backed into a corner, its fur bristling and claws unsheathed. Riley had no desire to antagonize her. Instead, he felt the urge to comfort her—and that astonished him. "Are you still angry because I saw the title of your book?" he asked.

"Furious." She slipped her steamed glasses to the end of her nose so she could see him above the frames.

"I didn't mean to make fun of you." She looked vulnerable, and he ignored the impulse to ask her first name. He didn't see her as a Jessica or a Jennifer. Possibly a Jacqueline.

"Why not make fun of me?" she flared. "Everyone else has . . . all my life. People have always thought I'm some kind of weirdo. I like books. I like to read." He saw tears in her eyes, and she twisted around so he couldn't look at her.

The instant the elevator doors parted, she escaped, her shoulders back, her head held high, and glided down the hall to her apartment.

Riley went to his own door, walking slowly. He withdrew the keys from his pocket with a frown, then wearily turned the lock and stepped into his dark apartment. A flick of the wall switch flooded the room with cheerless light. He threw his raincoat over the back of a chair and went into the kitchen to put a frozen dinner in the microwave.

Once again the little mouse, as he still thought of her, had fired to life, turning on him. Even cold and miserable, she'd walked out of the elevator with her chin raised. Her back was ramrod straight, and she moved with as much dignity as any princess. He smiled as he recalled the way her wet dress had clung to her, revealing full breasts, round hips and a trim waist. She had long legs, nicely shaped. He couldn't imagine why she chose to hide behind those generic business suits. The dress she wore today was the first he could remember seeing her in. The dark navy color wasn't right for her. With that chestnut hair and those large honey-brown eyes she should wear lighter shades. At least she'd had her hair down, which was a definite improvement. Although it had been wet and clinging, he just knew it was soft. Silky. He wanted to lift it in his fingers and—

Slumping into a chair, Riley shook his head. He didn't like the things Ms. J. Gilbert brought to the surface in him. It had been a lot of years since he'd given a woman this much thought. What he felt was pity, he assured himself. She was lonely. For that matter, so was he.

The microwave made its annoying sound, and he removed the tray, wondering what the country mouse was having for her dinner.

Holding a tissue to her nose, Jayne sneezed loudly. Her eyes itched, and her throat felt scratchy. A glance at her watch told her it would be another three long hours before she could go home and soak in a hot tub. Thankfully Gloria had offered to handle storytime today. While the preschoolers huddled around her friend, Jayne sat at her desk and cut out brightly colored letters for the June bulletin board. Her class reunion was only seven weeks away. Like the ominous approach of a thunderstorm, defeat settled over her. She wouldn't go. It was as simple as that.

"Could you tell me where you keep the biographies?"

She raised her eyes, and they met a familiar blue gaze. Riley Chambers . . . She clutched the scissors so hard that her thumb ached. "Pardon?" Stunned, she couldn't remember what he'd asked.

"The biographies."

In an effort to stall for time, she put the scissors down. Riley Chambers was on her turf now. "They're directly to your left."

"Could you show me where they are?"

"Yes, of course, but you look like a man who knows his way around."

"Not in this library," he mumbled.

She stood, pausing to push the glasses up onto her nose, then led him to the section he'd requested. "The area to the right is the children's fiction department for ages three to six. If you like, we'll stop here so you can browse."

Riley ignored that. He'd had one heck of a time finding out where she worked. Their apartment manager had to have the most closed mouth of anyone he'd ever known. Generally speaking, he approved of that, but with a lie about undefined but urgent "legal matters," he'd managed to get his answer. "The name Jayne suits you," he said. He'd seen the nameplate on her desk.

"As long as you aren't Tarzan."

"I don't live in a jungle."

"But you obviously speak the language." A smile tugged at the corner of her mouth.

After delivering Riley to the section he'd requested, Jayne watched as he took down several volumes and flipped through the pages. She studied him with helpless fascination. Riley Chambers was a cynical man who looked at the world through wary eyes. Nonetheless, she had a glimmer—more than a glimmer—of his sensuality. Horrified at her thoughts, Jayne quickly returned to her desk. She resumed her task, doing her best to pretend he wasn't anywhere around.

"I'd like to check these out," Riley said, setting two thick volumes on the corner of her desk.

"Do you have a library card?"

"Yeah. It's tricky borrowing books without one."

"You don't need me for that." Jayne didn't know why he'd

come. He probably wanted to throw her off guard. That wasn't going to work. Not in the library.

"I assumed that as a public employee you'd be willing to help me."

"Books are checked out at the front desk."

"I want you to do it."

"Why?"

"Why not?"

"I'm the children's librarian."

"That doesn't surprise me. You look like someone who'd prefer the world of make-believe and happy ever after."

"Is that so wrong?" she replied, her temper flaring.

"Just as long as you don't expect to find your heroes in a sleazy bar."

Color heated Jayne's already flushed face, and she glanced around, wondering if Gloria had heard him. Gloria raised her head long enough to wink encouragingly. "Why are you here?" Jayne whispered.

"You confuse me," he admitted after a minute. "Or maybe *disturb* would be a better word."

"Why?"

"I don't know. Probably because you look like an accident waiting to happen."

"I don't need a fairy godfather." Not when Gloria insisted on waving a magic wand over her head every morning.

"I know what you're after," he whispered back. "I saw the book, remember?"

Jayne bit her lip. Riley was playing with her, amusing himself at her expense. "I'm not looking for a husband. I . . . only need a man for one night."

"So that's it." The corner of his mouth edged up.

"No!" she cried at his knowing look. Her cry attracted the attention of the entire room. The library went silent as heads turned toward them. Embarrassed half to death, Jayne lowered her chin and pleaded, "Would you please just go away?"

Riley abandoned his books and stalked outside, berating himself with every step. Talk about stupid! What kind of game did he think he was playing? Earlier that afternoon the workload had gotten to him, and when he couldn't tolerate it anymore, he'd leaned back in his chair and closed his eyes. A picture of the alluring Jayne Gilbert, all sugar and spice, had immediately entered his mind. He didn't know why she fascinated him so much. Maybe it was because of her innocence, her gentle beauty and the goodness he sensed in her.

After a day like this one, he needed some of that innocence. It'd taken him the better part of an hour to get the information about her job out of the building manager. Discovering she was a librarian hadn't come as any surprise. It fit his image of her. But showing up here hadn't been one of his more brilliant ideas. He hadn't meant to browbeat Jayne and he'd been amused by her witty comebacks. She'd held her own.

Feeling angry and frustrated with himself, Riley went back to the office. He'd apologize to her later. Ms. Gilbert deserved that much.

By the time all the paperwork had been cleared from his desk, it was close to eight. He rubbed a hand over his face, feeling more tired than he'd been in years. He was getting too old for this work. Grabbing his jacket from the back of his chair, Riley tossed his empty paper cup into the garbage can. He hadn't had anything but coffee since early afternoon. The way things were going in this madhouse, it was a miracle he didn't have an ulcer.

Once he'd parked in the apartment lot and headed across the

street to the building, thoughts of Jayne flooded his mind. He sighed, unable to disperse them.

The elevator stopped on the ninth floor. He stood for a full minute outside her door before deciding it would be better to get this apology over with. He knocked once, loudly.

Jayne was miserable. Her throat felt like fire every time she swallowed. Her head ached, and the last thing she wanted was company. Housecoat cinched tight around her waist, she unlocked the door.

"You again?" she whispered, hardly caring. "What's the matter, didn't you have enough fun earlier?"

Riley disregarded her comment. "You look awful."

"Thanks."

"Are you sick?"

"No," she answered hoarsely and coughed. "I enjoy looking like this."

Without an invitation, Riley walked into her apartment and demanded, "Have you seen a doctor?"

Jayne stood by the door, holding it open and staring pointedly into the empty hallway. "Make yourself at home," she said with heavy sarcasm. As it was, she'd spent a good part of the afternoon explaining Riley's visit to Gloria. Somehow her friend refused to believe it was a coincidence that he'd come into the library. According to Gloria, Riley was definitely interested in Jayne. That suggestion only made her laugh.

"You might have a fever. Have you taken your temperature?"

"I was about to do that." The man appeared oblivious to her lack of welcome. She closed the door and turned around, leaning against it.

"Sit down," he said.

"Are you always this bossy?"

"Always."

Too weak to argue, Jayne did as he said.

"Where's your thermometer?"

She pointed to the kitchen counter and tucked her bare feet underneath her. "Why do you keep pestering me?"

He didn't respond, seemingly intent on reading the thermometer. Impatiently he shook it.

"Open your mouth," he ordered, and when she complied, he gently inserted it under her tongue.

Curious, Jayne followed his progress as he paced the carpet in front of her, checking his watch every fifteen seconds. He picked up a book from the coffee table, read the title and arched his brows. Replacing the book, he resumed his pacing.

"I came because I wanted to apologize for this afternoon. I had no business, uh, pestering you."

"Then why did you?" she mumbled, holding the thermometer in her mouth as she spoke.

"I don't know." His hand sliced the air. "Probably for the reason I mentioned earlier. You . . . disturb me."

"Why?" she asked again.

"If I knew the answer to that, I wouldn't be here."

"Then go away."

"I thought misery loved company."

"Not this misery."

"Too bad." Carefully he withdrew the thermometer and examined it.

"Well? What does it say? Will I live?"

"A little over ninety-nine. Got any aspirin?"

Jayne shook her head. "I'm never sick."

He studied her skeptically, and Jayne waited for a harangue that never came.

"I'll be back." He left her door slightly ajar, and Jayne felt too miserable to get up and lock him out.

Riley returned a couple of minutes later, his arms loaded with a variety of objects: soup can, a box of tissues, bottle of aspirin, frozen lemonade and the paper.

"Are you moving in?" she asked irritably. The other day she'd assumed that she couldn't meet a man in her own living room. Riley was proving her wrong.

He scowled and stalked wordlessly into her tiny kitchen. What an odd man he was, Jayne thought. He obviously felt *something* for her if he was going to all this trouble, and yet he didn't seem to want her company.

After a moment Jayne decided to investigate. Struggling to her feet, she paused in the middle of the room to sneeze and blow her nose.

Riley stuck his head around the corner. "Sit," he ordered, giving her a ferocious glare.

Jayne glared back at him. "What are you doing in my kitchen?"

"Making dinner. Don't be ungrateful."

"I'm not hungry," she said, advancing a step. Riley would never be able to figure out her organizational methods. He'd look in her cupboards and claim that even her groceries were filed under the Dewey decimal system.

"Is it feed a cold and starve a fever or the other way around?" Riley asked next.

He made quite a sight with his white shirtsleeves rolled halfway up his arms and an apron tied high around his waist. The top two buttons of his shirt were opened to reveal dark curling hair. Jayne couldn't help smiling.

"Now what's so funny?" His own smile was lazy.

"You."

"What?" He glanced down at his flowered apron. "What's the matter, haven't you ever seen a man working in the kitchen?"

"Not in mine."

"Then it's time you did." He turned away from her and took a saucepan from the top of the stove, then opened and closed her cupboard doors until he located glasses and bowls. "You should smile more often," he said casually as he worked, pouring equal amounts of soup into the wide bowls.

"I've got a cold. My head hurts, my throat feels raw, and there's a crazy man in my kitchen, ordering me around. Give me a day or two, and I'll find the humor in all of this." She didn't add that she had seven weeks to come up with a man who'd make heads turn when he walked into a room.

"Sit."

"Again? See what I mean?" she complained, but she did as he asked, pulling out the high-backed oak chair.

Riley brought her a bowl of hot soup, a steaming mug and two aspirin. Jerking the apron from around his waist, he took the chair across from her.

"What is it?" she asked, staring at the steaming bowl.

"Chicken noodle soup." He pointed to the bowl, then the mug. "And hot lemonade."

"Couldn't you be more original than that?"

"Not on short notice."

"Are you eating here, too?"

"What's the matter? Do you expect the help to eat in the kitchen?"

Jayne smiled again. "Why are you doing this?"

Riley shrugged. "Because I owe you. I didn't mean to make fun of you earlier."

"When?" To her way of thinking, he'd done it more than once.

"This afternoon. I shouldn't have come in and given you a hard time. I want to apologize."

"If you're in the mood to make amends, you might mention the other night, as well."

"No." He scowled briefly, letting his eyes drop to her lips. "You brought that on yourself."

Jayne set her spoon aside. "I don't know if I like you. I've never met anyone who confuses me the way you do."

"Then that makes two of us. Listen, I've lived most of my life without women, and I don't want a prim little country mouse messing things up at this late date." The words were harsher than he'd intended, but Jayne was stronger than her soft, vulnerable manner had led him to believe. She had an inner strength he was only beginning to recognize.

Jayne bristled, her hand gripping the spoon tightly. "I didn't invite you here." She'd have a heck of a time explaining this to Gloria if her friend ever found out.

"I'm aware of that."

The phone rang, jerking Jayne's attention across the room.

"Do you want me to answer it?" Riley asked.

"No," she answered, rising from her chair. "I will." She reached the phone on the fourth ring and grabbed it. "Hello," she said, slightly out of breath.

"Jayne, it's Mark Bauer. Do you remember me? We met at the art gallery last Saturday."

Three

"Hello, Mark, of course I remember you." Jayne leaned against the chair, trying to ignore Riley, who was standing behind her.

"You don't sound the same," Mark continued.

"I've got a cold." That had to be the understatement of the year.

"Not a bad one, I hope."

"Oh, no, I'll be fine in a day or two." Muffled sounds coming from behind Jayne made her tense. Riley was either pacing or fooling around in her kitchen. She wondered if he'd discovered how organized she was. Even her soup cans were stored in alphabetical order.

"Do you think you'd be well enough to go to a movie with me Friday night?" Mark asked.

Jayne was stunned. After behaving in such a ridiculous way,

she hadn't expected to hear from Mark again. Least of all to have him ask her out. "I'd like that, thank you."

"Shall we say seven, then?"

"Seven will be fine."

Jayne replaced the receiver and stared at the phone, dumbfounded. A prickly feeling attacked the base of her neck and slithered down her spine. The dumb act had worked once, but she doubted she could maintain it for any length of time. Keeping it up for the seven weeks until her class reunion would be impossible. And once they were in Seattle, she couldn't suddenly tell him: *Surprise! It was all an act. I'm really brilliant.* "I shouldn't have agreed to go." Jayne was shocked to realize she'd spoken aloud.

"Why not?"

Feeling a bit sick to her stomach, Jayne turned to face Riley, who was standing beside the kitchen table. One large hand rested over the back of the polished oak chair. Their eyes met. "I . . . don't know exactly what he looks like," she admitted honestly, but that wasn't the reason for her hesitancy. Someone like Riley would have instantly seen through her act. Unfortunately—or fortunately—Mark wasn't Riley.

"What do you mean?"

"When we met, I wasn't wearing my glasses." Jayne vowed that if Riley so much as snickered, she'd ask him to leave.

"If wearing glasses bothers you, why don't you get contacts?" he asked matter-of-factly, reaching for his spoon. That night at Soft Sam's she hadn't worn her glasses, he remembered and stiffened.

"I've tried but I can't. My eye doctor recommended a book on how to use them, but . . ."

"It didn't help you?"

Jayne lowered her hands to her lap. "Sadly, no."

"Where did you meet this Mark guy?" He struggled to keep his voice calm and disinterested. He'd been trained not to reveal interest or emotion. It should come easy, but with Jayne, for some reason, it didn't.

"At the art gallery last Saturday." She caught a sneeze with her napkin just in time. "One of those books said that was a good place to meet men."

Relaxing, Riley tried his first spoonful of lukewarm chicken noodle soup. He might not be an inventive chef, but this meager meal would take the edge off his hunger. The fact that Jayne was sitting across from him with her quiet wit and seductive eyes made even soup more appealing.

They ate in silence, but it was a companionable one as if they were at ease with each other for the first time. Jayne wasn't hungry, but she managed to finish her soup. Riley insisted on doing the dishes, and she didn't argue too strenuously. There were only a couple of bowls and a saucepan that he rinsed and tucked in the dishwasher.

"Is there anything else I can do for you?" Riley asked, standing by the door.

Jayne smiled shyly and shook her head. "No, you've been very kind. Thank you." He was an attractive man, and she didn't know why he was paying her so much attention. His concern was so unexpected that she didn't know how to categorize it. They were neighbors, and it would be good to have a friend in the apartment complex. Riley was probably thinking the same thing, Jayne mused. Their relationship was mutually beneficial.

"I'll see you later," he said.

"Later," she agreed.

The next morning, Jayne woke feeling a hundred percent better. The ache in her throat was gone, as was the stiffness in her arms and legs. Declaring herself cured, she dressed for work, humming as she moved around the bedroom. For several days she'd been dreading the approach of summer and her class reunion, but this morning things looked brighter. Mark had asked her out, and she was determined to keep his interest in her alive. That shouldn't be difficult with Gloria's coaching.

Although the day was predicted to be pleasantly warm, Jayne reached for her jacket on the way out the door. She half looked for Riley as she waited for the elevator, but she'd only seen him a few times in the mornings. Their paths didn't cross often. She would like to have told him how much better she felt and thank him again for his help.

Standing at the bus stop, she noticed that the clouds were breaking up. The air smelled fresh and springlike. Jayne had to remember that this was June, yet it felt more like April or early May. School would be out soon, and her section of the library would be busier than usual.

When a sleek black car pulled up by the curb, Jayne instinctively stepped back, then experienced a flush of pleasure when she recognized the driver.

Riley leaned across the front seat and opened the side door. "It might not be a good idea for you to stand out in the cold. I'll give you a ride downtown."

"I feel great this morning," she told him. "Thanks for the offer," she felt obliged to say, "but the bus will be here any minute."

Riley's grip tightened on the door handle. "I'll give you a ride if you want. The choice is yours." He said it without looking at her.

Jayne still didn't understand why he was so concerned about her health, but now wasn't the time to question his solicitude. She slid into the front seat, closed the door and fastened her seat belt. "You're going to spoil me, Mr. Chambers."

"I don't work far from you," he said, checking the side mirror before merging with the snarled traffic.

That explained why she and Gloria had seen him at lunchtime. Jayne studied him as he maneuvered the car. He might have offered her a ride, but he certainly didn't seem happy about it. His lips were pursed, and his forehead creased in a frown. Although traffic was heavy and sluggish, that didn't seem to be the reason for his impatience. She assumed it had something to do with her.

Jayne folded her hands in her lap, regretting that she'd accepted his invitation. She couldn't understand why he'd offer her a ride when her presence was clearly upsetting to him.

"You're quiet this morning," Riley commented, glancing her way.

"I was afraid to say anything." Jayne focused her gaze on her laced fingers. "You looked like you'd bite my head off if I did."

"When has that ever stopped you?"

"Today."

Riley's frown grew, if anything, fiercer. "What made you think I was angry?"

"You look like you ate rattlesnakes for breakfast," she replied.

"I do? Now?"

A quick movement—what Jayne termed an "almost smile"—touched his mouth.

"Your face was all scrunched up," she said, "and your expression was terribly intense. I was wondering why you're giving me a ride when it's clear you don't want me in the car with you."

"Not want you in the car?" he repeated. "That's not it at all. I was just thinking about a problem . . . at the office."

"Then your thoughts must be deep and dark."

"They have been lately." His face softened as he averted his eyes from the traffic to briefly look at her. "Don't worry, I've never been one to do anything unless it's exactly what I want."

Pleased by his response, Jayne relaxed and smiled. Riley was different from anyone she'd known before. Yet in certain ways they were alike. He was at ease with her quiet manner. In the past Jayne had felt it necessary to make small talk with men. Doing that had been contrary to her nature; finding things to talk about was always difficult, even with Gloria. Mark would expect it, and she'd make the effort for his benefit.

Riley stopped at a red light, and Jayne watched as his fingers loosened their grip on the steering wheel. He turned to her. "You're looking better this morning."

"Like I said, I feel wonderful. It was probably the soup."

"Undoubtedly," Riley agreed with a crooked grin.

"Thank you again," she said shyly, astonished by how much a smile could alter a man's appearance. The glow in his blue eyes warmed Jayne as effectively as a ray of sunlight. "You mentioned an office. What do you do?"

The hesitation was so slight that Jayne thought she must have imagined it.

"I'm an inspector."

"For the city?" Somehow his words didn't ring entirely true, but Jayne attributed that notion to reading too many thrillers and suspense novels.

"Yeah, for the city. I'll let you off at the next corner." Not waiting for her response, he switched lanes and stopped at the curb.

"I'm in your debt again," she murmured. Her hand closed over the door handle. "Thank you."

"Have a good day, Miss Prim and Proper."

Jayne flashed angry eyes at him. When she clenched her hands and stalked away, Riley grinned. Jayne Gilbert was easy to bait. Her reaction to teasing suggested she was an only child. That would also account for her quiet, independent nature. He appreciated that quality in her. Without realizing it, Riley smiled, his troubled thoughts vanishing in the face of a simple display of emotion. Who would've guessed a shy librarian could have that effect on him?

Jayne was watching the evening news two days later while a casserole baked in the oven, when Riley's image flitted into her restless mind. The news story relayed the unsavory details of a prostitution ring that had recently been broken. The blonde woman on the screen looked vaguely familiar, and Jayne wondered if she'd seen her that night in Soft Sam's, the night she met Riley. But she hadn't been wearing her glasses, and it was difficult to tell.

Jayne didn't know what made her think of Riley. She hadn't seen him for a few days. In fact, she'd been half looking for him. At first he'd made his views of her plain. Now she wasn't sure what he thought of her. Not that she expected to bowl him over with her natural beauty and charm. She didn't expect that from any man. She liked Riley, enjoyed his company, and that was rare. The fact was, Jayne didn't know what to make of her relationship with him. Perhaps it was premature to even call it a relationship. Friends—she hoped so. But nothing more. Riley wasn't the type of man she pictured walking into her class reunion. No, she'd reserve Mark for her classmates' inspection.

Riley was too . . . rough-edged. Mark seemed smoother. More sociable.

Shaking her head, Jayne felt guilty that her thoughts about Riley—and Mark, for that matter—could be so self-serving. After all, Riley had gone out of his way for her.

On impulse, she pulled the steaming casserole from the oven and divided it into two equal portions. With giant oven mitts protecting her hands, she carried the steaming dish down the hallway to Riley's apartment. She knocked at the door, balancing the casserole in one hand, and waited impatiently for him to answer.

The door was jerked open in an angry motion, but his frown disappeared as soon as he saw her. "Jayne?"

"Hi." Now that she was there, she felt like an idiot, but she'd been behaving a lot like one lately. "The library got a new cookbook this week. I read through it and decided to try this recipe."

"And you're looking for a guinea pig?"

"No." The comment offended her. "I wanted to thank you for fixing me dinner the other night and for the ride to work."

"It isn't necessary to repay me."

Jayne sighed. "I know that. But I wanted to do this. Now are you going to let me in, or do I have to stand here while we argue?"

"I don't know—you look kind of appealing like that."

"I didn't think men found 'prim and proper' appealing." She loved turning his own words back on him.

Riley grinned, and his whole face relaxed with the movement. The dark blue eyes sparkled, and Jayne was reminded that he could be devastatingly attractive when he wanted to be.

"Prim and proper women can be fascinating," he said softly.

Jayne sucked in her breath. "Don't play with me, Riley. I'm not good at games. The only reason I'm here is to thank you."

"I should be thanking you—this smells delicious." He stepped aside, and Jayne brought the dish to his kitchen. Riley's apartment was similar to her own, although Riley possessed none of her sense of orderliness. His raincoat had been carelessly tossed over the back of a living room chair, and three days' worth of newspapers littered the carpet.

"It's chicken tamale pie," she told him, feeling awkward without the dish in her hands.

"Will you join me?"

Jayne was convinced the invitation wasn't sincere until she remembered his claim that he never said or did anything without meaning it.

"No, my dinner is waiting for me. I just wanted—"

"—to thank me," he finished for her.

"No," she said mischievously. "I came to prove that prim and proper girls have talents you might not expect."

"Given half a chance, I'd say they'd take over the world."

"According to what I remember from Sunday school class, we're supposed to inherit it." She gave him a comical glance. "Or is that the meek and mild?"

"Never meek, Ms. Gilbert." Chuckling, Riley closed the door after her and sighed thoughtfully. He wasn't so sure Jayne was going to control the world as he'd teased, but he was genuinely concerned that he could be falling for her. And then, without much trouble, she'd end up ruling his heart and his life.

He swept a hand across his face, trying to wipe out the memory of her standing in his apartment. Instead, he realized how *right* it had felt to be with her, even if it was only for those few minutes. This woman was entering his life when he was least prepared to deal with it. He was in his thirties and cynical about the world. She was *much* too innocent for him, yet he found himself attracted to her. She touched a vulnerable part of him that Riley hadn't known existed, a softness he thought had vanished long ago.

For both their sakes, it would be best to avoid her.

Several times before her date with Mark, Jayne studied her dating advice books. With Gloria choosing her outfit, Jayne dressed casually, or what was casual for her—a plaid skirt and light sweater. She used lots of mascara and left her hair down. It fell in gentle waves to her shoulders and shone from repeated brushing. Rereading *How to Get a Man Interested in You* while she waited, Jayne mentally reviewed the discussion topics Gloria had given her and recalled her friend's tips on how to keep a conversation going. She hoped Mark would do most of the talking and all that would be required of her was to smile and bat her eyelashes. Granted, that felt a bit false, but she was starting to believe that social interactions, especially male-female ones, often were.

Mark arrived precisely when he said he would. Their evening together went surprisingly well. And fortunately she was farsighted so she had no trouble seeing the screen, even without her glasses. The movie was a comedy with slapstick humor.

After the movie, Mark suggested a cup of coffee.

Jayne agreed, and her hand slid automatically inside her pocket to the list of conversation ideas. But she didn't need them. Mark was a nice man with a huge ego. He spoke in astonishing detail about his position as an office manager. She didn't know why he felt the need to impress her with his importance, but as the books suggested, she fawned over every word, exhausting though that was.

In return she told him she worked for the city, but not in what capacity. Librarians were stereotyped. It didn't matter that she fit that stereotype perfectly. Later, as they went back to her apartment, Jayne thought wryly that Gloria needn't have worried about making up a list of topics to discuss. As she'd originally hoped, Mark had done most of the talking. She should've been relieved, even pleased, but she wasn't. With Mark she felt like . . . like an accessory.

Outside her apartment door, clenching her keys, Jayne looked up at him. "I had a lovely time. Thank you, Mark."

He placed his hand on the wall behind her and lowered his head. Jayne felt a second of apprehension. She wasn't sure she wanted him to kiss her. Nonetheless, she closed her eyes as his mouth settled over hers for a gentle kiss. Pleasant, but not earth-shattering. "Can I see you again?" he asked, his breath fanning her temple.

"Ah . . . sure."

"How about dinner Wednesday night? Do you like to dance?"

"Love to," she told him, wondering how quickly a book and CD could teach her. She had about as much rhythm as a piece of lint. The class reunion was bound to have some kind of dancing, and she'd need to learn sooner or later, anyway. She'd check out an instruction book and CD on Monday. Her motto should be *By the Book,* she decided with a satisfied grin.

Monday afternoon, when she was walking home from the bus stop, she heard Riley call her from the parking lot across the street.

"Hello," Jayne called and waved back, feeling unreasonably pleased at seeing him again. He carried his raincoat over his arm, and she wondered if he ever wore the silly thing. She'd only seen it on him once or twice, yet he had it with him constantly.

Checking both sides of the street before jogging across, Riley joined her in front of the apartment building and smiled roguishly when he noted the CDs poking out of her bag. "Don't tell me the books on manhunting didn't help and you're advancing to audio?"

Jayne studied the sidewalk between her shoes. "No, Mark asked me to go dancing, and . . . I'm not very good at it."

"Two left feet aren't uncommon." Riley resisted the urge to fit his hand under her chin and lift her gaze to his. He wanted to pull her hair free of that confining clasp and run his fingers through it. The thought irritated him. He didn't want to feel these things. This woman was like a red light flashing *trouble.* She didn't hide her desire to get married, or at least find a man, while Riley had no intention of settling down. Yet he was like a moth fluttering dangerously close to that very same light. The light warning there was trouble ahead . . .

"I went to a few dances in high school, but that was years ago," Jayne said. "Ten, to be exact, and I don't remember much. I don't think just shuffling my feet around will work this time."

"Do you want any help?" The offer slid from his mouth before he could censor it. Silently he cursed himself.

"Help?" Jayne repeated, surprised. "You'd do that?"

He nodded. Yes, he'd do that, just so she'd marry this Mark guy and get out of his life. He sighed. Who was he trying to kid? He'd do it so he could stop wondering how she'd feel in his arms.

"It *would* be easier with a partner," Jayne murmured. She saw Riley's eyebrows drawn together in a dark glower as if he already regretted making the offer. "If you're sure."

"I'll be at your place in an hour."

"Let me cook dinner, then . . . as a means of thanking you," she added hurriedly.

This cozy scene was going to be difficult enough as it was. "Another time," he said, putting her off gently.

Calling himself every kind of fool, Riley knocked on Jayne's apartment door precisely one hour later. He'd never felt more mixed up in his life. His arms ached for the warm feel of this woman, and yet at the same time he dreaded what that sensation would do to him.

Jayne opened the door, and Riley mumbled something under his breath as he stalked past. She couldn't understand what he was saying. She'd changed out of her "uniform" and into linen pants the color of summer wheat and a soft cashmere sweater. The instruction book that came with the CD was open on the coffee table.

"You ready?" Riley's voice had a definite edge to it.

"Yes, of course," she said too quickly, turning on the CD player. "The first part is a guide to waltzing. The book says . . ." Feeling ridiculous, Jayne placed her hands on her hips and boldly met his scowl. "Listen, Riley, I appreciate the offer, but you don't have to do this."

"I thought you wanted to learn how to dance."

"I do, but with a willing partner. From the looks you're giving me, one would assume you're furious about the whole idea."

Indecision showed in every weather-beaten feature of his face. "I don't want you to get the wrong impression, Jayne. I'm rotten husband material."

She valued his honesty. He wasn't interested in her, not romantically. They hadn't even gone out on a date. He didn't think of her in those terms, yet he'd made an effort to seek her out, talk to her, be with her. If he wanted to be just friends, it was fine with her. In fact, wasn't friendship what *she* preferred, too? "I think I realized that from the first time I saw you in the elevator. You'd make some poor girl a terrible husband, Riley Chambers. What I don't understand is why you've appointed yourself my fairy godfather."

A slow smile crept into his eyes. "If you turned into a pumpkin at midnight, that might be the best thing all the way around."

"You don't know your fairy tales very well, Mr. Chambers. The coach turned back into a pumpkin. Not Cinderella."

The sweet sounds of a Viennese waltz swirled around them. An instructor's voice rang out. "Gentlemen. Place one hand on the lady's waist . . ."

Riley bowed elegantly. "Shall we?"

Pretending to fan her face, Jayne batted her lashes and gave him a demure look. "Why, Rhett, you have the most charmin' manner."

Loosely Riley took Jayne in his arms. She followed his lead, and he could tell by the concentration on her face that this was difficult for her. "*One,* two, three. *One,* two, three," the instructor's voice chanted.

"Pretend you're enjoying yourself," he told her, "otherwise Mark's going to think you're in pain."

Jayne laughed involuntarily. She *was* trying too hard. "Don't be so anxious for me to step on your toes."

"I'm not!" Riley positioned his hands so the need to touch her was at a minimum. He adjusted his fingers at her shoulder and then at her hip, all to no avail. Each time his hands shifted, he became aware of the warmth that lay just beneath his fingertips. He tried desperately not to notice.

Swallowing, he concentrated on moving to the music and held his breath. Fairy godfather indeed! He should be arrested for the thoughts that were racing at breakneck speed through his head. This entire situation was ridiculous. Riley had held women far more intimately than he was embracing Jayne, and yet he was acting like a teenage boy on his first date. Briefly he wondered if she had any suspicion of what she was doing to him. He doubted it; knowing Jayne, she'd have to read about it first. Or maybe she had. Maybe this whole thing was an experiment, just like her visit to Soft Sam's. Gritting his teeth, Riley did his utmost to ignore the feel and the flowery scent of the woman in his arms—to ignore the texture of her soft skin, the way her body moved in perfect rhythm with his.

Jayne nodded happily to the music. *One,* two, three . . . This was going so much better than she'd imagined. Riley was obviously a good dancer, moving confidently with a grace she wouldn't have expected in a man his size. She felt a warmth where he positioned his hands at her waist, and forced her body to relax.

"How am I doing?" she asked after a while.

"Fine," he muttered. He was more convinced than ever that Jayne had no idea what she was doing to him. He had to endure this torture, so he'd do it with a smile. "When you go out with Mark, do you plan to leave your hair up?" He inched back to put some distance between them.

"Probably not."

"Then maybe you should let it down now. You know, to . . . uh, practice." He couldn't believe he was suggesting this, well aware that he was only making things worse.

"Okay." She reached up and took off the clasp; the dark length fell free.

"What about your glasses?" he asked next, resisting the urge to lift a strand of hair and feel its texture.

"Mark has never seen me in glasses."

"Then take them off."

"All right." She laid her glasses beside the hair clasp on the end table. A fuzzy, blurred Riley smiled down at her.

"No squinting."

"I can't see you close up."

"You won't see Mark, either, so it shouldn't make any difference."

"True," she agreed. But it *did* make a difference. She didn't need her glasses or anything else to know it was Riley's arms around her. When she slid into his embrace once again, it felt completely natural. His hold on her tightened ever so slightly, and when he pressed his jaw against the side of her neck, Jayne's eyes slowly closed. They danced, and she observed that they fit together perfectly.

Riley drew her closer, and Jayne's mind whirled with a confused mixture of emotions. She shouldn't be feeling this. Not with Riley. But she didn't want to question it, not now. . . .

"This feels good," she whispered, fighting the impulse to trace the rugged line of his jaw. He smelled wonderful, a blend of spicy aftershave and—what? Himself, she decided.

Riley smoothed her hair, letting his hand glide down the silky length from the crown of her head to her shoulder. Reluctantly he stopped when the last notes of the waltz faded away.

"Yes, it does feel good," Riley said, his voice husky. *Too good,* his mind added.

He dropped his arms, and Jayne thrilled at his hesitancy when he stepped back. "I don't think you'll have any problems with the waltz."

"I shouldn't have," she said. "Anyway, with Mark all I need to do is look at him with adoring eyes and bat my lashes, and he's happy."

Riley didn't like the idea of Jayne flirting with another man. He knew that didn't make sense, since he was helping her prepare for a date with this Mark guy. "That won't satisfy a man for long," he muttered.

"It'll satisfy Mark," she countered. "I'm not exactly a flirt, you know. I'm not even sure how most women do it."

"It seems to me you're doing a good job learning."

"What do you mean?"

"Just now—dancing. You were practically throwing yourself at me."

"I was not!"

"You sure were."

Jayne was too humiliated to argue. She vaulted across the room and removed the CD. Her hands shook as she returned it to the plastic case. "That was an awful thing to say."

"It's about time you woke up and realized what men are like."

"I've already told you I don't need a fairy godfather."

"You need *someone* to tell you the score."

Jayne glared at him angrily. "And I suppose you're the one to enlighten me."

"Yup. Someone has to. You can't go flaunting yourself the way you just did with me."

"Flaunting?" Jayne almost choked on the word.

"That's right—flaunting." Riley hated himself for the things he was saying. He was both furious and unreasonable—a bad combination.

"*You* were the one who offered to show me how to dance. I . . . I even told you—"

"You can't tease a man, Jayne," he interrupted, coming to grips with his emotions. "Not me, not Mark, not any man."

"And how many times do I have to tell you I'm not a tease? Honestly, look at me!"

"That's the problem. I *am* looking."

"And?" she whispered, shocked at the tightness of his voice.

"And . . ." He hesitated. "All I can think about is doing this." He reached for her, taking her in his arms and covering her mouth with his.

Jayne was too stunned to react. The kiss had the sweetest, most tantalizing effect, momentarily causing her to forget the angry censure in his voice.

Regaining her composure—or pretending to—she broke away. "What made you do that?"

The look he was giving her told Jayne he wasn't pleased about that kiss. "I don't know. It was a mistake."

"I . . . yes." And yet Jayne didn't want to think of it that way.

"You go out with Mark, and we'll leave it at that."

"But—"

"Just go out with him, Jayne."

She dropped her gaze to the carpet. "All right."

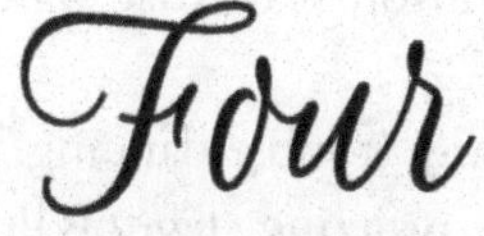

Four

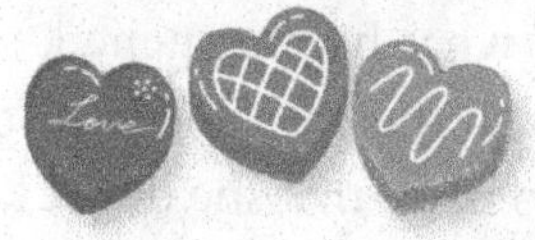

After she'd buzzed Gloria in, Jayne jerked open the apartment door. "What took you so long? Mark's due any minute."

Flustered, Gloria shook her head. "If you weren't so afraid to wear your glasses, you'd see exactly what he looks like."

Being the good friend she was, Gloria had volunteered to be there when Mark arrived so she could tell Jayne if he'd be an acceptable date for the high school reunion. Mark's image remained a bit fuzzy in her mind, but as the day of her reunion drew closer, Jayne discovered how badly she wanted to go. But she'd decided early on not to attend without a handsome man at her side. The problem was that Mark was her only likely prospect. And she didn't even know if he'd be interested!

"You look fantastic," Gloria commented, stepping back to examine Jayne's outfit. "Are you sure you can dance in that?"

Jayne had wondered the same thing. The silk blouse was

new, pale blue with a pleated front. The black skirt was standard straight fare, part of her everyday uniform. She'd spent what seemed like hours on her hair, but to no avail. It was too straight and thick to manage. In the end, she'd tied it at the base of her neck with a chiffon scarf that was a shade deeper than her blouse.

"I shouldn't have any trouble dancing." But then she hadn't graduated beyond the waltzing stage. Riley had left soon after their kissing fiasco, and she hadn't seen him since. Every time Jayne thought about what had happened, she grew angry . . . not with Riley, but with herself. She hadn't meant to flirt with him, but she wasn't so naive that she didn't know what was happening. Pride had demanded that she pretend otherwise. But she regretted the kiss. It had been so wonderful that four days later the warm taste of his mouth still lingered on hers. Nor could she erase the sensation of being held in his arms.

"You're sure I look okay?" Jayne raised questioning eyes to her friend. As it was, she had to drum up enthusiasm for this date.

"You look fine."

"Before, it was fantastic."

"Fantastic, then."

Straightening the chiffon scarf at her neck, Jayne closed her eyes. She had a bad feeling about tonight. If she was honest, she'd admit she'd rather be going with Riley. She felt comfortable with him. Except, of course, for that kiss. And it'd been . . . not comfortable but exciting. Memorable. However, Riley hadn't spoken to her in days. She wasn't entirely sure he even liked her; the signals she'd received from him were conflicting. It was almost as though he didn't want to be attracted to her but couldn't resist.

The buzzer went, and she cast a frantic glance in Gloria's direction and quickly tucked her glasses inside her purse.

"Calm down," Gloria said. "You're going to have a wonderful time."

"Tell me why I don't believe that," Jayne mumbled on her way to the door.

Riley Chambers pressed the button on his remote control to change channels. He'd seen fifteen-second segments of no fewer than ten shows. Nothing held his interest, and there was no point trying to distract himself. Jayne was on his mind again. Only she didn't flit in and out of his thoughts the way she had before. Tonight she was a constant presence, taunting him. Television wasn't going to help; neither was reading or the internet or any other diversion he could invent.

Standing, Riley paced to the window to stare at the rain-soaked street. He buried his hands in his pockets. So she was going out with this Mark character. Dinner and dancing. He shouldn't care. But he did. The idea of another man with his arms around Jayne disturbed him. It more than disturbed him, it made him completely crazy.

She'd felt so good in his arms. Far better than she had any right to. Days later, he still couldn't banish the feel, the taste, the smell of her from his mind. Avoiding her hadn't worked. Nothing had. She lived three doors down from him, yet she might as well have packed her bags and moved into his apartment. She was there every minute of every night and he didn't like it. What he really wanted to do was exorcise her from his life. Cast those honey-brown eyes from his memory and go about his business the way he was paid to do. *No.* He turned. What he really wanted to do was find out what Mark was like.

Before he could analyze this insanity, he grabbed his raincoat and stormed out the door.

"Hello, Mark." Jayne greeted him with a warm smile. "I'd like to introduce my friend Gloria."

"Hello, Gloria." Mark stepped forward to shake Gloria's hand, then held it far longer than necessary. His eyes caressed her face until Jayne noticed the pink color in her friend's cheeks.

"It's nice meeting you." Gloria pulled her hand free. "But I have to be going."

"No," Jayne objected. "Really, Gloria, stay."

Gloria threw her a look that could have boiled water. "No. You and Mark are going out. Remember?" The last word was issued through clenched teeth.

"The more the merrier, I always say." Mark was staring at Gloria with obvious interest, or what Jayne assumed was interest. She couldn't really tell without her glasses.

"No, I have to go," Gloria insisted.

"That's a shame," Mark said.

There was another knock at the door, and three faces glared at it.

"I'll get that," Jayne said, excusing herself. The few steps across the floor had never seemed so far. It could only be a neighbor, yet she wasn't expecting anyone. Least of all Riley.

"Riley." She breathed his name in a rush of excitement.

His gaze flew past her to Mark and Gloria. "I stopped by—" he paused, suddenly realizing he had to come up with a plausible excuse for his unexpected arrival "—to get the recipe for the casserole you made the other night. It was delicious," he said.

"Of course. Come in, please." Jayne stepped aside, trying to disguise her reaction, and Riley strolled past her.

"Riley Chambers, this is Mark Bauer and Gloria Bailey." Somehow she made it through the introductions without revealing her pleasure at Riley's unexpected visit.

"Pleased to meet you," Mark said stiffly, and the two men shook hands.

"Gloria." Riley nodded in the direction of Jayne's friend.

"Riley lives down the hall from me," Jayne felt obliged to add. "Gloria and I work together," she explained.

Riley nodded.

"I'll get you that recipe," Jayne told him.

"I'll help," Gloria said hurriedly, following her into the kitchen. "What's going on?" Gloria whispered the minute they were out of sight.

"I don't know."

"You don't really think he cares about that stupid recipe, do you?"

Jayne thought back to all the times she'd been with Riley. He bewildered her. He'd come to the library intent on harassing her, then had looked after her when she was ill. Most surprising had been his willingness to teach her to dance—which had turned into a scene that wouldn't soon be forgotten by either of them. "With Riley, I never know."

"He's here to check out Mark."

Jayne's eyes widened with doubt. "I have trouble believing that."

"Trust me, kiddo, the guy's interested."

"Two men at the same time? The girls of St. Mary's would keel over if they knew." Two men interested in her was a slight exaggeration. The minute Mark had met Gloria he couldn't stop looking at her.

"What are you going to do?" Gloria wanted to know.

"What do you mean?"

"From the look of things, Riley isn't leaving."

Jayne bit her bottom lip. "What should I do, invite him along?"

"Invite us both."

"But what will Mark think?"

"It won't matter. The way Riley's giving him the evil eye, Mark's not likely to risk life and limb by asking you out again."

"Oh, I can't believe this."

"Where's that cookbook?" Gloria whispered, glancing into the living room.

There wasn't any point in looking. "I returned it last week."

"Then tell him that, for heaven's sake!"

Back in the living room, Jayne found the two men sitting on the sofa, staring at each other like angry bears. It was as if one had invaded the other's territory.

Riley stood. Slowly Mark followed suit.

"I'm sorry, Riley, but I returned that book to the library. I'll see if I can pick it up for you, if you'd like."

"Please."

Gloria stepped forward, linking her hands together. "Jayne and I were just thinking that since the four of us are all here maybe we could go out together."

Jayne nodded. "Right," she said boldly. "We were."

"Not dancing." Riley categorically dismissed that.

"There's a new movie at the Lloyd Center," Gloria suggested.

"A movie would be fun." Jayne nodded, looking at Mark. After all, he was supposed to be her date. "We could always eat later."

"That sounds fine," Mark agreed with little enthusiasm.

For that matter, eagerness for this impromptu double date

was remarkably absent. The silence in Mark's car as they drove to the shopping complex grated on Jayne's fragile nerves. But she knew better than to even attempt a conversation.

At the theater Mark and Riley bought the popcorn while the two women found seats. The place was crowded and they ended up far closer to the front than Jayne liked.

"This isn't working," she whispered.

"You're telling me. The temperature in that car was below freezing."

"I know. What should I do?" Jayne could hear the desperate appeal in her own voice.

"Nothing. Things will take care of themselves." Gloria sounded far more confident than Jayne felt.

The two men returned, and to her delighted surprise, Riley claimed the seat beside her. Mark took the one next to Gloria. The women glanced at each other and shared a sigh of relief. Apparently Mark and Riley had settled things in the theater lobby.

For his part, Riley wasn't pleased. His instincts told him Jayne was going to be hurt by this guy. He'd seen the looks Mark was giving Gloria. Three minutes in the lobby, and the two men had come to an agreement. Riley would sit with Jayne, Mark with Gloria. If Jayne was out to find herself a decent man, he thought grimly, Mark Bauer wasn't the one. She should look elsewhere.

The theater darkened, and after the previews the credits started to roll. Jayne squinted, then pulled her glasses out of her purse. It was ridiculous to pretend any longer. She doubted Mark had even noticed.

Before they'd entered the theater, Jayne hadn't paid much attention to the movie they were about to see. She soon realized it was going to be filled with blood and gore. She swallowed uncomfortably.

"What's wrong?" Riley whispered and grinned when he noticed she'd put her glasses back on.

"Nothing." She couldn't think of a way to tell him that any form of violence greatly upset her. She detested movies like this where men treated life cheaply, and grotesque horror was all part of an intriguing plot.

At the first gory scene, Jayne clutched the armrests until her fingers ached and closed her eyes, praying no one was aware of her odd behavior.

"Jayne?"

Riley's voice was so low she wasn't even sure she'd heard him. Opening her eyes, she turned to look at him. "Are you all right?" he asked solicitously.

With a weak smile, she nodded. A blast of gunfire rang from the screen, and she winced and shook her head.

"Do you want to leave?"

"No."

Watching her, Riley wasn't surprised that she was troubled by violence. It fit with what he knew of her—all part of the innocence he'd come to like so much, the goodness he'd come to count on. He didn't want to fall for her, but he knew the signs.

His interest in the movie waned. Her hand still clenched the armrest in a death grip, and with a gentleness he hardly knew he possessed, Riley pried her fingers loose and tucked her hand in his, offering her comfort. She turned to him with a look of such gratitude that it took years of hard-won self-control not to lean forward and kiss her. He didn't like this feeling. Now wasn't the time to get involved with a woman, especially *this* woman. It was too dangerous. For him and possibly for her.

* * *

Thursday morning, Gloria was waiting for Jayne on the front steps of the library.

"Morning," Jayne muttered, feeling defeated. She'd been standing at the bus stop when Riley drove past. He hadn't even looked in her direction, and she'd felt as though a little part of her had died at the disappointment. "How did everything go with Mark?" Jayne's original date had taken Gloria home.

"Fine . . . I guess."

"Did he ask you out?"

"Yeah, but I'm not interested." Gloria wrapped her arms around her waist and shook her head. "I finally figured out what's wrong. Mark reminds me too much of my ex."

"Mark's off my list, as well."

"I would think so. Riley would probably skin him alive if he showed up at your door again."

"I don't understand Riley," Jayne murmured. "He barely even said good-night when he dropped me off. He wouldn't even look at me." And men claimed they didn't understand women! For all her intelligence, all the reading she'd done, Jayne was at a loss to explain Riley's strange behavior. She had thought they'd shared something special during that horrible movie, and then the minute they got outside, he treated her as though she had some contagious disease.

"Who would you rather go to the reunion with? Riley or Mark?"

Jayne didn't need to mull that over. "Riley."

"Then you need to change tactics."

"Oh, Gloria, I don't know. You make this sound like some kind of game."

"Do you want to attend the reunion or not?"

"I do, but . . ."

"So, form your plan and choose your weapons."

Jayne might not have needed to ponder which man interested her most, but tactics were something else. She liked Riley, and she sensed that her feelings for him could grow a lot more intense. But the opposite side of the coin was the reality that if she chose to pursue a relationship with this man, she could be hurt.

That evening, still undecided about what to do, Jayne was surprised to receive a call from Mark, asking her out again. Apparently the man didn't scare off as easily as Gloria and Riley seemed to think. Or it could be that Mark had noticed Riley's lack of interest following the movie. It didn't matter; she politely declined.

When she didn't see Riley the following day, either, Jayne was convinced he was avoiding her again. Only this time she was armed with ammunition and reinforcement from Gloria.

That evening, Jayne made another casserole from the Mexican cookbook—which she'd taken out again—and delivered it to Riley's door.

Surprise etched fine lines around his eyes when Riley answered her knock.

"Hello." Jayne forced a bright smile.

He frowned, obviously not pleased to see her.

"I brought you dinner." It had all sounded so simple when she'd discussed her plans with Gloria earlier in the day. Now her stomach felt as though a weight had settled there, and her resolve was weakening more every minute. "It's another casserole from the same cookbook you asked about the other night."

His hand remained on the door. "You didn't need to do that."

"I wanted to." Her smile was about to crumple. "You mentioned it the night Mark was by. . . . You do remember, don't you?" He still hadn't asked her into his apartment. She wasn't any good at this flirting business. Chagrined, she dropped her gaze to the floor. "I can see you're busy, so I'll just leave this with you."

Reluctantly he stepped aside.

Rarely had Jayne been more miserable. Things weren't supposed to happen like this. According to Gloria, Riley would appreciate her efforts and gratefully ask her to join him.

She moved into his kitchen and saw the box from a frozen microwave dinner sitting on the counter.

After setting the casserole on the stove she removed her oven mitts. "Don't worry about returning the baking dish." She didn't want him thinking she was looking for more excuses to see him. She had been, but that didn't matter anymore. Embarrassed and ill at ease, she gave him a weak smile. "Enjoy your dinner."

"Jayne." His hand on her shoulder stopped her, and when she raised her eyes to his, he pulled away, thrusting his fingers into his hair. "I wish you hadn't done this."

"I know," she said and swallowed miserably. "I won't again. I . . . I don't know what I did to make you so upset with me, but your message is coming through loud and clear."

"Jayne, listen. I saw those books you're reading. I'm not the man for you. I told you already—I'd make a terrible husband." He took a step toward her.

"Husband!" she spat. "I'm not looking for a husband."

"Then what *do* you want?" He knew his voice was raised, he couldn't help it. Jayne did that to him. He saw the tears in her eyes and watched as she tried to blink them away. "Then why are you reading those ridiculous books?" he asked.

With her fists clenched, Jayne met his glare. "I have my reasons."

"No doubt." The proud tilt of her chin tore at his heart. He didn't know what Jayne thought she was doing, but if she was serious about a relationship with him, the timing couldn't be worse. The dangers of this undercover assignment were many and real. He had enough to worry about without having his head messed up by a woman. But Jayne wasn't an ordinary woman. He'd known it the first time she'd flared back at him. She was genuine and sweet and, yes, naive. She was also smart and he sensed the passion beneath her demure exterior.

"What you think of me is irrelevant," she said, flexing her hands at her sides. "If you must know, all I really want is to attend my high school reunion. And I'm going even if I have to hire a man to go with me." Her voice rose with every word. "And furthermore, I'm going to learn to dance, and if you won't help me, fine. I'll find someone else who will."

"So *that's* what this is all about? And the casserole is in exchange for dancing lessons?" No way was he addressing the issue of a hired companion. But at least she hadn't mentioned Mark Bauer.

"Yes."

"Fine." He walked across the room and flipped on the radio. Soft music filled the apartment. "Come on, let's dance, if that's all you want."

The invitation held as much welcome as cold charity. Jayne's first response was to throw his offer back in his face, but she managed to swallow her pride. After all, finding a way into his arms was exactly the reason she'd come here tonight.

When she walked into his embrace, he held her stiffly. His

tense muscles kept her away from him, so there was only minimal contact.

"You didn't hold me like this the other day," she protested.

Gritting his teeth, Riley brought her closer into his arms. Eyes shut, he breathed in the scent of her hair. She reminded him of springtime, fresh and eager and so unbelievably trusting that it frightened him.

His hands sought her hair. Silky, glorious, just as he'd known it would be. He removed the clasp and let it fall to the floor. His fingers tangled with her hair as a tenderness for the woman enveloped him.

The music changed to an upbeat song with a bubbly rhythm, but their steps remained unchanged. Dancing was only an excuse to hold each other, and they both knew it.

Riley wrapped his arms around her. Their feet barely shifted as the pretense lost its purpose.

Jayne's arms were tight around his neck. She didn't dare move for fear her actions would break this magical spell. There was something strong and powerful about Riley that she couldn't resist. Her mouth found his neck, and her warm breath left a film of moisture against his skin. Lightly she kissed him there.

Riley stiffened, his whole body tensing at her seemingly playful kiss. "Jayne," he breathed. "What are you trying to do to me?"

"The same thing you're doing to me," she answered. Her own voice was weak. "I've never felt like this before. . . ."

The only response he seemed capable of was a groan.

"Riley, kiss me," she said urgently. "Please kiss me."

He angled her head to one side and slanted his mouth over hers with a desperate hunger that burned in him like a raging fire.

He kissed her again with an intensity that drove him beyond his will. His mouth sought hers until they were both weak and trembling.

"Jayne," he whispered harshly, "tell me to leave you alone. Tell me to stop."

"But I like it."

"Don't say that."

"But, Riley, it feels so good. *You* feel so good."

"Jayne," he pleaded, wanting her to stop him. Instead she arched into him, her mouth on his.

"I want to kiss you forever," she whispered.

"Don't tell me that," he said, fighting with everything that was in him and losing the battle with every breath he took.

Instinctively she moved against him, and Riley thought he'd die with the pleasure and pain. He lowered his hands to her waist. "No more of that. Understand?"

"I don't think I do. I never dreamed anything could feel this wonderful."

Riley didn't even hear her as he pressed his mouth to her cheek, her ear, her hair, anyplace but her lips.

"Jayne," he said a moment later. "We have to stop." He pressed his cheek to hers. His eyes were closed, and his breathing was labored as he struggled within himself.

Jayne moved so that her mouth found his, tasting, licking and kissing him until Riley feared she'd drive him mad.

"No more," he said harshly, breaking the contact. He held her away at arm's length, clasping her shoulder. "What's the matter with you?"

Jayne blinked.

"You're acting like a child with a new toy you've just discovered."

"But it feels so good." How flimsy that sounded, even to her.

"And just where did you think this kissing and touching would end?"

"I thought . . ." She didn't know what she thought.

Riley looked down into Jayne's bewildered face and cursed the anger in his voice. "Listen, maybe you'd better find someone else for these lessons you're so keen to learn."

Jayne swallowed down the hurt. She didn't consider Riley her teacher. She'd believed they were exploring those exquisite sensations together. Her face felt hot with shame.

"Maybe I should!" she cried. "I'm sure Mark would be willing."

"Oh, no, you don't. Not with Mark."

"Who then? It isn't like I've got hordes of admirers lined up, dying to go out with me." Dramatically, she flung out her arm.

"That's not my problem." He attempted a show of indifference. "Find whoever you want. Just stay away from me."

"Don't worry." After this humiliation, she had no intention of ever seeing him again.

She couldn't get out of his apartment fast enough. Once inside her own, she felt tears of hurt and anger burning for release. They rolled down her face, despite all her efforts to hold them back.

Sinking into the soft cushion of her sofa, she buried her face in her hands. She was a twenty-seven-year-old virgin, hurrying to catch up with life, and it had backfired. She'd behaved like an irresponsible idiot just as Riley had claimed.

A loud knock sounded on the apartment door.

Aghast, she stared at it. There wasn't anyone in the world she wanted to see right now.

"Jayne!" Riley shouted. "Open up. I know you're in there."

She was too shocked to move. Riley was the last person she expected to come to her now.

Riley gave a disgusted sigh. "The choice is yours. Either open that door, or I'll kick it down."

His threat was convincing enough to prompt her to unlatch the lock and open the door.

Riley stood in front of her and handed her the oven mitts. "You forgot these."

Wordlessly she took them.

The guilt he felt at the sight of her red eyes knotted his stomach. "I think we'd better talk."

Like a robot, she moved aside. Riley stalked past her and into the apartment. "You want to attend that reunion? Fine. I'll take you."

"Why?"

"Haven't you ever heard that expresion about not looking a gift horse in the mouth?"

"But why?"

"Because!" he shouted.

"That's not a reason."

"Well, it'll have to do."

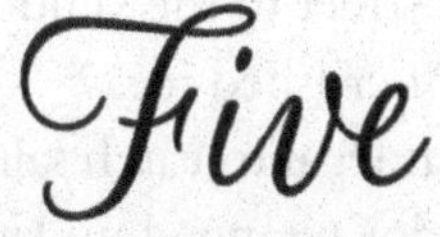

Five

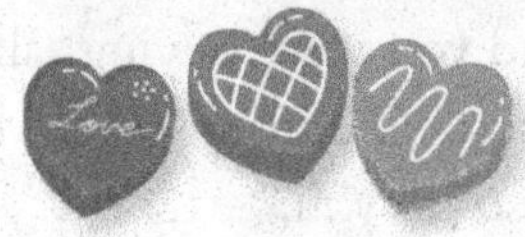

The glorious June sunshine splashed over the street, silhouetting the Burnside Bridge that towered above Riverside Park. The Saturday market was in full swing, and noisy crowds wandered down the busy street. Some gathered to watch a banjo player while others strolled past, their arms heavy with a variety of newly discovered treasures.

Jayne nibbled on a cinnamon-covered "elephant ear" pastry as she strolled from one booth to the next. Riley was at her side, carrying the shopping bag that grew increasingly heavy with every stop.

"I can't believe you've lived in Portland all these months and you didn't know about the Saturday market," she remarked.

"You do most of your shopping here?"

"Just the produce." Jayne offered him a bite of her elephant ear. "They're good, aren't they?"

Chewing, Riley nodded. "Delicious."

Finishing it off, Jayne brushed the sugar from her fingers and dumped the napkin in the garbage. Riley took her hand and smiled. "Where to next?"

"The fish market. I want to try a new salmon recipe." They strolled down the wide street to the vendor who displayed fresh fish laid out on a bed of crushed ice.

"I didn't know it was legal to catch salmon this small," Riley commented as the vendor wrapped up Jayne's choice.

"That's a rainbow trout," she said and laughed.

"I thought you said you were buying salmon."

"I changed my mind. The trout looked too good to resist."

"At the moment, so do you."

His lazy voice reached through the noisy crowd to touch her heart. Tears filled her eyes, and she quickly looked away, not wanting him to see the effect his words had on her.

The stout vendor handed Riley the fish, and he tucked it in the brown shopping bag. Before his attention returned to her, Jayne brushed the tears from her cheek.

"Jayne." Concern was evident in his tone. "What's wrong?"

She smiled up at him through her happiness. "No one's ever said things like that to me."

"Like what?" His brow compressed.

"That I'm irresistible."

"My sweet little librarian," he said, placing an arm around her shoulders, drawing her close to his side. "You tie me up in knots a sailor couldn't undo."

"Oh, Riley, do I really?" She felt excruciatingly pleased. "I owe you so much."

Despite his efforts not to, Riley frowned. He was grateful that Jayne didn't seem to notice. He wondered how this virtuous librarian, whom he'd once thought of as a prim and proper young woman, could inspire such desire in him. Over the years, he'd been with a number of women. None of them compared to her. None of them had meant to him what she did. At night, unable to sleep, he often lay awake imagining Jayne. This woman tugged, like a swift undercurrent, at his senses. Jayne in bed, soft and mussed, her hair spilling over the pillow. The image of her was so strong that it was a constant battle not to make it real. The intensity of his feelings for her shocked him even now, weeks after having accepted her into his life. This wasn't the time to be caught up with a woman. Losing sight of his assignment could be dangerous. It could cost him his life. But if he hadn't acted when he did, he could have lost *her,* and that thought was intolerable. As soon as this job was over, he was getting out. The time had come to think about settling down. Jayne had done that to him, and he realized for the first time how much he wanted the very lifestyle he'd previously shunned.

Therein lay the problem. Being with her had placed a burden on him. She made him ache with need; at the same time, he experienced the overpowering urge to protect her. This was a dilemma—because there was no one to protect her from him but his own conscience. The weight of that responsibility fell heavily on his shoulders.

"You're very quiet," Jayne commented when they reached the parked car. "Is something wrong?"

"No." He smiled down on her and was instantly drawn into those warm brown eyes.

"I'm glad you came with me."

Riley had to admit he looked for excuses to be with her. Carrying her bags was one, offering her a ride was another. Simple things to do, but they brought him pleasure out of all proportion to the effort they entailed.

They drove back to the apartment building in companionable silence. After parking in his assigned spot, Riley carried her purchases into the building.

"Will you come in?" she asked outside her door.

"Only for a minute."

Setting the shopping bags on the kitchen counter, Riley watched the subtle grace with which she moved around her small kitchen. "I'll have a surprise for you later," she announced.

"Dinner?"

"No. Not that." Every time Riley kissed her, he ended up pulling the clasp from her hair. Her surprise was an appointment with the hairdresser to restyle her hair so that when Riley held her again, he could do whatever he liked with it. "You'll have to come by this evening and see."

"I'll do that."

"Riley?" She turned to him and leaned against the counter, hands behind her back.

He looked at her intent face. "Hmm?"

"May I kiss you?"

"Now?" He swallowed; she didn't make keeping his hands off her easy.

"Please."

"Jayne, listen . . ."

"Okay." She moved to his side and slipped her arms over his chest to link her fingers behind his neck. Her soft body conformed to the hardness of his.

Riley groaned, finding it nearly impossible to maintain his resolve. He was convinced that she had no idea of the powerful effect she had on him.

"Do you like this?" She pressed her lips to his, and Riley felt his legs weaken. He was grateful for the support of the kitchen counter.

"Yes," he groaned.

She began to kiss him again, straining upward on her toes, but Riley quickly took charge. He kissed her with the hunger that ate at his insides.

Jayne moved restlessly against him, but he broke away.

"No," he said abruptly, his chest heaving. "That's enough."

Jayne hung her head as the heat of embarrassment colored her cheeks. "I'm sorry, Riley."

"Think next time, will you? I'm not some high school kid for you to experiment with. I told you that before." He hated to see the hurt he was inflicting on her, but she didn't seem to understand the stress she was putting him under.

Jayne took a step backward.

He plowed his fingers through his hair. "I'll talk to you later. Okay?"

"Sure."

The door closed, and Jayne winced. Oh, dear, she was doing everything wrong. Riley wanted to cool things down just when she wanted to really heat them up for the first time in her life. Several men had kissed her over the years, but she'd never responded to any of them the way she did to Riley. He didn't merely light a spark; Riley Chambers ignited a bonfire within her. Jayne was as surprised as anyone. She'd thought she was too refined, too shy, trapped with too many hang-ups to experience the very physical desires Riley evoked in her. He'd taught her differently, and now she was riding a roller coaster, speeding downhill ahead of him. If it wasn't so ironic, she'd laugh.

Listening to the radio, Jayne finished putting away the morning's purchases. She changed clothes for her hair appointment and left the apartment soon after one. The beauty salon was a good mile away, but the day was gloriously warm, and she decided to walk instead of taking the bus. She wanted time to think.

As she strolled along, it seemed as if the whole world was alive. She saw and heard things that had passed her notice only weeks before. Birdsong filled the air, as did the laughter of children in the park.

Jayne cut a path through the lush green boulevard, pausing to watch several children swooping high on the park swings. She recognized a little girl from the library's story hour and waved as she continued down the meandering walkway.

Looking both ways before crossing the street, Jayne's gaze fell on Soft Sam's. She gave an involuntary shudder as she remembered the desperation of that first visit. She'd been so naive, thinking that because the place was in her neighborhood it would fulfill her requirements. Now she couldn't believe she'd even gone inside. She could just imagine what Riley had thought when he first saw her there. He'd warned her about the bar several times since, but he needn't have bothered. People went into Soft Sam's with one thing on their minds, and it wasn't companionship.

Jayne started across the street, and as she stepped off the curb, Riley came into view. He was standing in the doorway of Soft Sam's. She raised her arm, then paused, not knowing if she should call out to him or not. Before she could decide, a tall blonde woman joined him, slipping an arm through his and smiling boldly up at him. Her face was familiar, and it took Jayne several troubled seconds to realize the woman was the same one she'd seen on the evening news.

The hand she'd raised fell lifelessly to her side. Jayne felt as though someone had kicked her in the stomach. The numbing sensation of shock and disbelief moved up her arms and legs, paralyzing her for a moment.

A car horn blared, and she saw that she was standing in the middle of the street. Hurriedly she moved to the other side. Pausing to still her frantically beating heart, she rested her trembling hand on a fire hydrant for support.

Hadn't she just admitted the reason men and women went to a place like Soft Sam's? Riley was there now, and it wasn't his first visit. He could even be a regular customer. And from the looks that . . . that woman was giving him, they knew each other well.

The pain that went through her was white-hot, and her eyelids fluttered downward.

"Are you all right, miss?"

Jayne opened her eyes to find a police officer studying her, his face concerned.

"I'm fine. I . . . just felt dizzy for a minute."

The young man smiled knowingly. "You might want to check with a doctor."

"I will. Thank you, officer."

He touched the tip of his hat with his index finger. "No problem. You sure you'll be okay?"

"I'm sure."

With a determination that surprised even her, Jayne squared her shoulders and walked in the direction of the beauty salon. She'd read about men like Riley. If there was a blessing to be found in this, it was learning early on that there was another side to him. One that sought cheap thrills.

Her hand was on the glass door of the salon when she hesitated. She wasn't having her hair done for Riley, she told herself;

she was doing it for the reunion. She wanted to go back looking different, didn't she? *None* of this was for Riley. None of it. It was for her.

Three hours later the reflection that greeted her in the salon mirror was hardly recognizable. Instead of thick, straight hair, soft, bouncy curls framed her face. Jayne stared back at her reflection and blinked. She looked almost pretty.

"What a difference," the hairdresser was saying.

"Yes," Jayne agreed. She paid the stylist and left a hefty tip. Anyone who could create the transformation this young woman had deserved a reward.

Jayne took the bus home. She sat staring out the side window, absorbed in what she'd witnessed earlier. For days she'd been planning this small surprise for Riley. Now she didn't care if she ever saw him again.

But perhaps that was a bit rash. If she was going to break things off, she'd wait until after the reunion. She knew she should be grateful to learn this about him, only she wasn't. The experience of undiluted love had been pure bliss.

Back inside her apartment, Jayne felt the need to talk to someone. She wouldn't mention what she'd seen. For that matter, she doubted she could put words to the emotions that simmered in her heart. She needed human contact so she wouldn't go crazy sitting here alone, thinking. She reached for the phone and called Gloria.

"Jayne, I'm so glad to hear from you," Gloria's voice boomed over the wire.

"Oh. Did something exciting happen?"

"I cannot believe my luck."

"You won the lottery!" It took effort to force some energy into her flat voice.

"Remember when you returned those how-to books about meeting men to the library?"

Of course she did. When Riley had said he'd attend the reunion with her, she hadn't seen any reason to keep them.

"Well, guess who checked them out?"

"Who?" The answer was obvious.

"Me. And, Jayne, guess what? They work! I met this fantastic man in the Albertsons store today."

"At the grocery store?"

"Sure," Gloria said. "Remember how that one book says the supermarket on Saturdays is a great place to meet men? I met Lance in the frozen-food section."

"Congratulations."

"We're going to dinner tonight."

"That's great."

"I have a feeling about this man. He's everything I want. We even like the same things. Looking through our grocery carts, we discovered that we have identical tastes."

"I hate to rain on your parade," Jayne said, smiling for the first time. "But there's more to a compatible relationship than both of you liking broccoli."

"It's not only broccoli, but fish sticks and frozen orange juice. We even bought the same brand of microwave dinners."

The thought of cardboard meals reminded Jayne of Riley's haphazard eating patterns. She did her best to dispel all thoughts of him, with little success.

"I didn't mean to jabber on. You must've called for a reason."

"I just wanted to tell you about my hair."

"Oh, goodness, I was so excited about meeting Lance that I forgot. What does Riley think?"

"He hasn't seen it yet."

"All right, how do *you* feel about it?"

"It's . . . different."

"I knew it would be," Gloria said with a laugh.

"Listen, I've got to go. I'll talk to you Monday, and you can tell me all about your hot date." On second thought, it had been a mistake to phone Gloria. Jayne's mind was in turmoil, and she wondered if she'd made any sense at all.

"Okay, see you then."

After a few words of farewell, Jayne hung up.

Riley—she assumed it was him—knocked on her door at about seven. Jayne had known he'd come by, but she didn't have the nerve to confront him with what she'd seen. There wasn't anything she could say. The hurt was still too fresh and too poignant.

Careful not to make any noise, she sat reading a new mystery novel. She could immerse herself in fiction and forget for a time.

After three loud knocks he'd left, and she'd breathed easier.

Sunday morning she went out early and returned late. She couldn't avoid him forever, but she needed to put distance between them until she'd dealt with her emotions. When they did meet, she didn't want what she'd learned to taint her reactions.

Early Monday afternoon Riley tossed an empty paper cup in the metal garbage can beside his desk. Jayne was avoiding him. He didn't blame her; he'd hurt her feelings by abruptly putting an end to their kissing. Someday, God willing, there wouldn't be any reason to stop. For now, he had to be in control and for more than the obvious reasons.

The report on his desk made him frown. He didn't like the sound of this. For that matter, he didn't like anything to do with

Max Priestly. The man was a slimeball; Riley always felt as though he needed a shower after being around him. How anyone like Priestly had been elected to public office was beyond Riley.

Standing, he reached for his coat. He'd dealt with enough mud this weekend. He needed a break. Only he wasn't going to get it. He missed Jayne, missed her fresh, sweet scent and the way he felt about himself when he was with her. She brought out the best in him. For the first time in recent memory, he was being noble. Twice now he could have taken what she was so freely offering, and he hadn't. She didn't know or even appreciate his self-control, but in time she would. And he could wait.

A glance at his watch confirmed that he could probably catch her at the library. He'd take her to lunch and ease her embarrassment. There was always the possibility that Priestly would see them together, but it was a relatively small risk and one worth taking. Pulling on his raincoat, he walked out of the office.

His steps echoed on the floor of the main library as Riley made his way to the children's department. He stopped when he found Jayne. At first he didn't recognize her. She looked fabulous. A beauty. She was holding up a picture book to the children gathered around her on the floor.

One small boy raised his hand and said something Riley couldn't hear. Jayne reacted by laughing softly and shaking her head. Leaning forward, she spoke to the group of intent young faces.

Just watching her with those children made Riley's heart constrict. He loved this woman with a depth that astonished him. *Loved her.* The acknowledgment felt right and true. Jayne closed the book, and the kids got up and surged closer, all chattering happily. Seeing her with these children created such intense desire in Riley that for a minute he couldn't breathe. Jayne was everything he could ever want. And a lot more than he deserved.

Gloria moved to Jayne's side and whispered in her ear. Instantly Jayne's gaze darted in Riley's direction. For a moment her eyes held a stricken look but that was quickly disguised. She stood, put the picture book down and said goodbye to the children, then walked over to him.

"Hello, Riley." Her voice held a note of hesitancy.

"Can I take you to lunch?"

She opened her mouth to tell him she'd already made other plans, when Gloria intervened. "Go ahead," Gloria urged. "You haven't had lunch yet. And if you're a few minutes late, I'll cover for you."

There was nothing left for Jayne to do but agree.

Riley's gaze held hers. He wasn't sure he understood the message he found there. Jayne looked almost as though she was afraid of him, but he couldn't imagine why. "I like your hair."

Self-consciously she lifted her hand to the soft curls. "Thank you."

"Where would you like to eat?"

"Anywhere."

Her lack of enthusiasm was obvious. "Jayne, is something wrong?"

Her stricken eyes clashed with his. "No . . . how could there be?" Immediately her right eye began to twitch.

Riley argued with himself and decided not to pursue whatever was troubling her. Given time, she'd tell him, anyway.

"There's a little restaurant on Fourth. A hole in the wall, but the food's excellent."

"That'll be fine," she said formally.

She knew that his hand at her elbow was meant to guide her.

Today it was a stimulation she didn't want or need. It wasn't fair that the only man she'd ever really fallen for preferred women who frequented a sleazy bar—and worse. Remembering the type of people at Soft Sam's, Jayne knew she could never be as worldly and sophisticated as they were. There was no point in even pretending. She wasn't that good an actress.

"You're quiet today." Riley led the way outside to his parked car and in a few minutes pulled into the busy afternoon traffic.

She managed a smile. "I sent in my money for the reunion this morning. It's less than a month away now."

"I'm looking forward to it." Riley studied her, growing more confused by the minute. Whatever was bothering her was more serious than he'd first believed. He forced himself not to pressure her to talk.

"So am I."

"I missed seeing you Saturday evening. You said you had a surprise for me." He found a parking space and pulled into it. "The restaurant's over there. I hope you like Creole cooking."

"That sounds fine."

He noted that she'd avoided responding to his first statement. "I recommend the shrimp-stuffed eggplant."

"That's what I'll order then." It would be a miracle if she could choke down any lunch.

They were seated almost immediately and handed menus. The selection wasn't large, but judging by the spicy smells wafting from the kitchen, Jayne guessed that the food would be as good as Riley claimed.

"I tried to call you Sunday," he told her, setting his menu aside. "I didn't leave a message."

"I rented a car and drove to Seaside for the day."

Riley knitted his brow. She'd left the apartment to get away from him. He would have sworn that was the reason. "You should've said something. I would have taken you."

Jayne lowered her eyes. "I didn't want to trouble you."

"It wouldn't have been any trouble. The trip could have been interesting. I've heard a lot about the Oregon coastline, but haven't had the chance to see it yet."

"It's lovely."

The waitress came, and they placed their order.

Jayne twisted the paper napkin in her lap, staring down at it, not looking at him.

"What did you do in Seaside all day?"

"Walked. And thought." She hadn't meant to admit that.

"And what were you thinking about?"

"You." No point in lying. Her eye would twitch, and he'd know, anyway.

"What did you decide?"

"That I wasn't going to let you hurt me," she whispered fervently.

He'd hurt her in the past and had discovered that any pain she suffered mirrored his own at having done something to upset her. "I would never purposely hurt you, Jayne."

He already had. Her napkin was shredded in half. "I'm different from other women you know, Riley. But being . . . inexperienced shouldn't be a fault."

"I consider your lack of experience a virtue." He didn't know where all this was leading, but they were on the right path.

A virtue! Jayne almost laughed. He'd gone from her arms to those of that . . . other woman without so much as a hint of conscience.

Their lunch arrived, and Jayne stared at the large pink shrimp that filled the crispy fried eggplant. She had no appetite.

"Why'd you change your hair?"

Jayne picked up her fork, refusing to meet his probing gaze. "For the reunion."

"Is that the only reason?"

"Should there be another one?"

"You said you had a surprise for me," he coaxed.

"Not exactly *for* you."

"I see." He didn't, but it shouldn't matter.

Tasting a shrimp, Jayne marveled at the wonderful flavors. "This is good."

"I thought you'd enjoy it."

They ate in silence for several minutes. Riley's appetite was quickly satisfied. He'd finished his meal before Jayne was one-third done. He saw the way she toyed with the shrimp, eating only a couple before laying her fork on the plate and pushing it aside.

"I guess I'm not very hungry," she murmured.

Riley crumpled his paper napkin. "Why is it so important for you to go to that reunion?" he asked bluntly.

Jayne had asked herself the same question over and over. Her hand went around the water glass. The condensation on the outside wet her hand, and she wiped her fingers dry on a fresh napkin.

"I'm not sure," she finally said. "I'd like to see everyone again. It's been a long time."

"You've kept in contact with them?"

"A few. Mainly a girl named Judy Thomas. She was the closest friend I had there."

"What about the boys?" They were the ones who worried Riley. Once her male classmates realized what an unspoiled beauty she'd turned out to be, they might give him a run for his money. He wouldn't relinquish this woman easily. He'd waited a lifetime for her.

"There weren't any. I attended a private girls' school."

Riley smiled at the unexpected relief that went through him. "That must have been tough."

"Not really. I attended a women's college, as well."

"So that's where you got your case of repressed relationship development." He tried to make a joke of it but saw quickly that his humor had fallen flat. Riley was baffled at the ready tears that sprang to her eyes.

"Jayne, I didn't mean that the way it sounded." His hand reached for hers.

Jayne jerked her fingers away. "Did you enjoy her, Riley?" The question was asked in such a small, broken voice that his face tightened with alarm. "Who?"

"The blonde from Soft Sam's."

Six

Regret went through Riley like a hot knife. Little wonder Jayne had been avoiding him. But how could he ever explain this to her? "You saw me?"

"I saw both of you," Jayne whispered. Her soft, pain-filled gaze held his, begging him to tell her it wasn't true. That she was mistaken, and it was only someone who resembled him.

Riley considered lying to her. She might have believed him, but Riley couldn't and wouldn't do it. "I wasn't with her for the reason you think."

Jayne closed her eyes for a moment. "What other reason could there be? I may be inexperienced, but I'm not stupid."

"We're friends." That was a huge exaggeration, but it wouldn't be wise to tell her any more than that for her own safety. Priestly had introduced him to the blonde, and later Riley had used his influence to get her off prostitution charges. By doing so, he'd gotten all the information she could feed him. He couldn't expect Jayne to understand any of this. For that matter, telling her the truth could put her in danger, and he refused to risk that.

"From the look of it, I'd say you were *very* good friends." To her humiliation, Jayne's voice cracked, but she continued speaking in a hoarse whisper. "How could you go to . . . her after the wonderful morning we shared? That's what hurts the most, knowing that you—"

"Jayne, I swear on everything I hold dear that I didn't touch her." His deep voice had a fervency she'd never heard from him.

Jayne desperately wanted to believe Riley, but she didn't know if she dared. He had the potential to hurt her more than anyone. Trusting him now could prove to be a terrible mistake later. "Then why were you with her?"

"I told you. She's a friend." His gaze didn't waver under the scrutiny of hers.

Jayne lowered her eyes to the lunch she'd barely tasted. "What does she have that I don't?"

"Jayne . . ."

"You went from my arms to hers with hardly a breath in between. Tell me. I want to know. What attracted you to this particular *friend* on this particular Saturday?"

Riley hedged. "The arrangements to meet had already been made. I would've met with her even if I hadn't been with you that morning."

"I see."

"I'm sure you don't, and quite honestly, I wouldn't blame you if you didn't believe me. But I'm asking you to trust me." He paused to study her tight features and silently cursed himself for the timing of this relationship. If he was going to fall in love, why did it have to be *now?* He felt torn. There was so much to live for with Jayne in his life. He had to get out of this business, and the quicker the better. For his sake as well as hers.

"I want to trust you." Indecision played across her face.

"Can you believe that I didn't touch her?" he asked.

In response, her eyes delved into his. "I believe you," she murmured. She had to trust Riley or go crazy picturing him in the arms of another woman. The image would destroy her.

"There's only one woman who interests me."

"Oh?"

"One exceptionally lovely woman with honey-brown eyes and a heart so full of love she can't help giving it away." He remembered finding her with the children in the library and again felt such overwhelming desire for her that he ached with it. As he watched her, he could picture her with their child. Until recently, Riley hadn't given much thought to a family. Because of his job, he lived hard, often encountering danger, even when he least expected it. No, that wasn't true; he *always* expected it. He'd seen other men, men with families, attempt to balance their two worlds, and the results could be disastrous. In an effort to avoid that, Riley had pushed any hope of a permanent relationship from his mind, and succeeded. Until he met Jayne.

"Come on," he said, standing. "Let's get out of here." He pulled his wallet from his back pocket and tossed a few bills on the table before waving to someone in the back kitchen. Then he led her outside.

When Jayne moved toward his car, Riley stopped her and directed her to a dark alley.

"I know this isn't the right time or place," he whispered, pressing her against the building's brick wall. His hands were on both sides of her face. "But I need this."

He kissed her hungrily, and Jayne responded the same way.

She couldn't get enough of him. She could feel his kiss in every part of her. Sensations tingled along her nerves. The doubts that had weighed on her mind dissolved and with them the pain of the past two days. Lifting her arms, she slid them around his middle and arched toward him.

"Oh, my sweet Jayne." His voice was raspy and filled with emotion. "Trust me, for just a little longer."

"Forever," she whispered in return. "Forever and ever."

Riley closed his eyes. With his current case he was going to demand a lot more of her trust. He wanted to protect her and himself and walk away from this part of his life and start anew. His prayer was that they could hold on to this moment for all time, but he already knew that was impossible.

When Jayne got back to the library, she was ten minutes late. Her lips were devoid of lipstick and her hair was mussed.

"Sorry I'm late," she said, taking her seat and avoiding Gloria's probing gaze.

"Where'd you go?"

"I . . . don't recall the name of the restaurant, but they serve Creole food. It's on Fourth."

"They must've been busy."

"Why?" Jayne's eyes flew to her friend.

"Because you're late."

"As a matter of fact, we were lucky to find a table." Her right eye gave one convulsive jerk, and she quickly changed the subject. "Have you heard from Lance?"

"I already told you we're going out again tonight."

"So you did," Jayne mumbled, having momentarily forgotten.

"He's wonderful."

"I'm really happy for you." Who would have believed that after months of searching, Gloria would finally meet someone in the frozen-food section of Albertsons?

"Don't be in too much of a hurry to congratulate me," Gloria said. "It's too soon to tell if he's a keeper. So far, I like him quite a bit, and we seem to have several common interests—besides groceries. But then that's not always good, either."

"Why not?" The more time Jayne spent with Riley, the more she discovered that they enjoyed many of the same things. They were alike and yet completely different.

"Boring."

Jayne blinked. "I beg your pardon?"

Gloria took a chair beside her and crossed her legs. "Sometimes people are so much alike that they end up boring each other to death."

"That won't be a problem with Riley and me. In fact, I was thinking that although we're alike in some says, we're quite different in others." Smiling, she looked at Gloria. "I like him, you know. I may even love him."

Gloria smiled back. "I know."

"I'm trying a new recipe for spaghetti sauce, if you'd like to come over for dinner," Jayne told Riley on Friday morning. He gave her a ride downtown most days now and phoned whenever he couldn't. His working hours often extended beyond hers, so she still took the bus home in the evenings. But things had worked out well. Since she arrived home first, she started preparing supper, taking pleasure in creating meals because it gave her an excuse to invite Riley over.

"I'll bring the wine."

"Okay." She smiled up at him with little of her former shyness.

"Jayne—" he paused, taking her hand "—you don't have to lure me to your place with wonderful meals."

Her eyes dropped. She hadn't thought her methods were quite that transparent. "I enjoy cooking," she said lamely.

"I just don't want you going to all this trouble for me. I want to be with you, whether you feed me or not. It's you I'm attracted to. Not your cooking. Well, not *just* your cooking."

"I like being with you, too."

Since their lunch on Monday, they'd spent every available minute in each other's company. Often they didn't do anything more exciting than watch television. One night they'd sat together, each engrossed in a good book, and shared a bottle of excellent white wine. That whole evening they hadn't spoken more than a dozen times. But Jayne had never felt closer to another human being.

Riley kissed her and touched her often. It wasn't uncommon for him to sneak up behind her when she was standing at the stove or rinsing dishes. But he never let their kissing get out of control. Jayne wasn't half as eager to restrain their lovemaking as Riley seemed to be.

That evening Jayne had the sauce simmering on the stove and was ready to add the dry spaghetti to the boiling water when Riley called.

"I'm going to be late," he said gruffly.

"That's fine. I can hold dinner."

"I don't think you should." His voice tightened. "In fact, maybe you'd better eat without me."

"I don't want to." She'd been having her meals alone almost every night of her adult life, and suddenly the thought held no appeal.

"This can't be helped, Jayne."

The city worked its inspectors harder than necessary, in Jayne's opinion. "I understand." She didn't really, but asking a flurry of questions wouldn't help. As it was, his responses were clipped and impatient.

He sighed into the phone, and Jayne thought she heard a car honk in the background. "I'll talk to you in the morning," he said.

"Sure, the morning will be fine. I'll save some dinner for you, and you can have it for lunch. Spaghetti's always better the next day."

"Great," he said. She heard a loud shout. "I've got to go," he said hurriedly.

"See you tomorrow."

"Right, tomorrow," Riley said with an earnestness that caused a cold chill to race up Jayne's spine. She held on to the phone longer than necessary, her fingers tightening around the receiver. As she hung up, a feeling of dread settled in the pit of her stomach. Riley hadn't been calling her from his office. The sounds in the background were street noises. And he was with someone. A male. Something was wrong. She could feel it. Something was very, very wrong.

Jayne didn't sleep well that night, tossing and turning while her short conversation with Riley played back in her mind. She went over every detail. He'd sounded impatient, angry. His voice was hard and flat, reminding her of the first few times she'd talked to him.

When she finally did drift off to sleep, her dreams were troubled. Visions of Riley with that woman from Soft Sam's drifted into her mind until she woke with an abrupt start. The dream had been so real that goose bumps broke out on her arms, and she hugged her blankets closer.

The following morning, Saturday, Riley was at her door early. Jayne had barely dressed and had just finished her breakfast.

"Morning." She smiled, not quite meeting his gaze.

"Morning." He leaned forward and brushed his mouth over hers. "I'm sorry about last night." He gently pressed his hands against the sides of her neck, forcing her to meet his eyes.

"That's okay. I understand. There are times I need to work late, as well." All her fears seemed trivial now. He was a city inspector, so naturally he didn't spend all his time in an office or on his own. She'd overacted. Her niggling worries about why he'd canceled melted away under the warmth of his gaze.

He broke away from her and walked to the other side of her living room. "This next week is going to be busy, so maybe we shouldn't make any dinner plans."

Jayne rubbed her hands together. "If that's what you want."

"It isn't."

He said it with such honesty that Jayne could find no reason to doubt him.

After a cup of coffee, they left for Riverside Park. Together they did the shopping for the week, making several stops. When they returned to the apartment building, their arms were filled with packages.

"I want to stop off at the manager's," Riley announced as they stepped into the elevator.

"I'll go on up to my place and put these things away." She didn't want the ice cream to melt while Riley paid his rent.

"I'll be up shortly."

The elevator doors closed, and Jayne watched the light that indicated the floor numbers. She smiled at Riley, recalling similar rides in times past and how she'd dreaded being caught alone with him. Now she savored the moment.

Riley smiled back. Their morning had been marvelous, he thought. It seemed natural to have Jayne at his side, and he'd enjoyed going shopping together like a long-married couple. He experienced a surge of tenderness that was so powerful it was akin to pain. He'd been waiting for this woman for years. He was deeply grateful to have her in his life, especially after the unsavory people he'd been dealing with these past few years. He loved her wry wit. Her sense of humor was subtle and quick. Thinking about it now made him chuckle lightly.

"Is something funny?" She raised wide inquisitive eyes to him.

"No, just thinking about you."

"I'm so glad I amuse you." She shifted her shopping bag from one hand to the other.

"Here." Deliberately he took her bag and set it on the elevator floor. Before she could realize what he was doing, he turned her in his embrace and slid his arms around her waist. "You're the most beautiful woman I've ever met, Jayne Gilbert."

"Oh, Riley." She lowered her gaze, not knowing how to respond. No man had ever said anything so wonderful to her. From someone else it would have sounded like a well-worn line, but she could see the sincerity in his eyes. That told her *he* believed it, even if she couldn't.

"Do you doubt me?"

She answered him with a short nod. "I've seen myself in plenty of mirrors. I know what I look like."

"An angel. Pure, good, innocent." With each word, he drew closer to her. Sweeping her hair aside, he brushed her neck with his mouth. She tilted her head, and the brown curls fell to one side. When his lips moved up her jawline, Jayne felt her legs grow weak. She leaned against the back of the elevator for support. Finally his mouth found hers in a long, slow kiss that left her weak and clinging to him.

The elevator stopped then, and Riley released her for a few seconds, closing the door again.

"Riley, that was our floor," she objected.

"I know." His eyes blazed into hers, and he leaned forward and kissed her again.

Jayne clung to him, awed that this man could be attracted to her. "I can't believe this," she murmured, and tears clogged her throat.

"What? That we're kissing in an elevator?"

"No," she breathed. "That you're holding me like this. I know it's silly, but I'm afraid of waking up and discovering that this is all a dream. It's too good to be true."

"You'd have a hard time convincing me that this isn't real. You feel too right in my arms."

"You do, too."

Her heart swelled with love. Riley hadn't said he loved her, but he didn't need to. With every action he took and every word he spoke, he was constantly showing her his feelings. For that matter, she hadn't told him how she felt, either. It was unnecessary.

Reluctantly he let her go and pushed the button that would open the elevator doors. "I'll be back in a couple of minutes." He grinned. "I need to go all the way down again."

"I'll start the spaghetti."

"Okay." He caressed her cheek. "I'll see you soon."

She stepped out of the elevator and instantly caught sight of a tall man. She didn't recognize him as anyone from her building and certainly not from the ninth floor. Judging by his age, as well as the leather he wore, he could have been a member of some gang. Jayne swallowed uncomfortably and glanced back at Riley. The elevator doors were closing, and she doubted he saw her panicked look.

Squaring her shoulders, Jayne secured her small purse under her arm and moved the shopping bag to her left hand. Remembering a book she'd read about self-defense, she paused to remove her keys from her purse and held the one for her apartment between her index and middle fingers. If this creep tried to attack she'd be ready. Watching him, Jayne walked to her apartment, which was in the middle of the long corridor. Her breath felt tight in her lungs. With every step she took, the young man advanced toward her.

His eyes were dark, his pupils wide. Fear coated the inside of her mouth. Whoever this was appeared to be high on some sort of drug. All the headlines she'd read about drug-crazed criminals flashed through her mind. Getting into her apartment no longer seemed the safest alternative. What if he forced his way in?

Jayne whirled around and hurried back to the elevator, urgently pushing the button.

"You aren't going to run away, are you?" The man's words were slurred.

In a panic, Jayne pushed the button again. Nothing.

He was so close now that all he had to do was reach out and touch her. Lifting one hand, he pulled her hair and laughed when she winced at the slight pain.

"What do you want?" she demanded, backing away.

"Give me your money."

Jayne had no intention of arguing with him and held out her purse. "I don't have much." Almost all the cash she carried with her had been spent on groceries, and she hadn't brought any credit cards. Or her cell phone . . .

He grabbed her purse and started pawing through it. When he discovered the truth of her statement, he'd be furious, and there was no telling what he'd do next. If she was going to escape, her chance was now.

Raising the bag of groceries, she shoved it into his chest with all her strength and took off running. The stairwell was at the other end of the corridor, and she sprinted toward it. Fear and adrenaline pumped through her, but she wasn't fast enough to beat the young man. He got to the door before she did and blocked her only exit.

Jayne came to an abrupt halt and, with her hands at her sides, moved slowly backward.

She heard the elevator door opening behind her and swung around. Riley stepped out. Jayne's relief was so great she felt like weeping. "Riley!" she called out.

Instantly her attacker straightened.

Riley saw the fear sketched so vividly on her face and felt an overwhelming instinct to protect. Wordlessly he moved toward her pursuer.

The man took one step toward Riley. "Give me your money."

Riley didn't say a word.

In her gratitude at seeing Riley, Jayne hadn't stopped to notice the lack of fear in him. With her back against the wall, her legs gave out, and she slumped helplessly against it.

Riley's face was as hard as granite and so intense that Jayne's breath caught in her lungs. The man who'd kissed her and held her in the elevator wasn't the same man who stood in the hallway now. This Riley was a stranger.

"Hey, buddy, it was just a joke," the young man said, reaching for the doorknob.

Jayne had never seen a man as fierce as Riley was at that moment. She hardly recognized him. Deadly fury blazed from his eyes, and Jayne felt cold shivers racing over her arms.

From there, everything seemed to happen in slow motion. Riley advanced on the young man and knocked him to the ground with one powerful punch.

The man let out a yelp of pain. Riley raised his fist to hit him again. Hand connected with jaw in a sickening thud.

Jayne screamed. "Riley! No more. No more."

As if he'd forgotten she was there, Riley turned back to her. Taking this unexpected opportunity to escape, the man propelled himself through the stairwell door and was gone.

Jayne forced back a tiny sobbing breath and stumbled to his side. She threw her arms around him as tears rained from her eyes. "Oh, Riley," she cried weakly.

Riley's body was rigid against hers for several minutes until the tension eased from his limbs and he wrapped his arms around her. "Did he hurt you?"

"No," she sobbed. "No. He was after my money, but I didn't have much."

His arms went around her with crushing force, driving the air from her lungs.

"If he'd hurt you—"

"He didn't, he didn't." No more words could make it past the constriction in her throat. Jayne realized it wasn't fear that had prompted this sudden paralysis, but the knowledge that Riley was capable of such violence. She didn't want to know what he might've done if she hadn't stopped him.

His hold gradually relaxed. "Tell me what happened," he said, leading her toward her apartment door.

"He wanted my money."

"You didn't do anything stupid like argue with him, did you?"

"No . . . I read in this self-defense book that—"

"You and your books."

She could almost laugh, but not quite. "I'm so grateful you got here when you did." She was thinking of her own safety, but also of the would-be mugger and what Riley would have done to him had he actually hurt her.

"I've never seen anyone fight like that," she murmured, stooping to pick up her purse and the groceries that littered the hallway.

"It's something I learned when I was in the military." Riley strove to make light of what he'd done. The last thing he wanted to do now was to fabricate stories to appease Jayne's curiosity.

He bent down to gather up some of the spilled groceries. Her hands trembled as she deposited one item after another in her bag.

"Are you sure you're all right?" Doubt echoed in his husky voice.

"Yes. I was more scared than anything."

"I don't blame you."

Her returning smile was wooden. "I surprised myself by how quickly I could move."

Getting to his feet, Riley brought the bag with him. "Let's get these things put away. I'll bet the ice cream is starting to melt."

Rushing ahead of him to unlock the apartment door, Jayne had the freezer open by the time he arrived in her kitchen. He handed the carton of vanilla ice cream to her; she shoved it inside and closed the door.

"Do you think we should call the police?" she asked, still shaking.

"No. He won't be back."

"How do you know?" His confidence was unnerving.

"I just do. But if it'll make you feel better, go ahead and call them."

"I might." She watched for his reaction, but he gave none. Maybe it was her imagination, but she had the distinct feeling that Riley didn't want her to contact the authorities.

Riley paced the floor. "Jayne, listen, I've got something to tell you."

"Yes?" She raised expectant eyes to him.

"I'm going away for a while."

"Away?"

"On vacation. A fishing trip. I'm leaving tonight."

Seven

"A fishing trip?" Jayne asked incredulously. Riley didn't know the difference between a salmon and a trout. "Isn't this rather sudden?"

"Not really. The timing looked good, so we decided to go now, instead of waiting until later in the summer." Riley opened the refrigerator and took out the bowl of spaghetti sauce, setting it on the counter.

Jayne moved to the cupboard and got a saucepan. She worked for the city, too, and knew from experience that vacation times were often planned a year in advance. One didn't simply decide "the timing looked good" and head off on vacation. "How long will you be gone?"

His eyes softened. "Don't worry. I'll be back in time for your reunion."

Jayne was apprehensive, but it wasn't over her high school reunion. This so-called vacation of Riley's had a fishy odor that had nothing to do with trout. Busy at the sink, she kept her back to him, swallowing down her doubts. "You must have had this planned for quite a while."

"Not really. It was a spur-of-the-moment decision." He didn't elaborate, and she didn't ask. Quizzing him about the particulars would only put a strain on these last few hours together.

She *should* ask him about these spur-of-the-moment vacation plans and how he'd arranged it with the city. From what he'd told her, Riley was a city inspector. But Jayne had doubts about that; she couldn't help it. Although he seemed to keep regular hours, he often needed to meet someone at night. She'd watched him several times from her living room window, seeing him in the parking lot below. She'd never questioned him about his late hours, though, afraid of what she'd discover if she pursued the subject.

She bit her bottom lip, angry with herself for being so complacent.

"You've got that look on your face," Riley said when she set the pan of water on the stove to boil.

"What look?"

"The one that tells me you disapprove."

"How could I possibly object to you taking a well-deserved vacation? You've been working long hours. You need a break. Right?"

"Right."

But he didn't sound as though he was excited about this trip. And from little things he'd let drop, Jayne suspected he didn't even know what a fishing pole looked like. He certainly didn't know anything about fish!

Standing behind her, Riley slipped his arms around her waist and pressed his mouth to the side of her neck. "A watched pot never boils," he murmured. "Jayne, listen—I shouldn't be gone any more than ten days. Two weeks at the most."

"Two weeks!" The reunion was in three. Turning, she hugged him with all the pent-up love in her heart. "I'll miss you," she whispered.

"I'll miss you, too." Tenderly, he kissed her temple, then tilted her head so that his mouth could claim hers.

Jayne marveled that he could be so loving and gentle only minutes after punching out a mugger. The whole incident had frightened her. There were depths to this man that she had yet to glimpse, dangerous depths. But perhaps it was better not to see that side of his nature. An icy sensation ran down her arms, and she shivered.

"You're cold."

"No," she said. "Afraid."

"Why?" He tightened his hold. "What do you have to fear?"

"I don't know."

"That mugger won't be back."

"I know." After what Riley had done to him, Jayne was confident the man wouldn't dare return.

Forcing down her apprehension, she smiled and raised her fingers to his thick dark hair, then arched up and kissed his mouth. She was being unnecessarily silly, she told herself. Riley was going on a fishing trip. He'd return before her reunion, and everything would be wonderful again.

Reluctantly breaking away from him, she sighed. "I'll get lunch started. You probably have a hundred things you need to do this afternoon."

"What things?"

"What about getting all your gear together?" She added the

dry noodles to the rapidly boiling water, wanting to believe with all her heart that Riley was doing exactly as he'd said.

"The other guy is bringing everything."

"But surely you've got stuff you need to do."

"Perhaps, but I decided I'd rather spend the day with you."

"When are you leaving?" One of her uncles was an avid sportsman, and from what Jayne remembered, he was emphatic that early morning was the best time for fishing.

"Tonight."

"Where will you be? Are you camping?"

He shrugged. "I don't know. I've left all the arrangements to my friend."

That sounded highly questionable, and her manufactured confidence quickly crumpled. Under the weight of her uncertainty, Jayne bowed her head.

"Honey." He tucked a finger beneath her chin, and her eyes lifted to his. "I'll be back in no time."

Despite her fears, Jayne laughed. "I sincerely doubt that." He hadn't even gone, and she already felt an empty void in her life.

"I know how important your reunion is to you."

Riley was more important to her than a hundred high school reunions. A thought went crashing through her mind with such searching impact that for a moment she was stunned. She wondered if she'd finally figured out why Riley paid her so much attention. "You seem awfully worried about my reunion."

"Only because I know how much you want to go."

With trembling hands she brought down two dinner plates from the cupboard. "I don't need your charity or your pity, Riley Chambers."

"What are you talking about?" His jaw sagged open in astonished disbelief.

Jayne's brown eyes burned with the fiery light of outrage. "It just dawned on me that . . . that all this attention you've been giving me lately could be attributed to precisely those reasons."

"Charity?" he demanded. "Pity? You don't honestly believe that!"

"I don't know what to think anymore. Why else would someone as . . . as worldly as you have anything to do with someone as plain and ordinary as me?"

Riley stared at her in shock. Jayne, plain and ordinary! Vivacious and outgoing she wasn't. But Jayne was special—more than any woman he'd ever known. He opened his mouth to speak, closed it and stalked across the room. What had gotten into her? He'd never known Jayne to be illogical. From her reaction, he could tell she wasn't falling for this fishing story of his. Telling her had been difficult enough. He hadn't wanted to do it, but there was no other option. He couldn't tell her the real reason for this unexpected "vacation," but he was lying to her for her own protection. The fewer people who were in on it, the better.

Jayne carried the plates to the table, feeling angry, hurt and confused; most of all, she was suspicious. How easily she'd been swayed by his charm and his kisses. She'd been a pushover for a man of Riley's experience. From the beginning she'd known that he wasn't everything he appeared to be. But she'd preferred to overlook the obvious. Riley was up to no good. She told herself she had a right to know what he was doing, and yet in the same breath, she had no desire to venture into the unknown mysteries he'd been hiding from her.

"Jayne, please look at me," he said quietly. "You can't accuse me of something as ridiculous as pitying you, then walk away."

"I didn't walk away . . . I'm setting the table." She turned to face him, her expression defiant.

"Charity, Jayne? Pity? I think you need to explain yourself."

"What's there to explain? I've always been a joke to people like you. Except that for a woman who's supposed to be smart, I've been incredibly stupid."

Riley was at a complete loss. His past dealings with women had been brief. In his line of work, it had been preferable to avoid any emotional ties. Now he discovered that he didn't know how to reassure Jayne, the first woman who'd touched his heart. He couldn't be entirely honest, but perhaps a bit of logic wouldn't be amiss. . . .

"Even if you're right and everything I feel for you is of a charitable nature," he began, "what's my motive?"

"I don't know. But then I wouldn't, would I?"

He took a step toward her and paused. He couldn't rush her, although every instinct urged him to take her in his arms and comfort her. "That's not what's really bothering you, is it?"

Tears clouded her eyes as she shook her head. "No."

He reached for her, but Jayne avoided him. "Honey . . ." he murmured.

She blanched and pointed a shaking finger in his direction. "Don't call me *honey.* I'm not important to you."

"I love you, Jayne." He didn't know any other way to tell her. The flowery words she deserved and probably expected just weren't in him. He could only hope she trusted him—and that she'd give him time.

Jayne's reaction was to place her hand over her mouth and shake her head from side to side.

"Well?" he said impatiently. "Don't you have anything to say?"

Jayne stared at him, her eyes wet. "You *love* me?"

"It can't have been any big secret. You must've known, for heaven's sake."

"Riley . . ."

"No, it's your turn to listen. I've gone about this all wrong. Women like moonlight, roses, the whole deal." He paced the kitchen and ran a hand through his hair. "I'm no good at this. With you, I wanted to do everything right, and already I can see it's backfiring."

"Riley, I love you, too."

"Women need romance. I realize that and I feel like a jerk because you're entitled to all of it. Unfortunately, I don't know the right words to tell you about everything inside me."

"Riley." She said his name again, her voice gaining volume. "Did you hear what I said?"

"I know you love me," he muttered almost angrily. "You aren't exactly one to disguise your feelings."

She crossed her arms over her chest with an exasperated sigh. "Well, excuse me."

"I'm not good enough for you," he continued, barely acknowledging her response. "Someone as honorable and kind as you deserves a man who's a heck of a lot better than me. I've lived hard these past few years and I've done more than one thing I regret."

Jayne started to respond but wasn't given the opportunity.

"There hasn't been room in my life for a woman. But I can't wait any longer. I didn't realize how much I need you. I want to change, but that's going to take time and patience."

"I'm patient," Jayne told him shyly, her anger forgotten under the sweet balm of his words. "Gloria says I'm the most patient person she's ever known. In fact, my father gets angry with me because he feels I'm too meek . . . not that meekness and patience are the same thing, you understand. It's just that—"

"Are you going to chatter all day, or are you going to come over here and let me kiss you?" His eyes took on a fierce possessive light.

"Oh, Riley, I love you so much." She walked into his waiting arms, surrendering everything—her heart, her soul, her life. And her doubts.

They kissed, lightly at first, testing their freshly revealed emotions. Then their lips stayed together, gradually parting as their mouths moved, slanting, tasting, probing.

Jayne whimpered. She couldn't help herself. There was so much more she longed to discover. . . .

His kisses deepened until he raised his head and whispered hoarsely. "Jayne. Oh, my sweet, sweet, Jayne."

"I love you," she said again and kissed him softly.

Riley tunneled his fingers through her hair and buried his face in the slope of her neck. But he didn't push her away as he had in the past. Nor did he bring her closer. His breath was rushed as he struggled with indecision.

"Riley . . ."

"Shhh, don't move. Okay?"

"Okay," she agreed, loving him more and more.

Gradually the tension eased from him, and he relaxed. But his hold didn't loosen, and he held her for what seemed like hours rather than minutes.

They spent the rest of the day together. After lunch they walked in the park, holding hands, making excuses to touch each other. Riley brought along a chessboard and set it up on the picnic table, and they played a long involved game. When Jayne won the match, Riley applauded her skill and reset the board. He won the second game. They decided against a third.

At dinnertime they ate Chinese food at a small hole-in-the-wall restaurant and brought the leftovers home.

Standing just inside her apartment door, Jayne asked, "Do you want to come in for coffee?"

"I've got to pack and get ready."

She nodded. "I understand. Thank you for today."

"No, thank *you.*" He laid his hand against her cheek, and when he spoke, his voice was warm and filled with emotion. "You'll take care of yourself while I'm gone, won't you?"

"Of course I will." She couldn't resist smiling. "I've been doing a fairly good job of that for several years now."

"I don't feel right leaving you." He studied her. He wished this case was over so he could give her all the things she had a right to ask for.

"You're coming back."

The words stung his conscience. There was always the possibility that he wouldn't. The risks and dangers of his job had been a stimulant before he'd fallen in love with Jayne. Now he experienced the first real taste of dread.

Fear shot through Jayne at the expression on Riley's face. She saw the way his eyes narrowed, the way his mouth tightened. "You *are* coming back, aren't you?" She repeated her question, louder and stronger this time.

"I'll be back." His voice vibrated with emotion. "I love you, Jayne. I'm coming back to you, don't worry."

Not worry! One glimpse at the intense look in his eyes, and she was terrified. From the way Riley was behaving, one would assume that he was going off on a suicide mission.

Riley smiled and brought his hand to her face. He touched her cheek, then her forehead, easing the frown between her brows. "I'll be back. I promise you that."

"I'll be waiting."

"I won't be able to contact you."

She nodded.

The story about his fishing trip was forgotten. Jayne didn't know where he was headed or why. For now, she didn't want to know. He said he was coming back, and that was all that mattered.

"Goodbye, my love," he said with a final kiss.

"Goodbye, Riley."

He turned and walked out the door, and Jayne was left with an aching void of uncertainty.

The library was busy on Monday morning. Jayne was sitting at the information desk in the children's department when the chief librarian approached, carrying a huge bouquet of red roses in a lovely ceramic vase.

"How beautiful," Jayne said, looking up.

"They just arrived for you." Her boss placed them on the desk.

"For me?" No one had ever sent her flowers at work.

Gloria walked across the room and joined her. "Who are they from?" she asked, then answered her own question. "It must be Riley."

"Must be." Jayne unpinned the small card and pulled it from the envelope.

"What's it say?" Gloria wanted to know.

"Just that he'll be home by the time these wilt."

"He must have sent them from out of town."

Jayne frowned. "Right." Except that the card was scrawled in Riley's own unmistakable handwriting. He could have ordered them before he went, or . . . or maybe he hadn't left Portland yet.

She squelched the doubts and possibilities that raced through her mind. She loved Riley and he loved her, and that was all that mattered. Not where he was or what he was doing. Or even whether he was fishing.

Without him, the days passed slowly. Jayne was astonished that a man she'd known and loved for such a short time could so effectively fill her life. Now her days lacked purpose. She went to work, came home and plopped down in front of the television. During the first week that he was gone, Jayne ate more microwave dinners than she'd eaten the whole previous month. It was simpler that way.

"You look like you could do with some cheering up," Gloria commented Friday afternoon.

"I could," Jayne murmured.

"How about if we go shopping tomorrow for a dress to wear to your reunion? I know just the place."

Jayne would need something special for the reunion, but she didn't feel like shopping. Still, it had to be done sooner or later. "All right," she found herself agreeing.

"And in exchange for my expert advice, you can take me to the Creole restaurant where you and Riley had lunch."

"Sure. If I can remember where it is. We only went there once." That day had been so miserable for Jayne that she hadn't paid much attention to the place or the food.

"You said it was on Fourth."

"Right." She remembered now, and she also recalled why she'd been so miserable. That was when she'd seen Riley with the blonde.

★ ★ ★

Gloria showed up at her apartment early Saturday morning. Jayne had no enthusiasm for this shopping expedition.

Gloria got a carton of orange juice from the refrigerator and poured herself a glass. "I checked out this new boutique, and it's expensive, but worth it."

"Gloria." Jayne sighed. The longer Riley was away, the more unsure she felt about the reunion. "I've probably got something adequate in my closet."

"You don't." Gloria opened the fridge again and peeked inside. "I'm starved. Have you had breakfast yet?"

Jayne hadn't. "I'm not hungry, but help yourself."

"Thanks." Pulling out a loaf of bread, Gloria stuck a piece in the toaster. "When you walk in the grand ballroom of the Seattle Westin, I want every eye to be on you."

"I'll see what I can do to arrange a spotlight," Jayne said.

"I mean it. You're going to be a hit."

"Right." In twenty-seven years, she hadn't made an impression on anything except her mattress.

"Hey, where's your confidence? You can't back down now. You've got the man, kiddo. It's all downhill from here."

"I suppose," Jayne said.

"I thought you should get something in red."

"Red?" Jayne echoed with a small laugh. "I was thinking more along the lines of brown or beige."

"Nope." The toast popped up, and Gloria buttered it. "You want to stand out in the crowd, not blend in."

"Blending in is what I do."

"Nope." Gloria shook her head. "For one night, m'dear, you're going to be a knockout."

"Gloria." Jayne hesitated. "I don't know."

"Trust me. I've gotten you this far."

"But . . ."

"Trust me."

Two hours later, Jayne was pleased that she'd had faith in her friend's judgment. After seeing the inside of more stores than she'd visited in a year, she found the perfect dress. Or rather, Gloria did—and not in the new boutique she'd been so excited about, either. This was a classic women's wear shop Jayne would never have ventured into on her own. The dress was a lavender color, and Gloria insisted Jayne try it on. At first, Jayne had scoffed; in two hours, she'd dressed and undressed at least twenty times. She was about to throw up her arms and surrender—nothing fit right, or if it did fit, the color was wrong. Even Gloria showed signs of frustration.

Everything about this full-length gown was perfect. Jayne stood in front of the three-way mirror and blinked in disbelief.

"You look stunning," Gloria breathed in awe.

Jayne couldn't stop staring at herself. This one gown made up for every prom she'd ever missed. The off-the-shoulder style and close-fitting bodice accentuated her full breasts and tiny waist to exquisite advantage. The full side-shirred skirt and double lace ruffle danced about her feet. She couldn't have hoped to find a dress more beautiful.

"Do we dare look at the price?" Gloria murmured, searching for the tag.

"It's lovely, but can I afford it?" Jayne hesitated, expecting to discover some reason she couldn't have this perfect gown.

"You can't afford not to buy it," Gloria stated emphatically. "This is *the* dress for you. Besides, it's a lot more reasonable than I figured." She read the price to her, and Jayne couldn't believe it was so low; she'd assumed it would be twice as much.

"You're buying it, aren't you?" The look Gloria gave her said that if Jayne didn't, she'd never speak to her again.

"Naturally I'm buying it," Jayne responded with a wide grin. Excitement flowed through her, and she felt like singing and dancing. Riley would love how she looked in this dress. Everything was working out so well. She'd shock her former classmates. They'd take one look at her in that gown with Riley at her side, and their jaws would fall open with utter astonishment. And yet . . . that didn't matter the way it once did.

"Now are you going to feed me?" Gloria fluttered her long lashes dramatically as though to say she was about to faint from hunger.

"Do you still want to try that place Riley took me to?"

"Only if we can get there quickly."

Smiling at her friend's humor, Jayne paid for the dress and made arrangements to have it delivered to her apartment later in the day.

She and Gloria chatted easily as they walked out to the street. Gloria drove, and with Jayne acting as navigator, they made their way down the freeway and across the Willamette River to the heart of downtown.

"There it is," Jayne announced as Gloria pulled onto Fourth Avenue. "To your left, about halfway down the block."

"Great." Gloria backed into a parking space. A flash of black attracted Jayne's attention. She glanced into the alley beside the restaurant and saw a sports car similar to Riley's. She immediately decided it wasn't his. There was no reason he'd be here—was there?

"I don't mind telling you I'm starved," Gloria said as she turned off the ignition.

"What's with you lately? I've never known you to show such an interest in food."

"Yes, well, you see . . ." Gloria paused to clear her throat. "I tend to eat when something's bothering me."

"What's bothering you?" Jayne instantly felt guilty. She'd been so involved with her own problems that she hadn't noticed her friend's.

"Well . . ."

"Is it Lance?" It had to be. Gloria hadn't talked about him all week, although the week before she'd been bubbling over about her newfound soul mate. "He's not turning out to be everything you thought?"

"I wish." Gloria reached for her purse and stepped out of the car door.

"What do you wish?"

"That he wasn't so wonderful. Jayne, I'm scared. Look at me." She held out her hand and purposely shook it. "I'm shaking all over."

"But if you like him so much, what's wrong?"

They crossed the street together and entered the restaurant, taking the first available booth. "I've been married once," Gloria told her unnecessarily. "And when that didn't work out, I was sure I'd never recover. I know it sounds melodramatic to anyone who hasn't been through a divorce, but it's true."

Gloria was right; Jayne probably couldn't fully understand, but she thought about Riley and how devastated she'd be if they ever stopped loving each other.

"Now I'm falling for another man and, Jayne, I'm so tied up in knots I can't think straight. Being with you today is an excuse not to be with Lance. Every time we're together, the attraction grows stronger and stronger. We're already talking about marriage."

"I guess it works that way sometimes," Jayne murmured, thinking she'd marry Riley in a minute. Gloria had met Lance only a couple of weeks after Jayne had started seeing Riley.

"We both want a family and we believe strongly in the same things."

"Are you going to marry him?"

Gloria shrugged. "Not yet. It's too serious a decision to make so quickly. Remember the old saying? Marry in haste and repent at leisure."

"And . . ."

"And I haven't told Lance. I know him, or at least I think I know him. He's just like a man."

"I should hope so." Jayne chuckled.

"Once he decides on something, he wants it *now.* I have this horrible feeling that I'm going to tell him I want to wait, and he's going to argue with me and wear me down. He may even tell me to take a hike. There aren't many men around as good as Lance. I could be walking away from the last opportunity I have to meet a decent man."

"If he loves you, he'll agree. And if he's too impatient, you'll have your answer, won't you?"

"No, because knowing me, I'll want him even more."

The waitress came with glasses of water and a menu. They ordered, ate lunch and chatted over several cups of coffee and cheesecake.

Glancing at her watch, Gloria said, "Listen, I've got to get back. Lance is picking me up in an hour."

Drinking the last of her coffee, Jayne stood. "Then let's get going."

Outside the restaurant, Jayne idly checked the alley for the black car as she crossed the street. It was still there. She could have sworn it was Riley's. But it couldn't be. Could it?

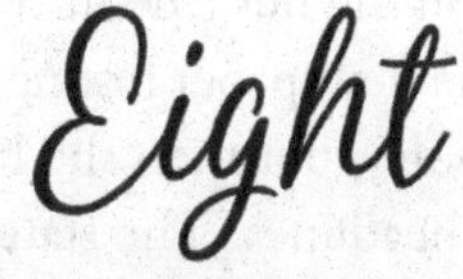

Eight

There had to be a thousand black sports cars in Oregon like the one Riley drove, Jayne told herself repeatedly over the next twenty-four hours. Probably more than a thousand. She was being absurd in even wondering if Riley's car was the one in the alley beside the Creole restaurant. He was fishing with friends. Right?

Wrong, said a little voice in the back of her mind. He'd lied about that; Jayne was sure of it. He'd never introduced her to any of his friends. He was new in Portland, having lived in the city for only a few months. He'd admitted there were things in his life he regretted. He'd said he wanted to change and that he wasn't good enough for her.

All weekend, Jayne's thoughts vacillated. Even if he'd lied about the fishing trip, it didn't automatically mean he was doing anything illegal, although those mysterious meetings in the parking lot weren't encouraging. And if he was doing something underhanded, she didn't want to know about it. Ignorance truly was bliss. If she inadvertently found anything out . . . She simply preferred not to know because then she might be required to act on it.

Monday morning on the bus ride into town, Jayne sat looking out the window, the newspaper resting in her lap. She hadn't heard anything from Riley, but then she hadn't expected to.

She glanced at the headlines. The state senator whom she'd met several months earlier had been arrested and released on a large bail. Apparently Senator Max Priestly, who'd lobbied heavily for legalized gambling in Oregon, had ties to the Mafia. She skimmed the article, not particularly interested in the details. His court date had already been set. Jayne felt a grimace of distaste at the thought that a public official would willingly sell out the welfare of his state.

Setting aside the front-page section, she turned to the advice column. Maybe reading about someone else's troubles would lighten her own. It didn't.

At lunchtime Jayne decided not to fight her uncertainty any longer. She'd take a cab to the Creole restaurant and satisfy her curiosity. The black sports car would be gone, and she'd be reassured, calling herself a fool for being so suspicious.

Only she wasn't reassured. Even when she discovered that the car was nowhere to be seen, she didn't relax. Instead she instructed the driver to take her to Soft Sam's.

The minute she climbed out of the taxi, Jayne saw the familiar black car parked on a nearby side street. Her heart pounded against her ribs as dread crept up her spine. Absently she handed the driver his fare.

Just because the car was there didn't mean anything, she told herself calmly. It might not even be his.

But Jayne took one glance at the interior, with Riley's raincoat slung over the seat, and realized it *was* his car.

Stomach churning, Jayne ran her hand over the back fender, confused and unsure. From the beginning of this so-called fishing trip, she'd suspected Riley was lying. She didn't know what he was hiding from her or why—she just knew he was.

Her appetite gone, Jayne backed away from the car and returned to the library without eating lunch.

That evening when she arrived at her apartment, Jayne turned on the TV to drown out her fears. The first time she'd ever seen Riley, she'd thought he looked like . . . well, like a criminal. Some underworld gang member. He wore that silly raincoat as if he were carrying something he wanted to conceal—like a gun.

Slumping onto the sofa, Jayne buried her face in her hands. *Could* he be hiding a weapon? The very idea was ridiculous. Of course he wasn't! She'd know if he carried a gun. He'd held her enough for her to have felt it.

The local news blared from the TV. The evening broadcast featured the arrest of Senator Max Priestly, who'd been caught in a sting operation. This was the same story she'd read in the morning paper.

Jayne stared at the screen and at the outrage that showed on Priestly's face. He shouted that he'd been framed and he'd prove his innocence in court. The commentator came back to say that the state's case had been damaged by the mysterious disappearance of vital evidence.

Deciding she'd had enough unsavory news, Jayne stood and turned off the TV.

In bed that night, she kept changing positions. Nothing felt comfortable. She couldn't vanquish her niggling doubts, couldn't relax. When she did drift into a light sleep, her dreams were filled with Riley and Senator Max Priestly. Waking in a cold sweat, Jayne lay staring at the dark ceiling, wondering why her mind had connected the two men.

Pounding her pillow, she rolled onto her side and forced her eyes to close. A burning sensation went through her, and her eyes opened with sudden alarm. She'd connected the two men because she'd seen Riley *with* Max Priestly. She hadn't met the state senator at the library, as she'd assumed. She'd seen him with Riley. But when? Weeks ago, she recalled, before she'd started dating Riley. Where? Closing her eyes again, she tried to drag up the details of the meeting. It must have been at the apartment. Yes, he was the man in the parking lot. She'd seen Priestly hand Riley a briefcase. At the time, Jayne remembered that Senator Priestly had looked vaguely familiar. Later, she'd associated him with the group of state legislators that had toured the library. But Max Priestly hadn't been one of them.

And Riley wasn't on any fishing trip. If he was somehow linked with this man—and he appeared to be—then he probably knew that Priestly had been arrested. Riley could very well have spent this "vacation" of his awaiting Priestly's bail hearing. No wonder he hadn't been able to give her the exact date of his return.

The first thing Jayne did the next morning was to rip through the paper, eagerly searching for more information. She didn't need to look far. Again Max Priestly dominated the front page. An interview with his secretary reported that the important missing evidence was telephone logs and copies of letters Max had dictated to her. They'd simply disappeared from her computer. When questioned about how long they'd been missing, the secretary claimed that their absence had been discovered only recently. After that, Jayne stopped reading.

The morning passed in a fog of regret. Jayne didn't know what her coworkers must think of her. She felt like a robot, programmed to act and do certain assignments without thought or question, and that was what she'd done.

When Gloria started talking about her relationship with Lance during their coffee break, Jayne didn't hear a word. She nodded and smiled at the appropriate times and prayed her friend wouldn't notice.

"Isn't it terrible, all this stuff that's coming out about Senator Priestly?"

Jayne's coffee sloshed over the rim of her cup. "Yes," she mumbled, avoiding Gloria's eyes.

"The news this morning said he has connections to the underworld. Apparently he was hoping to promote prostitution rings along with legalized gambling."

"Prostitution," Jayne echoed, vividly recalling the bleached blonde on Riley's arm that afternoon. She'd refused to believe he had anything to do with the woman, even though she knew what the woman was. Somehow she'd even managed to overcome the pain of seeing Riley with her. Now she realized that Soft Sam's was more than simply a bar. Riley had repeatedly warned her to stay away from it. She hadn't needed his caution; Jayne had felt so out of place during her one visit that she wouldn't have returned under any circumstances.

After her coffee break with Gloria, Jayne's day went from bad to worse. Nothing seemed to go right for the rest of the afternoon.

That evening, stepping off the bus, she saw Riley's car parked in his spot across the street. He was back. A chill went through her. She wouldn't tell him what she knew but prayed that he loved her enough to be honest with her.

She hadn't been inside the apartment for more than five minutes when Riley was at her door. Jayne froze at the sound of his knock. Squaring her shoulders, she forced a smile on her lips.

"Welcome back," she said, pulling open the door.

Riley took one look at her pale features and walked into the apartment. For nearly two weeks, he'd tried to put Jayne out of his mind and concentrate on his assignment. A mistake could have been disastrous, even deadly. Yet he hadn't been able to forget her. She'd been with him every minute. All he'd needed to do was close his eyes and she'd be there. Her image, her memory, comforted him and brought him joy. *So this was love.* He'd avoided it for years, but now he realized the way he felt was beyond description.

"I've missed you," he whispered, reaching for her.

Willingly Jayne went into his arms. She couldn't doubt the sincerity in his low voice.

"Oh, Riley." His name became an aching sigh as she wound her arms around his neck and buried her face in his chest.

Her tense muscles immediately communicated to Riley that something was wrong. "Honey," he breathed into her hair. "What is it?" His hand curved around the side of her neck, his fingers tangling with her soft curls. He raised her head the fraction of an inch needed for her lips to meet his descending mouth. He'd dreamed of kissing her for days. . . .

Jayne moaned softly. She loved this man. It didn't matter what he'd done or who he knew. Riley had said he wanted to change. Jayne's love would be the bridge that would link him to a clean, honest life. Together they'd work to undo any wrong Riley had been involved in before he met her. She'd help him. She'd do nothing, absolutely nothing, to destroy this blissful happiness they shared.

Their gentle exploratory kiss grew more intense. Riley lifted his head.

"Oh, my love," he moaned raggedly into the hollow of her throat. "I've missed you so much."

"I missed you, too," she whispered in return.

He buried his hands deep in her hair and didn't breathe. Then he mumbled something she couldn't hear and reluctantly broke the contact.

For days he'd dreamed about the feel of her in his arms, yet his imagination fell short of reality. Her lips were warm and swollen from his kisses, and he could hardly believe that this shy, gentle woman could raise such havoc with his senses. "Has anything interesting happened around here?" he asked, trying to distract himself.

"Not really." She shook her head, glancing down so her twitching eye wouldn't be so noticeable. "What about you?" She approached the subject cautiously. "Did you catch lots of fish?"

"Only one."

"Did you bring it back? I can fry up a great trout."

Riley hated lying to her and pursed his lips. He swore that after this case he never would again. "I gave it to . . . a friend."

"I didn't think you had many friends in Portland." Her voice quavered slightly.

"I have plenty of friends." He raked his hand through his hair as he stalked to the other side of the room. He'd broken the cardinal rule in this business; the line between his professional life and his personal one had been crossed. He'd seen it happen to others and swore it wouldn't happen to him. But it was too late. He'd fallen for Jayne with his eyes wide open and wouldn't change a thing. "So, nothing new came up while I was away?"

Sheer nerve was the only thing that prevented Jayne from collapsing into a blubbering mass of tears. She wanted to shout at him not to lie to her—that she *knew.* Maybe not everything, but enough to doubt him, and it was killing her. She loved him, but she expected honesty. Their love would never last without it.

"While you were gone, I bought a dress for the reunion."

His eyes softened. "Can I see it?"

"I'd like to keep it a surprise."

Unable to help himself, he leaned forward and pressed a lingering kiss to her lips. "That's fine, but you aren't going to surprise me with how beautiful you are. I've known that from the beginning."

Despite her efforts to the contrary, Jayne blushed. "You won't have any problem attending the reunion, will you?" If Riley was mixed up with Senator Priestly, then he probably wouldn't be able to leave the state.

Riley gave her an odd look. "No, why should I?"

"I don't know."

His eyebrows arched. "There's no problem, Jayne, and if there was, I'd do anything possible to deal with it." He wouldn't disappoint her. Not for the world. They were going to walk into that reunion together, and he was going to show her the time of her life.

The phone rang, and Jayne shrugged. "It's probably Gloria," she said as she hurried into the kitchen to answer it.

"I'm going down to collect my mail," Riley told her. "I'll be back in a minute."

"Okay."

Jayne was off the phone by the time Riley returned. He

started to sort through a variety of envelopes, automatically tossing the majority of them. "What did Gloria have to say?" he asked with a preoccupied frown.

Jayne poured water into the coffeepot. "It . . . wasn't Gloria."

"Oh?" He raised his eyes to meet hers. "Who was it?"

"Mark Bauer." She had no reason to feel guilty about Mark's call, but she did, incredibly so.

"Mark Bauer," Riley repeated, lowering his mail to the counter. "Has he made a habit of calling you since I've been gone?"

"No," she said. "Of course not."

Riley responded with a snort. He'd recognized Mark's type immediately. The guy wasn't all bad, just seeking a little companionship. The problem with Mark was that he had the mistaken notion that he was a lady-killer. He kept the lines of communication open with a dozen different women so that if one fell through there was always another. Only this time Mark had picked the wrong woman. Riley wasn't about to let that second-rate would-be player anywhere near Jayne.

"It's true, Riley," Jayne protested. Mark hadn't contacted her in weeks.

"What did he want?"

"He suggested a movie next Saturday."

"And?"

"And I told him I wasn't interested."

"Good." Reassured, Riley resumed sorting through ten days' worth of junk mail.

"But . . . I'd go out with him if I wanted. It just so happens that I didn't feel like a movie, that's all." If he could lie to her so blithely, she could do the same. Jayne wouldn't have gone out with Mark again, but she didn't need to admit that to Riley.

Swiftly, she retreated into the living room, grabbing the remote and flicking on the TV, hoping to catch the evening news. If the early broadcast gave more details about the Max Priestly case, she could judge Riley's reaction to it.

Riley stiffened as he watched Jayne walk away, her spine straight and defiant. So she'd go out with other men if the mood struck her? Fine. "Go ahead," he announced.

Jayne turned around. "What do you mean?"

"You want to go out with other men, then do so with my blessing." Anger quivered in his voice. He didn't know what game Jayne was playing, but he wanted no part of it.

"I don't need your blessing."

"You're right. You don't." His teeth hurt from clenching them so tightly. "Listen, we're both tired. Let's call it a night. I'll talk to you in the morning."

"Fine." Primly, she crossed her arms and refused to meet his gaze.

But when the door closed, Jayne's confidence dissolved. Their meeting hadn't worked out the way she'd wanted. Instead of confronting Riley with what she'd learned, Jayne had tried to test his love.

After ten minutes of wearing a path in her carpet, Jayne decided that she was doomed to another sleepless night unless they settled this. She'd go to him and tell him she'd seen his car parked at Soft Sam's when he was supposedly fishing with friends. She'd also tell him she remembered seeing him and Senator Priestly in the apartment parking lot. Once she confronted Riley with the truth, he'd open up to her. And they were desperately in need of some honesty.

Standing outside his door, Jayne felt like a fool. Riley didn't answer her first tentative knock. She tried again, more loudly.

"Just a minute," she heard him shout.

Angrily Riley threw open the front door. His quickly donned bathrobe clung to his wet body. Droplets of water dripped from his wet hair.

"Jayne," he breathed, surprised to see her. "I was in the shower."

She stepped into the apartment, nervously clasping her hands. "Riley, I'm sorry about what I said earlier."

His smile brightened his dark face. "I know, love."

Awkwardly she began pacing. "We need to talk." They couldn't skirt the truth anymore. It had to come out, and it had to be now.

"Give me a minute to dress." He paused long enough to kiss her before disappearing into the bedroom.

Feeling a little out of place, Jayne moved into the living room. "Would you mind if I turned on the television?" she called out. The evening newscast could help her lead into the facts she'd unwittingly discovered.

"Sure, go ahead" came Riley's reply. "Remote's on top of the TV."

As she walked across the room, Jayne caught sight of a reddish leather briefcase sticking out from under the TV. She froze. This was the case she'd seen Senator Priestly hand over to Riley that afternoon so long ago. At least it appeared to be. She hadn't seen many of this color and this particular design.

Trembling, Jayne sank to her knees on the carpet and pulled out the briefcase. Her heart felt as though it was about to explode as she pressed open the two spring locks. The sound of the clasp opening seemed to reverberate around the room. For a panicked second she waited for Riley to rush in and demand to know what she was doing.

When nothing happened, Jayne pushed her glasses higher on her nose and carefully raised the lid. The briefcase was empty except for one file folder and one computer flash drive. Her heart pounding, Jayne opened the file. What she saw caused her breath to jam in her throat. She lifted the sheet that was a telephone log—Senator Priestly's calls. Sorting through the other papers, Jayne discovered copies of the incriminating letters that were said to be missing. Riley had in his possession the evidence necessary to convict Priestly. The very evidence that the police needed.

Feeling numb with shock and disbelief, Jayne quietly closed the case and returned it to its position under the TV.

She was sitting with her hands folded in her lap while Riley hummed cheerfully in the background. She couldn't confront Riley with what she'd found. At least not yet. Nor could she let him know what else she'd learned. If she was going to fall in love, why, oh why, did it have to be with a money-hungry felon?

Hurriedly Riley dressed, pleased that Jayne had come to him. He didn't understand why she'd started acting so silly. It was obvious that they were in love, and two people in love don't talk about dating others. His hands froze on his buttons. Maybe Jayne had seen him with Mimi again. No, he thought and expelled his breath. Jayne wouldn't have been able to hide it this well. He'd known almost instantly that there was something drastically wrong the first time she'd been upset. Something was bothering Jayne now, but it couldn't be anything as major as seeing him with that woman.

Walking into the living room, Riley paused. Jayne's spine was ramrod straight, and tears streamed down her ashen face.

"Jayne," he whispered. "What is it?"

She came to him then, linking her arms around him. "I love you, Riley."

"I know, and I love you, too."

She sobbed once and buried her face in his shoulder.

"Honey, has someone hurt you?" he asked urgently.

She shook her head. "No." Breaking free, she wiped her cheeks. "I'm sorry. I'm being ridiculous. I . . . don't know what came over me." Immediately her right eye started twitching, and she stared down at the floor. "I just wanted to tell you I regret what happened earlier," she said in a low voice.

"I understand." But he didn't. Riley had never seen Jayne like this. "Are you hungry? Would you like to go out for dinner?" Showing himself in a public restaurant wouldn't be the smartest move, but they could find an out-of-the-way place.

"No," she said quickly, too quickly. "I'm not hungry. In fact, I've got this terrible headache. I should probably make it an early night."

Riley was skeptical. "If you want."

She backed away from him, inching toward the door. "Good night, Riley."

"Night, love. I'll see you in the morning."

Turning, she scurried across the room and out the door like a frightened mouse. More confused than ever, Riley rubbed his jaw. From the way Jayne was behaving, he could almost believe she knew something. But that was impossible. He'd gone to extreme measures to keep her out of this thing with Priestly.

Back inside her apartment, Jayne discovered that she couldn't stop shaking. The Riley Chambers she'd fallen in love with didn't seem to be the same man who'd returned from the fishing trip. Riley might believe he loved her, but secretly Jayne wondered how deep his love would be if he was aware of how much she knew.

Ignorance had been bliss, but her eyes were open now, and she had to take some kind of action. But *what* kind?

She'd refused to believe what the evidence told her about Riley; now she had to accept it. She didn't have any choice. No matter what the consequences, she had to act.

A sob escaped as she thought about that stupid class reunion, which had gotten her into this predicament in the first place. At this point, going back to St. Mary's was the last thing she wanted to do.

Tears squeezed past her tightly closed eyes, and Jayne gave up the effort to restrain them. She let them fall, needing the release they gave her. No one had ever told her that loving someone could be so painful. In all the books she'd read over the years, love had been a precious gift, something beyond price. Instead she'd found it to be painful, intense and ever so confusing.

Jayne didn't bother to go to bed. She sat in the darkened room, staring blankly at the walls, feeling wretched. More than wretched. The bitter disappointment cut through her. She didn't know what would happen to Riley once she talked to the police. If he hadn't already been arrested, they'd probably come for him after that.

Once again she entertained the idea of confronting him with what she'd discovered and asking him to do the honorable thing. And again she realized the impossibility of that request. Riley had lied to her several times. She couldn't trust him. And yet, she still loved him. . . .

As the sky lightened with early morning, Jayne noticed that the clouds were heavy and gray. It seemed like an omen, a premonition of what was to come.

Knowing what she had to do, Jayne waited until she guessed Riley was awake before phoning him.

"I won't be going to work today," she told him, unable to keep the anguish out of her voice.

Riley hesitated. It sounded as if Jayne was ready to burst into tears. "Jayne," he said, unsure of how much to pressure her right now, "honey, tell me what's wrong."

"I've . . . still got this horrible headache," she said on a rush of emotion. "I'm fine, really. Don't worry about me. And, Riley, I want you to know something important."

"What is it?" Momentarily he tensed.

"I care about you. I'll probably never love anyone more than I love you."

"Jayne . . ."

"I've got to call the library and tell them I won't be in."

"I'll talk to you this evening."

"Okay," she said hoarsely.

Ten minutes later, she heard him leave. She waited another fifteen and made two brief phone calls. One to Gloria at the library and another to a local cab company, requesting a taxi.

The cab arrived in a few minutes, and Jayne walked out of the lobby and into the car.

"Where to, miss?" the balding driver asked.

She reached for a fresh tissue. She hadn't put on her glasses because she kept having to take them off to mop up the tears. "The downtown police station," she whispered, hardly recognizing her own voice. "And hurry, please."

Nine

Lieutenant Hal Powers brought Jayne a cup of coffee and sat down at the table across from her. She supposed this little room was normally used for the interrogation of suspects. This morning she felt like a criminal herself, reporting the man she loved to the police.

"Now, Ms. Gilbert, would you like to start again?"

"I'm sorry," she murmured, brushing away the tears. "I told myself I wouldn't get emotional, and then I end up like this."

Lieutenant Powers gave her an encouraging smile. Jayne had liked him immediately. He was a sensitive man, and she hadn't expected that. From various mysteries she'd read, Jayne had assumed that the police often became cynical and callous. Lieutenant Powers displayed neither of those characteristics.

She gripped the foam cup with both hands and stared into it blindly. "I live in the Marlia Apartments, and I . . . have this neighbor. I suspect he may be involved in something that could get him into a great deal of trouble."

"What has your neighbor been doing?" the lieutenant asked gently.

"I think highly of this neighbor, and I . . . I don't want to say anything until I know what would happen to him."

Lieutenant Powers frowned. "That depends on what he's done."

Jayne took another sip of coffee in an effort to stall for time and clear her thoughts. "To be honest, I can't say for sure that . . . my neighbor's done anything unlawful. But he's holding something that he shouldn't. Something of value."

"Does it belong to him?"

Jayne's eyes fell to the smooth tabletop. "Not exactly."

"Do you know who it does belong to?"

With dismay in her heart, she nodded.

"Who?"

Jayne was silent. There'd never been a darker moment in her life.

"Ms. Gilbert?"

"What I found," she said as tears once again crept down the side of her face, "belongs to Senator Max Priestly."

The lieutenant straightened. "Do you know how your neighbor got this—whatever it is?"

"It's a briefcase with telephone logs and incriminating letters." Now that she'd finally spilled it out, she didn't feel any better. In fact, she felt worse.

"How did your neighbor get this briefcase?"

"I saw the senator give it to Ril—my neighbor." She hurried on to add, "He, my neighbor, doesn't realize that I saw the exchange or that I know what's inside."

"How *do* you know?"

Jayne's gaze locked with his. "I looked."

"I see." The lieutenant rose and walked to the other side of the room. "Ms. Gilbert—"

"Could you tell me what will happen to him?"

One side of his mouth lifted in a half smile. "I'm not sure. . . ." He appeared preoccupied as he moved toward the door. "Could you excuse me for a minute?"

"Of course."

Lieutenant Powers left the room, and Jayne covered her face with both hands. This was so much worse than she'd imagined. Her deepest fear was that the police would insist she lead them to Riley. She felt enough like an informer. A betrayer . . . If only she'd been able to talk to Riley, confront him—but that would've been impossible. Loving him the way she did, she would've been eager to believe anything he told her. Jayne couldn't trust herself around Riley. So she'd done the unthinkable. She'd gone to the police to turn in the only man she'd ever loved.

The door opened, and Lieutenant Powers returned. "I think you two have something you need to discuss."

Jayne suddenly noticed that the lieutenant wasn't alone. Behind him stood Riley.

Jayne's mouth sagged open in utter disbelief.

"I'll wait for you outside," Powers added.

"Thanks, Hal," Riley said as the lieutenant walked out the door.

"Oh, Riley!" Jayne leapt to her feet. "I'm so sorry I had to do this!" she cried through her tears.

"Jayne . . ."

"No." She held up her hand to stop him. "Please, don't say anything. Just listen. I told you this morning that I love you, and I meant that with all my heart. We're going to get through this together. I promise you that I'll be by your side no matter how long you're in prison. I'll come and visit you and write every day until . . . until you're free again. You can turn your life around if you want. I believe in you." She spoke with all the fervency of her love.

Riley's mouth narrowed into a hard line.

"You told me once that you wanted to change," Jayne reminded him. "Let me help you. I want to do everything I can."

"Jayne—"

Her hand gripped his. "Riley, I beg you, please, please tell them everything."

He pulled his hand free. "Jayne, honestly, would you stop being so melodramatic!"

Melodramatic? She blinked, unsure that she'd heard him correctly. "What do you mean?"

"There's no need for you to write me in prison."

"But . . ."

"Jayne, I'm with the FBI. I've been working undercover for six months." Witnessing her distress, Riley cursed himself for not having told her sooner. He also realized that he *couldn't* have told her. Doing so could have put the entire operation in jeopardy. Breaking cover went against everything that had been ingrained in him from the time he was a rookie. But seeing the anguish Jayne had suffered was enough to persuade him that he had to explain.

"Honey, I couldn't tell you."

Stunned, Jayne managed to nod.

"I would've put you in danger if I had."

She continued staring at him. Riley, her Riley, worked for the FBI. She waited for the surge of relief to fill her. None came.

"Why do you have the evidence needed to convict Senator Priestly?" Her voice sounded frail and quavering.

"I'm working undercover, Jayne. I can't really say any more than that."

She didn't understand what being undercover had to do with anything. Then it dawned on her. "You're trying to catch someone else?"

Riley nodded.

"Doesn't that put you in a dangerous position?"

He shrugged nonchalantly. "It could."

Hal Powers stuck his head inside the door. "You two got everything straightened out yet?"

"Not quite," Riley answered for them.

"You want a refill on that coffee?" Powers asked Jayne.

She looked down at the half-full cup. "No, thanks."

"What about you, Riley?"

Riley shook his head, but Jayne noticed the look of respect and admiration the other man gave him.

"This isn't the first time you've done something like this, is it?" she asked.

"She doesn't know about Boston?" Hal stepped into the room, his voice enthusiastic. He paused to glance at Riley. "You've got yourself a famous neighbor, Ms. Gilbert. We even heard about that case out here. Folks call it the second French Connection."

Riley didn't look pleased to have the lieutenant reveal quite so much about his past.

"If you're working undercover, what are you doing here, in the police station?"

"He came to talk to you," Powers inserted.

Riley tossed him an angry glare. "I said I wasn't interested in coffee," he stated flatly.

Powers didn't have to be told twice. "Sure. If you need me, give me a call."

"Right." Riley crossed the room and closed the door behind the other man.

Given a moment's respite Jayne blew her nose and stuffed the tissue inside her purse. Her hand shook as she secured the clasp. She'd made a complete fool of herself.

"How did you know about the briefcase?" Riley asked, turning back to her.

"You were careless, Riley," she said in a small voice. "The corner was poking out from under your TV."

Riley didn't bother to correct her. The briefcase was exactly where it was supposed to be.

"What made you check the contents?" Jayne wasn't the meddling type. She must have suspected something to have taken it upon herself to peek inside that briefcase.

"I saw Max Priestly give it to you weeks ago . . . before I knew you. It was late one Saturday afternoon, in the parking lot."

Riley frowned. "Since you seem to have figured out that much, you're probably aware that my fishing trip—"

She gave a tiny half sob, half laugh. "I know. You don't need to explain."

Riley doubted she really knew, but he wasn't at liberty to elaborate. "I didn't want to lie to you. When this is over, I'll never do it again."

Jayne stood up. All she wanted to do now was escape. "I was obtuse. If I hadn't been so melodramatic, as you put it, I would have guessed sooner."

"You did the right thing. I know how difficult coming here must have been."

Jayne didn't deny it. She was sure there'd never be anything more physically or mentally draining—except telling Riley goodbye. Her hand tightened around the strap of her purse as she prepared to leave. "I . . ."

"Let's get out of here." Riley took her hand and raised it to his lips. "I'm sorry for having put you through this."

She quickly shook her head. "I put myself through it."

"We're done in here," Riley told Lieutenant Powers on the way out the door. He slipped his arm around Jayne's waist. "Where do you want me to drop you off?"

"But . . . you don't want to be seen coming out of here, do you?"

"Having you with me would make an explanation easier if the wrong person happens to see me. Do you want to go home?"

"Yes, please. I didn't sleep well last night."

Again Riley felt the bitterness of regret. Unwittingly he'd involved Jayne in this situation and put her through emotional distress. Once he was through with the Priestly case, he planned to accept a management position in law enforcement and work at a desk. He'd had enough risk and subterfuge. More than enough. He wanted Jayne as his wife, and he wanted children. He pictured a son and daughter and felt an emotion so strong that it seemed as though his heart had constricted. Jayne was everything honest and good, and he desperately needed her in his life.

The ride back to the apartment building was completed in silence. Although she'd been awake all the night, Jayne didn't think she'd be able to sleep now. Her mind had shifted into double time, spinning furiously as she sorted through the facts she'd recently learned.

When Riley parked the car and walked her into the building, Jayne was mildly surprised. She hadn't expected him to be so solicitous. Besides, she'd prefer to be alone, for the next few hours anyway.

She paused outside her apartment door, not wanting him to come in. "I'm fine. You don't have to stay."

She didn't look fine. In fact, he couldn't remember ever seeing her this pale. "Do you need an aspirin?" he asked, following her inside.

"No." Jayne couldn't believe that he hadn't noticed her lack of welcome. Too much had happened, and she needed time alone to find her place in the scheme of things—if she had a place. Everything was different now. Nothing about her relationship with Riley would remain the same.

"There's aspirin in my apartment if you need some."

"I'm fine," she said again. "Really."

He helped her out of her jacket and glanced at the heap of discarded tissues on the coffee table. The evidence that Jayne had spent a sleepless night crying lay before him. "Honey, why didn't you say something when you found the briefcase?"

She shrugged, not answering.

"You must've been frantic." He picked up the wadded tissues and dumped them in the kitchen garbage. The fact that Jayne had left a mess in her neatly organized apartment told him how great her distress had been. Riley wanted to kick himself for having put her through this.

"I was a little worried," was all she'd admit.

"I can't understand why you wouldn't confront me with

what you knew." He'd raised his voice, but his irritation was directed more at himself than at Jayne. Riley didn't know what his response would have been had she come to him, but at least he could have prevented this night of anxious tears.

"I couldn't!" she cried angrily. She pulled another tissue from the box.

Riley frowned tiredly. "Why not?"

"It's obvious that you don't know anything about love," she said sharply. "When you love someone, it's so easy to believe the excuses he or she gives you—because you want to trust that person so badly. You've lied to me repeatedly, Riley. . . . You've had to. I understand that now. But . . . but—" She paused to inhale a deep breath. "I couldn't tell you *before* I knew that. I couldn't have counted on you telling me the truth, and worse, I couldn't have trusted my own response."

"Oh, my love." Riley wrapped her in his arms, fully appreciating her dilemma for the first time.

The pressure of his hands molded her against him, and her hands slipped around his neck. Her pulse thundered in her ears when he raised her chin and then she felt the warmth of his mouth on hers. His kiss melted away the frost that had enclosed her heart.

When the kiss was over, Jayne reeled slightly. His hands steadied her. "I've got to get back," he said.

She took a step away from him, breaking all physical contact, trying to put distance between them. It was far too easy to fall into his arms and accept the comfort of his kiss. "I understand. Don't worry about me, Riley. I'll go to bed and probably sleep all day." At least she hoped she would, but something told her differently.

"I'll call you this afternoon."

"Okay," she told him and walked him to the door. He kissed her again briefly and was gone.

Standing in the hallway, Riley felt like ramming his fist through the wall. He would've given anything to have avoided this. She looked so small and lost, her face drained, her expression shocked. He'd thought Priestly and his accomplice would've made their move by now. He'd been waiting days for this thing to be over. Jayne's reunion was this coming weekend; he'd make sure all the loose ends were tied up by then.

Putting on her glasses, Jayne wandered over to the living room window and watched from nine floors above as Riley, carrying the briefcase, approached his car. He got in and pulled out of the lot and onto the street. Still standing at the window, Jayne saw another car pull out almost immediately after and follow him. Her heart jumped into her throat when she realized that he was being tailed.

Craning her neck, she saw the blue sedan behind him turn at the same intersection. Nervously she rubbed her palms together, wondering what she should do. She had no way of contacting Riley. The only phone number she had was for his apartment, not his cell.

Running into the kitchen, she called the police and asked for Lieutenant Powers, saying it was an emergency.

"Powers here," she heard a moment later.

"Lieutenant," Jayne said, fighting down her panic. "This is Jayne Gilbert. Riley dropped me off at my apartment, and I saw someone follow him."

"Listen, Ms. Gilbert, I wouldn't worry. Riley's been working undercover a lot of years. He can take care of himself."

"But . . ."

"I doubt anyone would tail Riley Chambers without him knowing about it."

"But he's concerned about me. He may not be paying attention the way he should. Could you please contact him and let him know?" She raised her voice, trying to impress the urgency of her request on him.

"Ms. Gilbert, I don't think—"

"Riley's life could be in danger!"

She could hear the lieutenant's sigh of resignation. "If it'll reassure you, then I'll contact him."

"Thank you." But Jayne wasn't completely mollified; she was also worried about how Riley would react. He wouldn't appreciate her warning. He might even be insulted. As Powers had claimed, Riley had been around a long time. He knew how to take care of himself.

Sagging onto the sofa, Jayne found that her knees were trembling. She couldn't help imagining Riley caught in a trap from which he couldn't escape. Forcefully she dispelled the images from her mind. This wasn't Riley's first case, she reminded herself, and it probably wouldn't be his last. That knowledge wasn't comforting. Not in the least. Loving Riley Chambers wasn't going to work. Could he really change the way he lived? He'd tasted adventure, lived with excitement; a house with a white picket fence would be so mundane to someone like him.

Jayne woke hours later, shocked that she'd managed to sleep. She rubbed a hand along the back of her neck to ease the crick she'd gotten from sleeping with her head propped against the sofa arm. Brilliant sunlight splashed in through her open drapes, and a glance at her watch said it was after five. She suddenly realized that Riley hadn't called. She wouldn't have slept through the ringing of the phone.

Pushing the hair away from her face, she swallowed down the fear that threatened to overtake her. Fleetingly she wondered if Powers had warned him about the blue sedan. She doubted it. It was obvious from their conversation that the lieutenant thought she was overreacting. Maybe she was.

In an effort to calm her fears, Jayne looked out her window. His parking space was empty, she noted sadly, and then felt a surge of relief when his car made a left-hand turn a block away. She also took consolation from the knowledge that there wasn't a blue car anywhere near Riley's.

But her relief quickly died when Jayne noticed a blue sedan parked on the side street. It might not have been the same one, but the resemblance was close enough to alarm her. Jayne was undecided—should she do anything?—until she saw a man climb out of the car. He paused and looked both ways before crossing the street to head in Riley's direction.

Jayne's heart flew into her throat when she watched him step behind a parked car, apparently to wait. It occurred to her that he could be planning to ambush Riley. Instantly she knew she was right. Jayne could sense it, could feel the threat. She had to get to Riley and warn him.

Without another thought, she raced out of her apartment and down the hall. For once, the elevator appeared immediately. By the time the wide doors opened into the lobby, Jayne was frantic.

She ran outside and came to an abrupt halt. She couldn't run up to Riley. She might be putting him in even greater danger if she intervened now. The thing to do was remain calm and see what the man planned to do—if anything.

Walking into the lot, Jayne saw Riley standing beside his car with the briefcase. He wasn't moving. The other man faced him and had his back to her. Approaching the pair at an angle, Jayne caught a flash of metal. The man had a gun trained on Riley.

Tension momentarily froze her, but she knew what she had to do. She broke into a run.

Riley saw her move, and terror burned through him. A scream rose in his throat as he called out, "Jayne . . . no!"

Ten

Jayne saw the way Riley's face had become drawn and white as she'd started to run. She didn't know much about martial arts, but after the incident with the mugger, she'd read a wonderfully simple book filled with illustrations. When she'd finished the book, Jayne had felt fairly confident that she could defend herself, if need be. Seeing a gun pointed at Riley's heart was all the incentive she needed to apply the lessons she'd learned.

Unfortunately her skill wasn't quite up to what she'd hoped it would be, and her aim fell far below his chest, possibly because she wasn't wearing her glasses. But where her foot struck caused enough pain to double the man over and send him slumping to the pavement. The gun went flying.

Riley recovered it. His face was pinched and drawn. "For crying out loud, Jayne. I don't believe you." He rubbed a hand over his face. "You idiot! Couldn't you see he had a gun?"

Feeling undeniably proud of herself, Jayne smiled shyly. "Of course I saw the gun."

"Did it ever occur to you that you might've been shot?" he shouted.

She shrugged. "To be honest, I didn't really think of that. I just . . . acted."

The man she'd felled remained on the ground, moaning. From seemingly nowhere, a uniformed officer appeared and forced him to stand before handcuffing his wrists.

Riley paced back and forth, and for the first time Jayne noticed how furious he was. The self-satisfied grin faded from her face. The least Riley could do was show a little appreciation. "I saved your life, for heaven's sake."

"Saved it?" He shook his head, momentarily closing his eyes. "You nearly cost us both our lives."

"But . . ."

"Do you think I'm stupid? I knew that Simpson—Priestly's campaign manager and accomplice—was in the parking lot. We were surrounded by three teams of plainclothes detectives. In addition, a squad car was parked on the other side of the building."

"Oh," Jayne replied in a small voice.

"You scared me half to death." He groaned. "And you're the one who hides her eyes during movies." He raked his fingers through his hair. "How do you think I'd feel if something happened to you?" Some of the harsh anger drained from his voice.

"I did what I thought I had to," Jayne returned, feeling faintly indignant.

Riley shook his head again. "I don't think my system could take another one of your acts of heroism. Where did you learn to leap through the air like that?"

"In a book . . ."

"You mean to tell me you learned that crippling move from something you read?"

"The illustrations were excellent, but I have to admit I was off a bit. I was actually aiming for his chest."

Riley just rolled his eyes.

"Under the circumstances," she said, trying to maintain her dignity, "I thought I did rather well."

Briefly his gaze met hers, and a reluctant grin lifted his mouth. "You did fine, but promise me you'll never, *ever* interfere again."

"I promise." Now that everything was over, reaction set in, and Jayne began to tremble. She'd seen Riley in terrible danger and responded without a thought for her own welfare. Riley was as incredulous as the policemen who milled around, shaking their heads in wonder at this woman who'd downed an armed man.

"Are you all right?" he asked, draping an arm around her shoulders and pulling her close. He savored the warmth of her body next to his.

"I'm fine." She wasn't, but she couldn't very well break down now.

"I've got to go downtown and debrief, write my report. But I'll be back in a couple of hours. Will you be all right until I return?"

"Of course."

Riley hesitated. Jayne was putting on a brave front, but he could tell that she was frightened now that she'd realized what could have happened. He didn't want to leave her, but it was unavoidable.

"I'll walk you to your apartment," he said, wanting to reassure her that everything was under control.

"I'm fine," she insisted in a shaky voice. "You're needed at the station."

"Jayne," he said, then paused.

"Go on," she urged. "I'll be waiting here. I'm not going anyplace."

He dropped a quick kiss on her mouth. "I love you, Jayne." And he did love her—so much that he doubted he could have survived if anything had happened to her.

As he left, Jayne went back to her apartment, telling herself Riley was safe, and that was what mattered most.

An hour later, Jayne reached her decision. It wasn't so difficult, really. She'd known it would come to this sooner or later, and she'd prefer it to be sooner. Again, as she had in the parking lot, she was only doing what she had to.

By the time Riley appeared, she was composed and confident. She opened her door and stepped aside as he entered her apartment. He bent to kiss her, and she let him, savoring the moment.

"We need to talk." She spoke first, not giving him a chance to say anything.

"You're telling me," Riley said with a grin. "I still can't get over you." If he lived for another century, Riley doubted he would forget those few seconds when Jayne had come running toward Simpson. And she'd done it to protect *him*—Riley Chambers. Naturally, she'd been unaware that he wasn't in any danger. All the way back from the jail, Riley was lost in the memory of those brief moments. He'd found himself an exceptional woman. And he wasn't going to lose her. He'd already started looking at diamond rings. On the night of her reunion he was going to ask her to marry him.

"Riley, about the reunion."

"What about it?"

"I've asked Mark to take me."

"*What?*"

"I want you to know I appreciate the fact that you were willing to attend it with me, but—"

"Jayne, you're not thinking straight," Riley countered, still not believing what she'd said.

She forced out a light laugh. "Actually, I've been giving it some thought over the past few days. This wasn't a sudden decision. When I went to the police this morning, I knew there was every likelihood that you wouldn't be able to go to Seattle with me."

Riley frowned. "So you asked Mark?"

"Yes." Her right eye remained still. Riley had taught her several things, and one of those was how to lie. The smoothness with which she told him this one was shocking. What a sad commentary on their relationship, Jayne mused unhappily. She'd love Riley forever, and years from now, when the hurt went away, she'd be able to look back on their weeks together and be glad she'd known and loved him—however briefly.

Riley clenched his fists. "Something's not right here. You're lying."

"I'm not the expert in that department. You are." She stalked into the kitchen. "Here," she said, handing him the telephone receiver. "If you don't believe me, call Mark."

Riley stared at the phone in utter astonishment. "Jayne . . . don't do this." His gut instinct told him she was lying.

"How was I supposed to know you weren't some crook? I couldn't take that chance. So . . . I asked Mark."

"Then unask him."

"I won't do that."

"Why not?" Riley was becoming angrier with every breath.

"Because I'm not sure you're the type of man I'd want to go with—the type of man I want to be with." The pain of what she was doing was so powerful that Jayne reached out to hold on to the kitchen counter. "I'm sorry, Riley, I am. I've known for some time that things weren't working out."

"Not sorry enough." Abruptly he swiveled around. "I'd suggest you have fun, but I doubt you will with Mark Bauer."

"I'm sure I'll have a perfectly good time," she lied, but the effort to hold back her tears made the words unintelligible.

"Jayne, darling, let me look at you." Dorothy Gilbert held her daughter by the shoulders and shook her gray head. Jayne's parents had met her at the train station. "You look fabulous."

Jayne smiled absently. The train had arrived on time. She was afraid to fly, but she beamed proudly at the thought of the one shining moment in her life when she'd ignored her fear and attacked a gunman. Such ironies were common with her.

"The new hairstyle suits you."

"Thank you, Mom." But the happiness she felt at seeing her parents didn't compensate for the emptiness inside her after that last confrontation with Riley. From her mother's arm, Jayne moved forward to receive her father's gruff embrace.

"Good to see you, sweetie," Howard Gilbert said.

"Thank you, Daddy."

Slowly they walked toward the terminal where Jayne was to collect her luggage.

"That Thomas girl arrived this morning from California. You might want to call her at her parents' house," Dorothy told Jayne as she put an arm around her waist. "She's already called to ask about you."

"I . . . I'd like to talk to her."

"She's married and has two daughters."

"How nice." Jayne wasn't married. Nor did she have children. She was the prim and proper woman Riley had accused her of being. It was what she'd been destined to be from the time she'd graduated from high school. She had been a fool to believe otherwise. Angry with herself for the self-pitying thoughts, Jayne smiled brightly at her mother.

"Judy said the reception at the Westin starts about eight."

"They mailed me a program, Mom." Jayne had decided she'd attend the reunion alone. Her dream had been to arrive with Riley at her side, but that was out of the question. So, as she'd done most of her life, Jayne would pretend. She'd walk into the reception with her head held high and imagine everyone turning toward her and sighing with envy.

She hadn't seen Riley. Not once since that fateful afternoon. For all she knew he could have moved out of the building. She was grateful he'd accepted her lies, making it unnecessary to fabricate others. She'd purposely hurt him to be kind. She wasn't the right woman for him, and his life was too different from hers.

She'd read about the charges against Priestly and Simpson. The articles and news reports gave an abbreviated version of Riley's part in all this, mentioning only that an FBI agent had worked with police departments statewide to destroy Priestly's organization.

Her father collected her suitcase, and then the three of them walked to the car parked across from the King Street Station.

"I have a lovely new dress," Jayne said.

"I'm so pleased you're attending this reunion, Jayne. I'd been worried you might not want to go." She stared intently at Jayne.

"I wouldn't miss it, Mom."

"Those girls never appreciated you," her father commented, placing Jayne's suitcase in the trunk of the car.

"Nonsense, Dad, I had some good friends."

"She did, Howard."

They chatted companionably on the drive toward Jayne's childhood home on Queen Anne Hill.

Once she got home, Jayne phoned her high school friend, Judy Thomas, and they chatted for nearly an hour.

"It's so good to talk to you again," Judy said. "I can hardly wait to see you."

"Me, too."

"I think I'd better get off the phone. Dad's giving me disapproving looks just like he did ten years ago."

"I guess we'll always be teenagers to our parents."

"Unfortunately." Judy giggled.

Jayne smiled when her mother stuck her head around the corner. "Don't you think you should start to get ready?"

Jayne contained a smile. Judy was right. They would always be teenagers to their parents. "Okay, Mom, I'll be off in a minute."

"See what I mean?" Judy said.

"Oh, yes. Listen, I'll see you tonight."

"See you then."

Jayne spent most of the next hour preparing for the reunion. Her mother raved about how the dress looked on Jayne. Gazing at her mirrored reflection, Jayne's astonishment was renewed. The dress was the most beautiful one she'd ever owned.

Adding the final touches to her makeup, Jayne heard her mother and father whispering in the background.

"We'd like to get some pictures of you and your young man," her father said when Jayne stepped out of her bedroom.

"Pardon me, Dad?"

"Pictures," he repeated, taking his camera from the case. "Go stand by the fireplace."

"All right." She went into the living room and stopped cold. Before her stood Riley. Tall, polished, impeccable and so incredibly good-looking in his tuxedo that she felt as though all the oxygen had escaped her lungs.

"Riley . . . what are you doing here?"

"Taking you to the reunion."

"But how did you know—"

"I believe your father wants to take a few pictures." Gently he took her lifeless hand in his and tucked it into his elbow.

Smiling, Dorothy and Howard Gilbert moved into the living room.

"Oh—Mom and Dad, this is Riley Chambers."

Riley came forward and shook hands with her parents. "Glad to see you again, Howard. And good to meet you, Dorothy."

Gruffly, her father motioned for the couple to stand in front of the fireplace while he took a series of photos.

"I believe these young people need a few minutes alone."

"Daddy—"

"You need to talk to your fiancé," Howard said, taking his wife by the arm and leading her into the kitchen.

Jayne didn't move and barely breathed, and she couldn't seem to speak.

"Having her father announce it isn't the most romantic way to tell the woman you love that you want to marry her," Riley said once her parents had left.

"Oh, Riley, please don't."

"Don't what? Love you? That would be impossible."

"No," she whispered miserably, hanging her head. "Don't ask me."

"But I am. Maybe it was presumptuous of me, but I bought a ring." He pulled out a jeweler's box from his inside pocket. "I don't know why you lied about inviting Mark. I don't even care. I love you, and we're going to have a marvelous life together."

"Riley." She swallowed a sob. "No, I won't marry you."

He put the jeweler's box on the mantel behind him and stared at her, his look incredulous. "Why?"

"Because I'm me. I'll never be anything other than a children's librarian. That's all I've ever wanted to be. You live life in the fast lane, while I crawl along at a snail's pace—if you'll forgive the clichés."

"But, Jayne, I'm sick of that life . . ."

"For how long? A year? Maybe two?"

"Jayne, I've already accepted a job—a desk job—with the Portland police. My undercover days are over."

"Riley, are you sure that's what you want?"

"I've never been more sure of anything." His eyes held a determination that few would challenge. "I've waited half my life for you, Jayne Gilbert, and I'm not taking no for an answer."

The blunt words took Jayne aback. Her lips tightened as she shook her head.

"Do you love me so little?" he asked in a voice that was so soft she could hardly hear it.

"You know I love you!" she cried.

"Then why are you fighting me?"

"I'm . . . afraid, Riley."

He took a step toward her, extending his hand. "Then put

your hand in mine. No man could ever love you more than I do. I'm ready for everything you have to give me. I've been ready for a lot of years."

Jayne couldn't fight him anymore. Tentatively, she raised her hand and placed it in his.

"I believe we have a reunion to attend."

"It isn't necessary. You know that, don't you? All I've ever needed is you." She blinked back tears. "Now, don't make me cry. It took me ages to get this makeup right."

"You're beautiful."

She laughed and reached up to kiss him. "Thank you, but I have trouble believing that."

"After tonight, you won't. I'll be the envy of every man there."

"Then it's true," Jayne said with a trembling smile. "Love is blind."

Riley turned to retrieve the jeweler's box and offered it to her. Smiling tremulously, she let him slide the engagement ring on her finger.

"What would you say to a fall wedding?"

Before Jayne could respond, Howard and Dorothy reappeared, and Dorothy protested, "Oh, no, that's nowhere near enough time!"

"It's fine, Dorothy," Howard said. "The only thing that matters to me is whether our daughter's marrying the right man. And I'm convinced she couldn't find anyone better than Riley." He winked at his wife. "I know you, of all people, can pull off a wedding in four months."

Dorothy gave a resigned sigh. "Have fun, you two," she murmured.

"We will, Mom."

On the way down the sidewalk to Riley's parked car, Jayne gave him an odd look. "When did you talk to my father?"

"A couple of days ago when I asked his permission for his daughter's hand."

"Riley, you didn't!"

He raised his eyebrows. "I did. I told you before that I was going to do everything right with you. We're going to be married as soon as possible—in a church before God and witnesses. We're going to be very happy, Jayne."

A brilliant smile curved her lips. "I think we will, too," she said.

A half-hour later, Riley pulled into the curved driveway of the downtown Westin where the reunion was being held. He eased to a stop, and an attendant opened Jayne's door and helped her out.

They walked through the hotel lobby and took the elevator to the Grand Ballroom.

"Ready?" Riley asked as they approached.

Her breath felt tight in her lungs. "I think so."

One step into the room, and Jayne felt every eye on her. The room went silent as she turned and smiled into the warmth and love that radiated from Riley's gaze.

Whispers rose. And the girls of St. Mary's sighed.

★★★★★